CHIEF INSPECTOR, THE BEGINNING

U.S. MARSHALS CONFRONT THE WORST CRIMINALS IN 1860

Ken Berquist

I wish to express my appreciation to all of those of whom were helpful in creating this work.

To, Gail, my loving and very patient wife who understands, when I get into the 'writing mindset', it ultimately results in a periodic slippage into hibernation.

TABLE OF CONTENTS

FOREWORD

During the 1840s, the United States saw a significant number of emigrants fleeing from the island of Ireland as a result of The Great Famine of Ireland. The four years following the famine produced significantly more emigrants than during the four years of the famine.

Irish citizens were also facing discrimination in the United Kingdom based on their religion, and were burdened with increasing rents and evictions. Evictions only increased after the repeal of the British Corn Laws in 1846 and the new Encumbered Estates Act in 1849, as well as the removal of existing civil rights. These new laws were created to crush terrorism from the Irelanders against their crooked landlords. All hope for change evaporated with the death of the Irish political leader, Daniel O'Connell, in 1847, and the failed rising of the Young Irelanders in 1848.

In 1848, gold was discovered in California and the United States saw increased emigrants from all over Europe seeking riches. Overwhelmed in the Atlantic ports of Boston, New York, Philadelphia, Washington and Miami, the United States leaked in Irish, Britons, French, Germans, Spanish, Swedes and more.

This is the story of one Irish emigrant family, who arrived in Philadelphia in 1848. Not seeking gold, they came seeking a better life of religious freedom, democratic government, safety and the ability to control their own destiny.

Shaun deBláca, his wife of fourteen years, Grace, and their twelve-year-old son, Liam, all from County Kildare in Ireland, arrived in the Port of Philadelphia on September 21, 1848. The day was bright with sun and few clouds, and the late summer temperature was unseasonably warm. It was a fitting start to a new life in a new land. Shaun was a man of some means, having been a successful gunsmith and rancher in his native Ireland, and the family, being well dressed and in good health, cleared the customs and immigration process without incident.

Having no family nor friends in the United States made getting settled a challenge. Determining where to settle was the first major decision as new immigrants. After consulting with several local immigrants of experience, Shaun settled on the nation's capital, which required several additional days of traveling to cover the one hundred and thirty-mile trek due south. He procured a suitable Calistoga heavy duty freight wagon and a team of four Morgan mares and then contracted help to load the assorted creates containing his gunsmithing tools and machinery along with several pieces of family luggage. He was advised to stay with the old road from Philadelphia through Baltimore, all the way to Washington as it would be the safest and would also have periodic roadhouses, providing food and shelter that would make the trip easier.

Along the way, and in the roadhouses, the evidence of James K. Polk, the current President of the United States and his Vice President George M. Dallas actively campaigning for the re-election that they would ultimately lose to the US

Army Major General, Zachery Taylor, and his running mate, Millard Fillmore. Both Shaun and Grace were excited to see the open political discourse without the brutality that was so common in Ireland. One could share one's opinion in spirited debate without recourse or violence.

The deBláca family was greeted warmly by the staff at the Willard City Hotel on Pennsylvania Avenue in Washington, ten days after disembarking from their vessel in Philadelphia. Liam was wide eyed with wonder, astonished by the many buildings, their immense size and the number of well-dressed men, women and children bustling about the streets and buildings. At the impressionable age of twelve, these early memories begin to form the man that will become the center of this story. Liam was a most inquisitive young man, much more mature than his age. He was unusually bright, well read, and multi-lingual, speaking and reading English and French, as well as his native tongue, Irish Gaelic. Liam had an unquenchable thirst for knowledge. His interests included mechanics, physics, animal husbandry, and law and was rarely found without a book on the subjects close at hand.

Shaun was granted a meeting with Henry A. Willard, co-owner of the Willard City Hotel, to ask advice regarding establishing his business. Henry took an immediate liking to the ease with which Shaun carried himself and the intelligence, energy and commitment to establishing a long term successful business. Henry's advice proved invaluable to selecting the location and in making the right business connections.

The Black Arms Company was established on November 2, 1848, with its principle place of business a medium-sized windowed shop near the U.S. Marine Barracks, on the corner 8th and I Streets, in Southeast

Washington. Shaun had brought more than just the tools and machinery he needed to build and repair firearms. He also brought the family name 'deBláca' which means 'black', frequently associated with the black powder needed for firearms and explosives.

Placing the shop near the Marine barracks was his first of many brilliant business decisions. Marines frequented the shop, purchasing unique rifles and hand guns as well as seeking repairs and supplies. The Black Arms Company soon took its place as *the* source of quality, expertise and fairness, and was frequently involved in lucrative consultation with the Colt, Henry, and Winchester companies representing the United States Marines' best interests.

The success soon provided the notoriety and additional wealth needed to send Liam to the George Washington University Law School, at the corner of 20th and H Streets in the Foggy Bottom neighborhood.

The story now opens in 1858, as Liam approaches graduation from Law School while working part time at the Black Arms Company. In the political backdrop, James Buchanan is in his third year as the President of the United States, while Senate hopeful Abraham Lincoln, through a series of debates in 1858, gave national visibility to his opposition to the expansion of slavery. Though Lincoln lost the Senate race to his archrival, Stephen A. Douglas, he plans to continue campaigning in the hopes of securing the Republican Party presidential nomination in 1860.

CHAPTER ONE

1858

The Yankton Sioux Tribe of South Dakota, a tribe of Yankton Dakota Sioux (Ihanktonwan Dakota Oyate), located in South Dakota sign a peace treaty with the United States.

Minnesota is admitted as the 32nd U.S. state.

The gold seekers known as the "Fifty-Niners" stream into the Rocky Mountains of the western United States during the Pike's Peak Gold Rush.

The first of the seven Lincoln–Douglas debates is held.

Fordyce Beals patents his six shooter revolver, which would later be produced by E. Remington & Sons, Ilion, N.Y as the Remington Model 1858.

Denver is founded.

U.S. President James Buchanan inaugurates the new trans-Atlantic telegraph cable by exchanging greetings with Queen Victoria. However, a weak signal forces a shutdown of the service in a few weeks.

Rain mixed with sleet pelted the large multi-paned window, sounding as if a discontented child was peppering the bullet glass with pebbles. That, of course, would be impossible as the window was several floors up in Washington's Willard City Hotel where the deBláca family had taken up residence at the invitation of the hotel co-owner, close friend and business adviser, Henry A. Willard. Wind blew against the casement window, rattling the sash as the raindrops distorted the lantern lights from the street below as they slid down the glass pane.

Liam, standing at the window's center, was looking down at the street below mindlessly watching the many carriages and pedestrians with umbrellas as they traveled to their homes or places to visit. The thick clover-green velour drapes were parted in the middle, held by matching decorative rope tiebacks. He could hear the horses' metal-shoed hooves clap against the cobblestoned street, recently installed at the request of the hotel in an effort to keep their guests free of the mud so prevalent on rainy days.

Today was a day of celebration and feasting, a day for giving thanks, reflection and prayer. It was Christmas in 1858, more than ten years after Liam and his family had arrived from County Kildare, Ireland, in search of a better life, free from British persecution. The deBláca family had much to be thankful for, and joined in prayer thanking God for their good fortune. As the head of the family, Shaun deBláca led the prayer, with his wife Grace and their only son Liam joining hands with him and with each other, along with their housekeeper and cook, Martha. Years of struggle and hardship in Ireland had made them a very close and loving family, and during the prayer Grace shed tears of joy for the men and the good fortune in her life.

"Liam, would you please carve the roast?" Shaun asked, while handing him the carving knife and fork.

"Father, that honor is always given the head of the house. It was you who planned our immigration. It was you who convinced mother and me that it was in the best interests of our family, and it was you who rebuilt our heritage as United States citizens. No, I respectfully decline. This remains and will always be your honor, Father."

The roasted goose that was placed by Martha on the dining room table was permeating the air with its fragrance along with the aromas from the roasted vegetables, potatoes and breads. It was a warm and comfortable room, rich in décor although not overly opulent. The four-post mahogany table was covered by a clover-green tablecloth, matching the velour drapes, and combined with the bone-colored china, silver flatware, and crystal glassware to add to the festive mood. The late afternoon was darkened by the storm clouds outside and the many multi-colored candles placed around the dining room added to its coziness. The fireplace crackled and blazed and radiated warmth, adding the slight sent of hickory and cedar in the air.

"Shaun, I believe that you and Liam are as anxious to taste this goose as am I," Grace said, suggesting that he should proceed with the carving in all due haste. Grace had the elegance and confidence that came with her nearly forty years of age, and beauty that belied her difficult early years in Ireland. Her chestnut shoulder-length hair was fashioned up, framing her apple-shaped face, drawing attention to deep forest green warm eyes. Grace had been a schoolteacher in Ireland and continued her profession in Washington. She was dressed in a pale green dress that hung to her raised-heel laced shoes and buttoned to the neck, always a proper woman.

"Yes, Father. Remember, I am still a growing boy!"

"No, Liam my son, you are a young man, no longer a boy, and I am proud of what you have accomplished in your twenty-two years of life," Shaun added as he reached for the carving knife and fork. Dressed formally in a black broadcloth suit, with a white shirt opened at the neck where a red ascot completed his ensemble, he decided to remove his top coat to prevent it being soiled by accidental drippings. The gold chain that was attached to the pocket watch tucked neatly into his black vest caught on a button of the coat and pulled the watch from the pocket.

Lifting the watch, Shaun caressed it with distant memories flooding his face. Coming back to the present, he said, "Liam, this watch was passed to me by my father. It was passed to him by his father and, in time, it will be passed to you by me. It is an ever-present reminder of family, of our heritage. I trust that you will cherish it as have I and pass it on to your son."

Liam smiled and nodded.

With the goose now carved, with pieces placed on the bone-colored serving platter, Shaun, Grace and Liam sat around the table and began their Christmas feast. As families do, they conversed as they dined.

"Liam, have you given more thought of what you will do now that you have earned your law degree?" Grace asked casually. There had been several discussions over the month's past, and Liam had not yet determined what he wanted for his life. He was torn. He loved working at the Black Arms, learning more about firearms every day, contributing to the company's growth and having a feeling of accomplishment that comes from working with one's hands as well as mind. However, he loved the practice of law, and from the depths of his soul he believed in the need for the institution of law, having experienced firsthand the effect of a lawless and corrupt society. He had graduated top of his class and had completed a very unusual and challenging curriculum that included mechanical engineering as well as the full law prerequisites, a demanding double major.

Liam, taking after his father Shaun, was dressed in a black broadcloth suit and white shirt, as was his practice, thinking for several long seconds before responding. Looking at his mother lovingly, Liam responded, "If father will have me, I would like to continue to work at the Black Arms Company, at least for a while. I am quite interested in the new cartridge revolver designs."

Shaun was delicately slicing a piece of goose breast and took a small bite and a sip of red wine before commenting. "Liam, you will always be welcome at the Arms, for as long as you wish. You could also organize and manage our legal affairs. Many of the contracts with the Marines are very complicated and your training in contract law would be most helpful. However, and this is important so hear me well. If at any time should you find your destiny elsewhere, you must follow that destiny. Your mother and I want you to have a life of happiness, challenge and fulfillment. Will you agree to that stipulation, Son?"

The sounds of cutlery filled the room's silence while Liam formulated his response. Law school had taught him several lessons, including thinking through a response thoroughly before verbalizing it. He took a sip of the dense red wine, aware of the eyes upon him while awaiting his thoughts.

"I am a most fortunate young man, as you put it Father, to have the love and respect of this family. I can never repay you for the gifts given me but I must and will continue to try. You know that the study and now the practice of law has become an important part of me. So, yes father, I agree. And I thank you both from the bottom of my heart."

"Good. That is settled and I am more pleased than I am able to express in words. Now, the Marines have asked for assistance with the new Spencer carbine. It appears that they are having difficulty with accuracy and feel the prototypes may have a flaw. You are the most accurate marksman I know of in the city. In point of fact, you are the best I have ever seen with both pistols and long guns on either side of the Atlantic. Would you be interested in adding that to your challenges?"

The pre-production prototype Spencer carbine was quite different from any other firearm used by the Marines. It was accurate, fired rapidly, had a long effective range, and held seven metallic cartridges unaffected by moisture that commonly caused misfires with older percussion cap and ball firearms. It could be fired more rapidly than their current models and reloaded in one-tenth the time. All of which will be critical assets should there be a war between the north and south. It had not yet been released to production by the Spencer Arms company and the Marines marksman unit had been issued the prototypes for testing before a large contract for the production models could be issued.

"That sounds interesting. I am in your debt yet again."

"Excellent. Colonel Haas is in charge. Contact him tomorrow, Son. I will send a note to him this evening advising him to expect you."

Martha was quietly watching the roast goose entrée being enjoyed, preparing to bring the warm apple pie before the family adjourned to the sitting room for brandy. She felt more a part of the deBláca family than an employee because she was treated that way, with the love and respect that was not normally given to a woman of color or a woman in family service. Martha enjoyed the long kitchen talks with Grace over tea, and frequently helped her grade her students' test papers, learning in the process. It was during these kitchen talks that Martha learned of the discrimination and persecution the deBláca family suffered in Ireland. Martha came to understand that they had much in common.

***

The storm had cleared by morning, leaving the streets and walks wet and icy in places, but the unseasonably warm temperature began to melt the ice likely turning it all to water before mid-morning. Liam left the residence in the Willard dressed in his black broadcloth suit, tie, derby hat, warm gray wool overcoat and gray wool gloves. He carried with him a leather valise containing the Marine consulting contract as well as the complete specifications for the new Spencer carbine. He decided to walk directly to the Marine headquarters in search of Colonel Haas and begin working with him and the Marine marksmen to solve their accuracy problem.

There was a slight cool breeze shaking the few remaining brown leaves from the oak trees lining Pennsylvania Avenue. His black leather-soled shoes slipped at times on the wet leaves and ice, caused him to walk a bit slower than his usual brisk pace. There was a hint of brine, sea water, in the air which he interpreted as a wind to the west. He mindlessly watched the carriages and men on horseback, traveling the street while remembering the power of familial love that enveloped him the night before. He could see in his mind's eye his mother's smile... she smiled warmly.

As he approached the street corner, Liam noticed the small knot of men holding signs and passing out handbills. The signs were simple wood boards, painted black with bold white lettering. The words imprinted "We want slavery" made clear the opinion on slavery and angered Liam. As he walked toward the small group of men, he speculated to himself that the black painted background with the bold white lettering fronting the sign was testimony to why he despised the practice of owning another human being. The group of men intentionally blocked Liam's passage. They were dressed in working-class clothing, more western in style. They all had work boots, denim trousers, deep navy wool coats, and western hats. The apparent leader's posture, western booted legs spread with arms folded across his chest, telegraphed hostility.

His path blocked, Liam stopped directly in front of the leader and they locked eyes. Liam, at six feet two inches tall, was easily four inches taller than the man he fronted. Wordlessly, they sized up each other.

Then the leader spoke, "What is your position on slavery, friend?" Several of the other men protesting stopped and turned to observe the confrontation. The leader's eyes couldn't remain still, yet they had intensity and menace about them. He slowly unfolded his arms and Liam noticed the butt of a pistol tucked in his belt.

Tension continued to increase as Liam continued looking down at the leader, their eyes locked, and the leader eventually side stepped, allowing Liam to walk by the group, making no comment. He made a conscious effort to lock the leader's image into memory, sensing the leader could be a very dangerous man.

The leader spewed in bitter anger to Liam's back, "We will meet again. And when we do, you will show me some respect!"

Entering the Marine barracks, Liam was met by the burly First Sergeant who noted that he was expected and escorted him to the barracks meeting room. With a meeting in progress, he removed his derby hat and stood in the rear until Colonel Haas noticed him.

Colonel Haas had just finishing addressing his team when Liam appeared, and knowing him by sight, asked him to address the team before calling for adjournment.

Liam thanked him with a warm handshake and turned to face the ten-member Marine marksman team that were seated on oak benches, dressed in full battle uniform, each with a Spencer placed uniformly on its shoulder stock with muzzle facing to the ceiling, trigger guard facing in, held with their left hand and nearly touching their left thigh.

Liam looked at each member individually before speaking. He was impressed with their bright and determined eyes as well as their focus. He was also conscious of the likely question each harbored about how a twenty-two-year-old "young" man would be able to provide the help they needed to improve their shooting accuracy.

"Gentlemen, Marines, you are the best trained fighting men in the world. I know that and the world knows that. More importantly, you know that. You have trained for years and the results with the Colt carbine is proof of that. Some of you may even remember using the old flint lock single shot rifles with a ball projectile. Those that do also remember the changes required to obtain the accuracy when changing to the Colt. The same degree of change is needed when moving to the modern Spencer. But the type of change is quite different. The Spencer uses, as you all know, a cartridge and the projectile is conical shaped. The muzzle velocity is seven hundred sixty feet per second and the recoil is significantly stronger due to the larger powder charge. This means that the adjustment for elevation is quite different than the Colt, as is the adjustment for windage. The rifle bore has striations that are designed to spin the projectile while it travels through the barrel providing, with the proper adjustments, significantly more accuracy. The only thing I need to and will accomplish today is to help each one of you make those adjustments. Questions?" There were none spoken aloud though it was likely that many harbored private thoughts. The room was silent.

Colonel Haas stepped up, sensing that the marksman team were skeptical about how such a young man could help them solve their accuracy problem, and said "I will give $50 to any marksman that can out shoot Mr. deBláca at one hundred yards right now, without any practice, and using your Spencer. So, there you are men, no risk to you at all and I know you all would like to take my money. Let's go to the range. Dismissed". There were murmurs and rumblings as the marksman team left the barracks meeting room and headed to the range, but what they were Liam couldn't make out.

Liam then turned to Colonel Haas and said, "Colonel, you are taking quite a risk with that challenge."

"No son. No I am not, not at all. I have known your father for nine years. He is the best gunsmith I have ever known. I trust he has taught you everything he knows about firearms. In addition, you graduated top in your class with diplomas in both mechanical engineering and law. If there is a mechanical issue, you'll correct it. I also know that you won the last long-range target shooting competition, and by a wide margin if I remember correctly. No, there is no risk at all and demonstrating your capability quickly will earn for you the respect we need to solve this problem quickly." He didn't even attempt to hide the wry grin framed by his neatly trimmed graying beard.

"Come; let me escort you to the range."

Liam was a solidly built young man, standing six feet two inches and weighing just shy of two hundred pounds. He, unlike most men of his acquaintance, didn't sport facial hair, which gave the appearance of a man younger than his age. His coal black hair, thick and wavy like his father's, accented the forest green eyes, like his mother's. He easily stood four inches over the heads of the tallest marksman, but didn't press his size and height to advantage or intimidation.

The range was well constructed at about four hundred yards deep and fifty yards wide. To the rear and left and right sides, there were thick, planked walls with earth built up to their full ten-foot height to prevent a stray ball or bullet from ricocheting and causing damage or injury. The walls also partially sheltered the range from wind. However, the walls also acted as a windbreak that could cause a squirrely wind that can be difficult to factor at longer range. There was a wind flag placed in each of the target areas to help the marksmen adjust for accuracy.

Each marksman went directly to their station. Each station consisted of a mat to lie on and a tripod on which to rest and balance the Spencer's long barrel and a cartridge box. They were marked one through ten on the cedar posts that supported the protective roof. The stations were paced five yards apart. Each station had its own target downrange that was a sand-filled canvas body-shaped form with a head, torso and legs. The head and body had separate target paper with five circles, the bull's eye center circle being four inches and solid black. The head target was about six inches' square while the torso target was twelve inches' square.

"Mr. deBláca, why don't you start in reverse order. You must understand, the station numbers indicate the proficiency of the marksman," Colonel Hass stated, "the best marksman being in position number one. It is an honor to be the best and each marksman strives to improve his standing to get there, and then, to stay there."

"As you wish, Colonel".

"Corporal Sweets, please ready your firearm and proceed with your best effort to the one-hundred-yard target," the Colonel commanded.

Corporal Sweets, following his orders with efficiency, lay on his mat, rested the Spencer on the tripod, adjusted his rear sight for one hundred yards, levered a cartridge, and slowed his breathing. He moved his finger from the trigger guard to the trigger, adjusted the sides of his feet flat on the mat and took a deep breath, sighted the target, exhaling slowly. When he had fully exhaled and sighted the bull's eye carefully, he gently pulled back on the trigger.

Colonel Haas, using his folding telescope, announced, "Torso target hit outside the fifth circle at six o'clock."

Corporal Sweets showed signs of relief in his face that he hit the target, although he acted as if he was disappointed that it wasn't a center hit.

"Mr. deBláca, would you please assume the temporary responsibility of Corporal Sweets' firearm and proceed with your best effort?"

Liam approached the corporal and was presented with the Spencer. Knowing where the bullet hit the target and looking at the placement of the rear sight gave him the needed knowledge. He correctly assumed Corporal Sweets was a competent marksman. To the surprise of the marksman team, Liam did not use the tripod and did not lie on the mat. Instead, he shouldered the Spencer, standing in the proper firing position, and levered a cartridge into the breach. Taking aim and looking at the wind flags, he stopped and adjusted the rear sight. Taking aim once again and moving his finger from the trigger guard to the trigger, he fired.

Colonel Haas, again using his folding telescope, announced, "Torso target hit inside the bull's eye."

The entire marksman team stared in disbelief. They assumed the firearm was at fault and now they had been proved wrong. They now knew that they were the problem. Liam recognized that this could be demotivating, and not wanting to do this from station nine all the way to one made a suggestion.

"Gentlemen, this Spencer is the finest carbine available today. I was able to accomplish this level of accuracy not because I am better than you, because surely I am not. It is because I know something that you do not and I am here to share that knowledge. One more demonstration if you please, Colonel. Let me go directly to station number one and use the four-hundred-yard target. This will help prove the solution to the accuracy problem." Liam walked briskly to station number one with the Colonel struggling to keep pace behind him. All eyes were on the pair as they covered the forty-five yards to the first station. The temperature was still cold enough to see their breath crystalize as they exhaled and the walk's pace was evidently having its impact on the older Colonel.

The colonel, after catching his breath, was the first to speak upon arriving at station number one. "Sergeant Flannigan, please ready your firearm and proceed with your best effort using the four-hundred-yard torso target."

As the marksman team encircled the station, Sergeant Flannigan repeated precisely the same routine demonstrated by Corporal Sweets. When he pulled the trigger, all eyes went immediately to Colonel Haas for confirmation of the shot. The Sergeant was the best shot of all on the team.

Colonel Haas, again using his folding telescope, announced, "Torso target missed." The team, almost in unison, groaned and one member quietly muttered, "That can't be."

Liam walked over to the sergeant and said, "Sergeant Flannigan, your next shot will be a target hit, I assure you, all of you. Your fundamentals are perfect. Only one thing is keeping you from hitting the four-hundred-yard head bull's eye, and that one thing is this: You think you are shooting with percussion cap and projectile, and you are intuitively adjusting for distance with that thought. We must remember, the muzzle velocity of the Spencer is far greater, meaning the bullet is moving much faster. But, more important is the projectile's shape. It is conical and has up to five times less wind friction. And the striations within the barrel are causing the bullet to spin. This is what that means." Liam knelt, pulled the mat to the side and drew with his finger in the sand that filled the floor of each of the shooting stations. First he drew a half oval and then what was almost a straight line.

Pointing to the oval, Liam explained, "With the ball you sight for a trajectory like this half oval. It is similar to throwing a rock at a distant target. But with that Spencer round, you sight for a trajectory like this small arc. Sergeant Flannigan, may I adjust your rear sight and request you take another shot at the four-hundred-yard torso? Also, remember that the conical shape of the bullet and its higher velocity means it is less affected by wind." Liam, having adjusted the rear site for the sergeant, handed him the Spencer with the muzzle facing the blue cloudless sky. He held it as the sergeant reached to take the rifle, their eyes locking; Liam gave a brief reassuring nod and released the rifle stock.

The marksman team crowded the station and the Colonel asked them to step back. Everyone was as anxious as they were intrigued. Everyone, that is, except Liam. Liam was confident that the sergeant would have a good showing.

Sergeant Flannigan replaced his mat, covering Liam's diagram in the sand, and lay in the shooter's position. He repeated the same ritual having committed it to muscle and mind memory long ago. His finger now on the trigger and completing an exhale, he fired.

Colonel Haas, again used his folding telescope, focused on the four-hundred-yard target and announced, "Torso target hit, second ring and very close to the bull's eye." The marksman team cheered and threw their hats in the air. The sergeant stood slowly, eyes again locking on Liam's, and offered his hand which Liam gladly accepted. Shaking, they both smiled and laughed a little.

"Sergeant, I think you can make those adjustments for the rest of the team without my help, yes?"

"Yes, sir, and if I can return the favor at any time, you send for me. A question, if you don't mind, are you as competent with a hand gun?" The sergeant didn't wait for a response. He removed his revolver and handed it to Liam, butt first.

Liam, smiled and accepted the challenge, walked into the station, chose the twenty-five-yard target, and fanned off five rounds in a few short seconds.

Colonel Haas, for the last time today, used his folding telescope, focusing on the twenty-five-yard target and announced, "Torso target hit, all five rounds in the bull's eye, grouped in a perfect circle."

There was complete silence from the team. Hitting a target at twenty-five yards with a pistol was a real challenge, but five direct hits in a matter of seconds was beyond their comprehension. The Colonel simply smiled a knowing smile as Liam thanked them for the attention, turned, and walked from the range.

The following months passed with Liam working at the Black Arms Company both as the legal department director as well as assisting in the design of custom firearms. He could not recall being happier, ever. Being with his father, and still learning a few new techniques and well-kept secrets continued their bonding, father and son, inseparable. They walked together to the Arms every morning, worked side by side, never happier or more fulfilled.

He designed and built his personal firearms. His favorite was a six shot double action .44 caliber pistol with a top-break for easy replacement of an empty cylinder with a fully loaded cylinder. He built two as a matched pair and had the saddlery build a customized black leather holster notched deeper than normal in the front for a quicker draw. Liam opted not to nickel plate the weapon because it would reflect light and could be easily seen. He opted instead to have it blued and dark. It had an eight-inch barrel for improved accuracy with one pinched sight and the handle grips made of dark bull horn. These pistols he carried in the leather holster, butt rear facing for a quick draw.

Liam also carried a custom made five shot double action .38 caliber top-break with a three-inch barrel in a shoulder holster. The shoulder holster was designed to carry the pistol near his heart, butt down and to the right for easy access. Where the .44s were not worn regularly, the .38 was on his person every waking moment, hidden from sight when wearing a coat or vest.

For hunting, Liam designed a rifle that was very similar to the Henry, designed by Benjamin Tyler Henry and build by Oliver Winchester. The improvements Liam designed included a loading chamber on the right hand side of the receiver, a barrel that was three inches longer that helped increase the capacity to twenty-two .44 caliber rounds. What impressed his father most was that these weapons were designed and crafted for functionality and reliability, not for show.

Liam was born to the woodlands and at the young age of eight in Ireland began to live on the range with small herd of cattle they raised for additional living money as well as food, moving them daily to better graze and hiding them from poachers, especially the British Army. His experience as a woodsman was exhibited in the firearm designs for functionality.

It was now late 1859, and tensions were building between several southern states and the northern states over the issue of slavery. The elections would be held next year, and citizens were becoming more vocal about their views on slavery. It was not uncommon for the vocal expression to turn violent and Liam continued to carry his custom .38 in his concealed shoulder holster. He never left home without it.

It was well known that the deBláca family was firmly anti-slavery. They didn't press their views on others, but didn't back away from a spirited debate on the subject either. Liam worried about his mother walking to and from the schoolhouse six blocks away. He pleaded for her to carry a derringer, just in case. But, Grace firmly rejected the idea. She would not walk armed anywhere. Period. It stood in stark contrast to the family business, but to Grace firearms were the providence of men not a female schoolteacher.

Arriving back at the Willard residence, Liam paused before opening the door, hearing voices inside. The voices of his father and mother he recognized with ease, but the other voice, deeply toned and educated, was only familiar. He knew he had heard it before but even with intense thought, he could not associate a name or face to it. Their voices hinted at a casual acquaintance, maybe a bit more. They were discussing the slavery issue and seemed to be of one mind. Grace was equally involved. He opened the door and entered his home.

"Welcome home son," Shaun boomed. "Come in and say hello to Mr. Jeremiah Black. He will be appointed Attorney General should the Republicans win the election, and I believe they will." Liam walked directly to Mr. Black and took his extended hand.

"I am very pleased to meet you, Mr. Black". Grace approached him, giving him a mother's loving embrace and a peck on the cheek, then motioning for him to give her his coat as she handed him a glass of wine.

"I know something of your background, Mr. deBláca. And, I am so pleased to finally make your acquaintance." Jeremiah was well into his fifties, with a full head of curly gray hair, trim and unusually fit for a man of his age.

"Please, call me Liam."

"Only if you address me as Jeremiah."

"If you insist sir."

Martha summoned the group to the dining room where she had just placed the roast. She was proud of the presentation, the steaming large roast of beef surrounded by pan roasted carrots, potatoes and greens. She paused by the dining room table with a beaming smile, waiting for comments from the man of the house. But Grace was the first to comment, "Martha, you have outdone yourself tonight! It looks smashing and smells even better. Simply splendid, Martha. Thank you so much." And Martha beamed a beautiful smile, displaying perfect white teeth contrasting her dark chocolate cheeks.

The fire roaring in the brick and fieldstone fireplace warmed the room and added to the ambience. The cedar cast off scents that enhanced the aromas from the roast and flooded the dining room walls with colors of cranberry and sky blue.

Once everyone was seated Jeremiah broke the silence. "Liam, you may have heard your father, mother and I discussing the politics surrounding the slavery issue as you came in. I know you are firmly against slavery as well but I would like to hear your own views. Would you mind?"

Liam sensed, accurately, that there was a motive at play here, what motive he didn't yet know, however, so he took his time formulating the response to Jeremiah's query. What seemed like several minutes was in reality only a minute, no more than two before responding. Again, as it had many times before, his attorney's mind engaged. He was capable of lightning-quick action when the situation called for it, but this situation required organized and insightful thought.

"Jeremiah, you are most likely aware that my family immigrated from Ireland in 1848. But, you may not be aware of the severity of the British rule from which we fled. In many ways the British treated the Irelanders as their slaves in addition to persecution and the removal of our religious freedom and civil rights. We know from firsthand experience the impact of slavery on a person and on their families. I believe that God created all people equally. All people have hearts and minds and dreams. All people have the right to be free to pray as they wish, work as they wish and fulfill their dreams as they wish. All people breathe the same air and drink the same water. I believe that no person has the right to subjugate another," Liam responded with genuine passion.

Liam went on, "I also believe that the southern states that embrace slavery damage all of society, not only those pressed into slavery, but those that do the pressing. The slavers don't know the value of a hard day's work, which results in a discontented, disconnected and morally bankrupt middle and upper class. It also skews the economy to unrealistic profits as a result of the lack of labor costs that misrepresents the American dream of success. Jeremiah, the Constitution of the United States reads 'we the people' not we the white people or we the red people or we the black people. If I had the ability to wipe the curse of slavery off the face of this earth, I would do so this very second!"

Shaun, Grace and Jeremiah let Liam's statements and his passion seep into their minds. Martha had listened to every word and came over his right shoulder to top off his wine. As she bent over to fill the glass a tear fell from her cheek to Liam's arm. Having filled the glass, she hugged his shoulder, giving him a few loving pats. Martha was a proud of Liam as she was of her own son, Joel.

Jeremiah, nodding his confirmation, looked to Shaun and Grace and asked, "May I?"

They both nodded in unison and Liam sensed he was now to hear the motive that had eluded him so far this evening.

"Liam, what do you know about the United States Marshals Service?"

"Not that much, only what I learned in law school. I know it is the oldest law enforcement agency within the United States. I know that it falls under the supervision of the Attorney General and takes direction from the courts. But that is about all."

"You are accurate, but allow me to fill in a few more important details. The agency was formed by the Judiciary Act of September 24, 1789. The U.S. Marshals are responsible for the protection of court officers and buildings, under the operation of the judiciary, as you implied. The service also assists with court security and prisoner transport, serves arrest warrants, and seeks fugitives. The Marshals Service is part of the executive branch of the United States government, and today is the enforcement arm of the federal courts."

Jeremiah paused and sipped his wine and then added, "If Abraham Lincoln is elected as President, I will be appointed as the Attorney General, and I would like you to head the United States Marshals Service. Your background in law, your moral compass and intelligence, and your knowledge of firearms will congeal to make you the perfect selection. The question I have for you is this: are you interested?"

The quiet was deafening. The Grandfather clock seemed to be shooting bullets for every second's tic. Pops and crackles sounded from the fire. No person spoke. No one was eating. The candle flames danced. Martha stood in the kitchen doorway, clutching her apron in anticipation of Liam's response. Everyone was focused on the young man from Ireland. And the young man was stunned, struggling to search the depths of his mind for an answer. He was an Irish immigrant who had graduated from George Washington University, and was now offered a very senior position within the United States government. He was stunned but, as was his practice, maintained his composure.

"I am very interested, yes, very interested. I can't express my thanks adequately for your consideration, Jeremiah," he said softly, obviously still turning the offer over in his mind. "Jeremiah, what company does the government work with for the US Marshals firearms?"

Jeremiah chuckled and said, "I see where you are going, Liam, and good for you. You will need to contract with a company that provides the type and quality of firearms needed and at a competitive price. If the Black Firearms Company can compete, as I suspect they can, they can be your provider of choice. It will be your decision and your budget to manage."

"Then, Mr. Attorney General, I accept your offer… contingent, of course, that Mr. Lincoln and the Republican Party take the White House and that I have the blessings of my father and mother."

.

CHAPTER TWO

1860

The Pony Express begins its first run from Saint Joseph, Missouri to Sacramento, California, traveling through Indian Territory.

Abraham Lincoln is selected as the U.S. presidential candidate for the Republican Party.

U.S. presidential election: Abraham Lincoln beats John C. Breckinridge, Stephen A. Douglas, and John Bell and is elected as the 16th President of the United States, the first Republican to hold that office.

Texas Rangers defeat a band of Comanche's at the Battle of Pease River; Cynthia Ann Parker is recaptured and returned to her family after 24 years.

South Carolina becomes the first state to secede from the United States.

The American South has an estimated 4 million slaves.

Abraham Lincoln was raised in a poor family on the western frontier. Even though Lincoln was mostly self-educated, he became a successful country lawyer, a Whig Party leader, an Illinois state legislator during the 1830s, and a one-term member of the United States House of Representatives during the 1840s.

Lincoln participated in a series of debates in 1858 that gave national visibility to his steadfast opposition to the expansion of slavery, his quick mind and his ability to communicate with all walks of society. He secured the Republican Party presidential nomination in 1860 and with almost no support in the South due to his firm position against slavery, Lincoln swept the North and was elected president in 1860.

However, his election caused seven southern slave states to declare their secession from the Union and form the Confederacy. The departure of the Southerners gave Lincoln's Republican Party firm control of Congress; however, no formula for compromise or reconciliation with the southern states was found. Lincoln explained in his second inaugural address:

"Both parties deprecated war, but one of them would make war rather than let the Nation survive, and the other would accept war rather than let it perish, and the war came."

Jeremiah Black was indeed appointed Attorney General and one of his first appointments was Liam deBláca as the Director of the United States Marshals Service. Liam was just twenty-five years of age and one of the youngest currently in the Marshals Service.

Liam's appointment earned the attention of all the major newspapers. Many of the papers played up his law and firearms experience as well as his and his immigrant family's firm opposition to slavery. It seemed that he was a direct Abraham Lincoln protégé. It was common for him, while in route to his new office, to be congratulated by those who were also against slavery as well as to be harassed by those that supported slavery.

At times the harassment went beyond shouting comments to outright physical challenges. Liam's six-foot-two and nearly two-hundred-pound stature was intimidating to the average person, and as a result the challengers typically numbered two or three, or even four at a time. He was able to overcome the challengers so far but he sensed in his soul that could change at any time.

In Liam's absence, Grace had begun to fill in for some of the bookkeeping and contract analysis at the Black Firearms Company. Liam was comforted that his mother was with his father and the workers at the arms company with the tensions rapidly rising and the prospect of war on the horizon. The streets and pubs were electric with discourse and the local police were stretched beyond the capacity of maintaining safety. The jails were overpopulated with prisoners that had been charged with assault, civil disobedience, and murder. The United States was unwinding from within and President Abraham Lincoln, the congress, and senate were challenged to stalemate.

Martha and her young son Joel had taken up residence at the deBláca's for safety. They shared the single guest bedroom. The evening supper conversation was saturated with the slavery and southern states' secession issues. Shaun and Grace were divided on Shaun's suggestion that the family move to the Philadelphia area to gain distance from the apex of trouble. It had been the only time that Liam had witnessed sharp words between his father and mother. They both recognized the severity of the problem,

Shaun thinking of the family's safety and Grace thinking that it would appear they were abandoning their adopted country. Liam privately agreed with his father's need for caution but recognized his mother's steel. Like the congress and senate, the deBláca family was at a stalemate.

Martha had placed a breakfast of fried eggs, bacon, diced potatoes and freshly baked bread on the dining room table. Joel was sitting at the table when Shaun and Grace entered the room.

"Good morning, Joel, Martha," Grace said as she went to her chair. "The bread smells heavenly, Martha!"

"Would you like coffee now, ma'am?"

Shaun was the first to respond "Yes, that would be just what the body needs, Martha."

"Good morning everyone," Liam announced as he walked into the dining room. He was wearing his coat as if ready to leave for the Marshals Service office immediately.

"Liam, are you not enjoying breakfast with us this morning?" Shaun asked.

"Sorry, Father, I need to be at the service early this morning. We are swearing in fifteen new deputy marshals. With the extensive discontent, the courts are overloaded and there are several outlaws that have escaped to the western territories that need to be brought to justice. If war breaks out, we will have more than we can handle." Then, pausing and looking at Joel, "Joel, if you keep up with your studies, I will hire you when you graduate. And, I will make this promise — if you keep your grades up in school, I will fund your university education. We need strong and educated young men and you have the talent. I have seen it!"

Joel was stunned into speechlessness but beamed with appreciation, as did Martha.

***

Liam exited the Willard briskly, walking to the post where his horse was tied earlier by the Willard's stable master. He had begun riding as it was the most convenient way to get around to the many government buildings during the working day, and his horse enjoyed being out of the stable. He had been an accomplished rider and woodsman since as a boy in Ireland riding the challenging hills and valleys. It had broken his heart to leave his Creena in Ireland, but he knew the horse could not handle the long ocean voyage to America. He had given Creena to his best childhood friend, knowing he would be well cared for.

Releasing the reins from the post, Liam stepped to the left of his horse and placed his left foot into the stirrup and swung effortlessly into the western saddle. The horse was enormous at over seventeen hands, broad in the shoulders and coal black with the exception of four white stockings. He had named this horse Creena, as well — Irish for love, after his love left in Ireland.

As Creena broke into a trot, Liam noticed a large group that spanned the Pennsylvania Avenue, walking in his direction. They were an aggressive mob, sporting black boards with bold white lettering making clear their support for slavery. Screams from the protestors seemed amplified by the drums and sticks banging against the boarded signs. Pedestrians in the street were pushed aside while carriages and horsemen turned in haste and sprinted away from the oncoming mob. A policeman trying to aid a young lady's escape from the protesting mobs path was, himself, now under attack. Thankfully, the young lady was now safe. Liam pressed heels into Creena's flanks, galloping to the policeman's aid. Some in the mob gave way to the huge horse but when he slowed to pull the policeman up onto Creena's back, several tried to pull him down to the ground. It was then he recognized the man in western-style clothing and remembered he had been the leader of the confrontation months ago.

The leader grabbed for Creena's reins and pulled hard causing the bit to dig into the horse's gums. Creena whined and head butted the leader, causing him to fall on his back, stunned. That gave Liam a few seconds to pull the policeman up onto Creena and begin turning out of the mob. The leader, back on his feet, was again grabbing for Creena's reins. Liam, recognizing that he needed to get free of this mob quickly, pulled his .38 pistol from the shoulder holster, aimed directly at the leader's head and pulled the hammer back.

The mob leader stood about five feet ten with broad shoulders and intense dark eyes. His deep-set black eyes were wild, darting from right to left and screaming with hate, insanity. His chiseled, unshaven face was creased with weathered lines, and the darkened skin suggested years of sun exposure. Greasy dark brown hair protruded from his western-style hat and there was graying evident in his handlebar mustache. He was snarling and baring his tobacco stained and uneven teeth as if in extreme pain.

Liam screamed, "Let go of the reins, now!" No one in the vicinity doubted his intention to pull the trigger if needed.

"You are going to regret pulling that gun on me," the leader responded. His face was contorted into an insane frenzy and his eyes were bulging, as if trying to escape their sockets. As he let the reins fall from his grip, he threatened, "Remember this face deBláca, you'll be seeing me again."

Liam put heels into Creena's flanks once again and galloped away from the leader and the rest of the mob, carrying the policeman to safety. How did that crazy man know my name, he wondered?

Well away from the mob, Liam slowed and then stopped to let the policeman down.

"Sir, thank you. They surely would have killed me if you hadn't come to my aid. I am in your debt. May I ask your name, sir?"

"My name is Liam deBláca. I am the Director of the U.S. Marshals Service. And it is I who thank you for coming to the aid of that young lady without thought to your personal risk. Good job, Officer."

"That man grabbing for your horse is Van Cooper, a real hard case, so watch your back. They will be calling in the Marines to disband that mob soon if they haven't already," the policemen said. As if on cue, shots could be heard coming from the direction of where the mob had progressed, accompanied by the screams of frightened people. "I fear that war will be upon us very soon."

"Yes, I am afraid you may be right. I'll be off now," Liam said, as he turned Creena and trotted toward his office.

Later that afternoon, Van Cooper, carrying a large carpetbag and his black board with white letters, walked toward the Black Arms Company entrance. Still insanely angry over the confrontation with Liam that morning and the humiliation of failure witnessed by his men, his only thought was revenge. He despised the rich for no other reason than he didn't have what they had. He didn't have a permanent home, didn't have a leisurely life, and didn't have anything but the clothes on his back. His assets included a very strong horse, his Remington six-gun, and his Henry rifle. He carried only the Remington forty-four with him now, angry with himself that he had left the Remington in his rented room this morning.

Leaving the sign resting against an oak tree outside, Van entered through the front door of the Black Arms Company and walked to the counter that separated the machine works from the store area.

In the machine works, several laborers dressed in rough work clothes covered with shop aprons were working with a few gunsmiths dressed in black broadcloth suits. There was the distinctive odor of gun oil in the air as well as the sounds of machines. The store area featured several wood-framed glass cases with a variety of weaponry on display. Off to the left were several desks, all but one occupied by men with their heads down writing in ledgers or reading various documents. At the other desk sat an attractive middle aged woman that Van recognized as Mrs. Grace deBláca. She looked up as Van entered and offered a brief smile before lowering her head and returning to her work.

Van placed the large carpet bag on the floor and pushed it against the counter where it wouldn't be seen by anyone on the other side of the counter. It was Shaun deBláca that left his desk and approached the counter.

"Good afternoon, sir. How may I be of assistance?"

"A box of forty-four shells," Van responded briskly.

Reaching underneath the counter to a recessed shelf, Shaun pulled a new box of shells and placed them on the counter. "That will be one dollar fifty."

Van, reaching into his denim pocket, pulled out a small group of coins and counted out the exact change on the counter, "Obliged."

Shaun sensed that the man standing on the other side of the counter was agitated, perhaps had been drinking. Something wasn't quite right but he couldn't place it. "May I be of additional assistance, sir?"

From the contorted face, Van snapped, "No." Then he began to turn as if heading to the door and Shaun turned as well, heading back to his desk. In that brief moment Van stopped, squatted down behind the counter, struck the

Lucifer he had held in his palm, and lit the short fuse that extended from the large carpet bag. Seeing the fuse lit and hearing it hiss, he double-timed to the door, leaving the black board with white letters resting against the oak intentionally and sprinted down the street.

Liam visited the Attorney General's office, as he frequently did before the day ended. The office was a beehive of activity caused by all the legal actions relating to the separation of the southern states. There were legal actions against each of the seven states comprising the Confederacy, and it was the administration's distant hope that they could prevent war. Although the odds were heavily against the prevention of war through legal action, Lincoln worked tirelessly on all options.

"Jeremiah, this city is a powder keg and the fuse is lit," Liam said. Liam was seated in a horsehair stuffed chair covered in supple brown leather in front of the large oak desk behind which the Attorney General sat.

"Yes and the fuse is burning down quickly. You took quite a risk today, Liam. You could have been hurt or killed by that mob." Jeremiah then drew heavily on his cigar and exhaled a plume of blue smoke that swirled to the ceiling.

Liam was just about to respond to Jeremiah when his thoughts were interrupted by an extraordinary loud explosion. This was no simple cannon fire, that much was certain to them both. He could tell the explosion wasn't very close, so it is likely not within the government grounds. It appeared to come from the direction of the inner city of Washington. A feeling of dread began to consume his body. He couldn't explain why his arms and legs were trembling but he knew he must get to the location of the explosion.

"Jeremiah, I need to go. Something isn't right!"

"Please be careful!"

Liam nearly sprinted from the office and down the hall to the rear exit where he had picketed Creena on some graze. Looking to the sky, he immediately saw the dense black smoke coming from deep within Washington proper. As he tightened the cinch spanning Creena's belly and looked up, it appeared to be coming from the general area of the Willard Hotel. He released the picket rope and dropped it to the ground in one motion as he swung into the saddle. Creena sensed and then responded to the urgency, and horse with rider was at full gallop toward the city.

Creena sensed his master's increased urgency and invested his immense strength and speed to surge past carriages, pedestrians and other horsemen. He could hear the first brigade's bells and knew they were on the way, or at the explosion site already. Liam's anxiety grew with every minute of travel. The closer he came to the origin of the black smoke, the more the dread enveloped him.

He pulled the reins, stopping Creena abruptly as he saw the fire billowing out of the shattered front windows of the Black Arms Company. He was overcome and in shock. Coming quickly to his senses, he heeled Creena again rushing to the building, or what was left of it, in the hope of saving lives. The fire brigade was already there and the firefighters were hopelessly standing outside as the flames and heat were overpowering and life threatening. Firemen pumped water into the hoses as long tongues of flame stabbed through the broken glass of the front windows. The door itself was missing, having been blown clean off its hinges. Soot was slowly covering the Black Arms Company hanging sign above the door. There was no sign of life, no possibility of life within the crumbling walls of his family's business.

Liam jumped from Creena without tying his reins and ran to the front door, but was repelled by flames and heat. Several of the firefighters tried to restrain him for his own safety. He fought them off while screaming for his father and mother, even while knowing — yet not accepting — that no one could survive such a blast and fire. He fell to his knees holding his face as the tears flowed from his eyes through his hands to the ground. He couldn't move. He was frozen in time. Thoughts of his childhood flooded his conscious. He was paralyzed, overwhelmed, lost.

The fire was out, the cold blackness of night upon him, yet he was still on his knees. In his mind, Liam was reliving the long voyage from Ireland, the creation of the Black Arms Company, the many meals and conversations shared with his father and mother, all pleasant memories subconsciously keeping his mind intact to be able to face the worst tragedy of his life. He slowly became aware of what was happening around him when Jeremiah's voice penetrated his consciousness as if it were miles away, just barely audible at first.

"Liam, Liam,… can you hear me?" Jeremiah was squatting beside him, cradling his shoulders. He became aware that someone had placed a wool blanket over his back. The sight of the burned-out husk of a building where he had worked alongside of his father, where his mother worked to keep the accounting records current and accurate, was terrifying. Small puffs of smoke puffed out from the cavity like fleeing ghosts and water dripped from the few remaining pieces of brick walls. Liam was slowly beginning to realize, but could not yet accept, that all was lost.

"Liam, I am here with you. Can you hear me?"

Slowly the words began to form within his mind and traveled ever so slowly to his lips. He was covered in soot and grime. His throat was raspy from the dryness of the flames, smoke and heat, parched. Finally, Liam responded in a whisper, "Yes, I can hear you, Jeremiah."

"Liam, I am so sorry. This is a terrible accident. The firefighters suspect a keg of black powder must have ignited. There was only one survivor."

That last comment brought Liam to full alert. "One survivor? Who? Who was it Jeremiah?"

"Liam," Jeremiah said softly while caressing Liam's shoulders. "I am sorry, your father and mother are gone. The survivor was a gunsmith that was standing at the rear door when the powder keg exploded. He was blown outside the building and only has minor cuts. He will be okay. He's here, waiting to talk with you. It is Hank. You remember him, don't you?"

"Yes, a good man. Where is he?" Liam's voice raspy and dry.

"Hank, Liam would like to talk with you." Jeremiah said while helping Liam to his unsteady feet.

Liam extended his hand as Hank approached from his right. Hank noticed he was a bit shaky and when they grasped each other's hand, he could feel it trembling a bit. It was cold and lacked its typical strength.

"Mr. deBláca, my deepest sympathies for the loss of your father and mother, and the loss of the eighteen other workers. This is a tragedy, sir, a tragedy." Hank was recovering from shock as well and looked intermittently from Liam to the burned-out building. "But this was no powder keg, sir. We were not working with cartridges this afternoon. Not at all. This was somethin' else sir. Somethin' else."

"What do you mean Hank, something else?" Liam's mind slowly engaging.

"Sir, just don't know. The explosion happened at the counter. It was the last thing I could see as I was blown clear out da' back door. That counter being torn up. Somethin' was in that counter!"

Liam then stood and began walking to the front door, stutter-stepping, appearing half dead, unsteady. He walked into the space through where the door once was, stepping on broken glass, burned firearms, and bits of charred wood. All that remained upright were the brick side walls that had prevented the fire from spreading to the adjoining buildings and some of the machinery. The counter, desks, and workbenches were all ashes now. The machines were toppled with only the iron and steel pieces remaining. It smelled of char, smoke and burned flesh. And, it smelled of acrid black powder. The firefighters had removed the human remains but the unmistakable horrible stench of burned flesh and hair remained.

Near where the counter would have been, Liam's eyes were drawn to a black circular object. He stared at it for a moment and then turned away. Something inside asked him to turn his gaze back and he bent down to touch the object. Touching it left the soot on his finger and a shiny gold color emerged. His heart began to race as he picked up the gold watch that his father was given by his father, and hugged it longingly to his chest realizing that his father's body must have shielded it from damage. Family. Heritage. *"And someday I will give it to you and you will in turn give it to your son."*

Liam had no tears left. He was near collapse from physical and emotional exhaustion and needed to escape this place. Turning, he noticed a black board sign with white lettering leaning against the tree by the street and in that instant he knew what had happened. He knew who was responsible for this carnage. He knew who had killed, no *murdered* his father, mother, and the eighteen loyal employees of the Black Arms Company. He knew and he vowed right there as he looked upon that sign that he would find Van Cooper and avenge this tragedy. Van Cooper would die a painful death, and he would watch the life drain from his ugly insane eyes.

It was a gray morning, cold, cloudless, and raw, and it aligned Liam's temperament.

Liam felt as if he didn't belong as he walked through the Marshals Service building entrance. It had been nearly two weeks since he had buried the remains of his father and mother. He had insisted that the eighteen employees be included in a single service, thinking that the surviving mothers and children could be of support to one another, and he had paid all of the costs. He also provided a stipend to each family to help them cope with the loss of their husbands and fathers.

As he entered the building he was confident he had made the right decision. The connection had been lost, fallen through the large hole in his broken heart. Liam seethed with anger. It flooded his every thought. It lived in his dreams. He was never alone without his need to find Van Cooper. Once found, he was unsure that his deep and unrelenting respect for the law would prevent him from extracting vengeance, painful vengeance, slow and painful vengeance.

Liam walked to the office of his boss, friend and confidant, Jeremiah Black, Attorney General of the United States. He found Jeremiah seated, thoroughly engrossed in several documents blanketing his mammoth oak desk. So engrossed, Jeremiah hadn't realized that Liam had entered his office and seated himself in the supple horsehair leather chair that fronted his desk.

"Good morning, Jeremiah."

"Oh my God, I didn't hear you enter! I am so happy to see you Liam. Welcome back, son." Jeremiah stacked his papers as he rose and quickly stepped around the desk to Liam. His arms were outstretched, signaling to Liam to rise and accept his embrace. The men embracing and the pats on the backs filled the office with love and respect.

Standing face to face, Jeremiah asked, "Liam, how are Martha and her son Joel adjusting?"

"That is part of the reason for my visit this morning, Jeremiah. They are slowly coming to accept the loss of my father and mother. As you know, they are like family, all the family I have left. I have asked Martha to move into the master bedroom so that Joel can make her old room his own. He is getting older and should have more privacy."

"But son, you should move into the master bedroom. You are the master of the house now."

"Jeremiah, the other and more important reason for my visit is to resign my post with the Marshals Service effective today." Liam was not emotional, but monotone in voice, the dead seriousness and determination evident in his eyes.

Jeremiah was not surprised. In fact, he had suspected this would be precisely how Liam would respond. He had been preparing over the last two weeks for just this discussion.

"Liam, I will ask you one question, and ask it as a friend, a friend to you and your father and mother. But, this question does not come from this office. Therefore, you will be able to answer this question honestly and without hesitation." Jeremiah leaned against his desk, paused, and looked intently into Liam green red-rimmed eyes.

"Liam, is your decision to resign motivated by your need to find Van Cooper?"

Liam didn't flinch. He remained eye locked with Jeremiah. The question penetrated his soul. It was carefully worded. He had used *"find"*, not arrest, not hunt down and kill. It was a question that didn't conflict with his commitment to and respect for the law, and was therefore easy to answer honestly.

"Yes, it has everything to do with my decision. I must find him Jeremiah. His face is imprinted in my consciousness. It haunts my dreams. He is a dangerous man, a man that will be at the forefront of more carnage. I don't know what my life will bring once he is found and brought to justice, but I do know that I will have no life worth living unless and until I do find him. I feel to blame Jeremiah, for the deaths of my father and mother and the eighteen people of Black Arms. I was the one who challenged Cooper and caused him to enact revenge for his humiliation. Jeremiah, surely can you understand?"

A brief smile appeared on Jeremiah's face. Not a smile of happiness, but a smile of recognition and acceptance. He turned from Liam and picked up a document from his desk. Holding the document and now facing Liam, he said, "Liam, I have a proposition for you and I would appreciate that you seriously consider it."

"Of course I will, Jeremiah." Liam said, somewhat intrigued.

"You are probably not aware that your father asked me to mentor you. He wanted me to watch out for you, to keep your best interests in mind. It is because of that and my respect and love for you that not only do I understand what you need to do, I have found a way to help you find that animal, Van Cooper, and bring him to justice. There is a position within the United States Marshals Service, a commission actually, that has not had an appointment since the service began back in 1789. The commission is entitled Chief Inspector. I have activated this commission with your name, reporting directly to me."

Liam was stunned into silence and slowly sat back in the leather chair. His mind was awhirl as he considered the possibilities. He would still be with the Service, but what would be his responsibilities?

"Jeremiah, you obviously have given a great deal of thought to this and I am grateful, very grateful. What are the responsibilities of the Chief Inspector, and how would it help find Van Cooper?"

"Not just Van Cooper, Liam, but it would start with that murdering renegade. You know that there is a lack of coordination between law officials of different states, counties, cities and towns. Nowhere is this problem more pronounced that in the western territories. The Marshals Service is weakly staffed there, as you have pointed out many times. The lack of budget has prevented direct oversight of your Marshals in the field and, as a result, lawlessness abounds. Marshals are empowered within their state' districts, and outlaws knowing this cross state lines to wreak havoc — rob, rape, murder — and then cross back into another state. The Chief Inspector has no such limitation and is empowered by the full might of the United States government. This is a dangerous undertaking, Liam, make no mistake about it. But, you are the perfect candidate. You not only know the law, but believe in it to your very core. You can ride better than most, are a competent woodsman, and are the best man with firearms in the entire eastern states. And you are driven, you have a just cause. I want you to find Van Cooper first, see to it that he is brought to justice, and then find others like him, bringing them to justice. When you are in a state, the marshals of those districts are at your command. You can start tomorrow. The decision is yours, Liam."

The grandfather clock standing on the right wall of Jeremiah's office clicked the seconds by. It was the only sound in the office for several minutes as Liam considered each variable. He would be employed, although that was not a major consideration as the insurance settlement and his family's small fortune would keep him in comfort for the rest of his life, as well as Martha and her son Joel. He would be enforcing the law that he so richly believed in, and in the process helping the territories become a safer place to live. That would encourage western migration, increasing the number and size of settlements. All of the variables were positive. He could think of no downside and actually found a sense of excitement growing within.

"Jeremiah, I am in your debt once again. Thank you, sir. Yes, yes indeed. I accept your proposal. It is the first good thing to happen to me since…" His eyes were distant and unfocused, deep in thought. "Are you sure that I won't be needed here with the outbreak of war so imminent?"

Jeremiah opened a wooden mahogany box that was resting on the surface of his desk, reached in with his left hand, and palmed an item. Then, turning to Liam and extending his right hand, he answered, "No Liam. You can best serve your country by focusing westward. Congratulations, Mr. Chief Inspector. Let me pin this star on your chest and induct you properly." The five pointed star was engraved with United States Marshal on the top rim and Chief Inspector on the bottom rim.

"Do you agree to uphold the laws of the United States of America to the best of your ability?"

"I do."

"Well then Mr. Chief Inspector, I have something else for you. Over the last ten days I took the liberty of assigning a few of your Marshals here in Washington to investigate the whereabouts of one Mr. Van Cooper. Cooper was being paid by someone in South Carolina to work up the anti-slavery crowds here in Washington. We have determined that he left the city two days after the Black Arms bombing. He was seen boarding the Baltimore and Ohio railroad to Baltimore, where we have tracked him to Parkersburgh, Ohio. We believe he is heading to St. Louis, but we cannot be sure. Here are your tickets for departure on tomorrow's train, and we have made arrangements for Creena in the baggage car. These are documents, signed by me and President Lincoln, who by the way, fully endorses your appointment, to enable you to draw funds as you need them from any bank or U.S. Army fort. There is also a warrant for the arrest of Van Cooper and twenty-five John Doe warrants. I will have wires sent to all Marshals advising them of your appointment and their requirement to support you in any way you see fit. Now, you have much to do in preparation. Wire me periodically with updates."

Then the two men embraced and Jeremiah said, "Son, I will miss you terribly. Please use caution and take care of yourself."

Teary eyed, Liam said, "Jeremiah, you have been like a father to me, and a dear friend to my parents. I will do everything to honor you and them and I will miss you as well. But I will be back. I am more grateful than words can express. Thank you."

CHAPTER THREE

1861

American Civil War: Delaware votes not to secede from the Union. Mississippi becomes the second state to secede from the Union, preceding the American Civil War. Florida secedes from the Union. Alabama secedes from the Union. Georgia secedes from the Union.

Jefferson Davis resigns from the United States Senate.

Louisiana secedes from the Union.

Kansas is admitted as the 34th U.S. state.

Texas secedes from the Union.

Delegates from six seceded states meet at the Montgomery Convention in Montgomery, Alabama.

The Confederate States of America adopts the Provisional Confederate States Constitution.

Jefferson Davis is elected the Provisional President of the Confederate States of America by the Weed Convention at Montgomery, Alabama.

The U.S. House unanimously passes a resolution guaranteeing non-interference with slavery in any state.

In Montgomery, Alabama, Jefferson Davis is inaugurated as the provisional president of the Confederate States of America.

President-elect Abraham Lincoln arrives secretly in Washington after an assassination attempt in Baltimore, Maryland.

Colorado is organized as a United States territory.

Nevada is organized as a United States territory.

President Abraham Lincoln takes office, succeeding James Buchanan.

The Stars and Bars is adopted as the flag of the Confederate States of America.

The Confederate States Constitution is adopted.

The American Civil War begins at Fort Sumter, South Carolina with its surrender to Southern forces.

Missouri's secession from the Union bill is signed by Governor Claiborne Fox Jackson.

Kentucky is accepted into the Confederate States of America.

Liam was comfortably seated in his first class rail car padded seat. The coach seating consisted of wooden straight-back benches, which were very hard on the long distance travelers. However, everyone had to endure the rocking, the endless clacking, steam engine noise, and of course, the thick black soot floating from the engine, seemingly ignoring the winds direction. Still, it was a far better form of transportation compared to stagecoach or horseback, and about eight times as fast.

The trip to Parkersburgh, Ohio on the B&O provided Liam the time for introspection. His thoughts were constantly of his loving parents, Shaun and Grace. He had aged years in the last few weeks, from a partially dependent son to a fully independent man. He would need that independence and self-reliance for what also occupied his thoughts, the capture of Van Cooper, and seeing that justice prevailed. The image of the burned-out husk of what had been the Black Arms Company haunted him, as did the brief memory of the morning he had last seen his parents alive. He had forgone breakfast with his family to arrive at his Marshals office early. He silently berated himself for placing his family behind his official duties.

He could not escape the blame, or perhaps he didn't want the escape. If he had left the Willard five minutes earlier or five minutes later and not had the confrontation with Cooper, his father and mother would be alive today, as would eighteen Black Arms employees. If he had pulled the trigger when he had his .38 pointed at Cooper's head…

Anger stabbed at his heart, an anger that could only be quenched by bringing Van Cooper to justice. But, could he control his anger or would vengeance overwhelm him? He was unsure.

Before leaving, he had arranged for Martha to maintain the Willard residence and provided a stipend to cover her and Joel's monthly living expenses and more. There was a tear-filled goodbye with the only family he had left, and he promised to return as soon as it could be managed.

Each day after breakfast, luncheon, and supper Liam would venture to the baggage car where Creena was stabled. He would stop at the meal service car first to pick up some sugar, an apple, or some oats to spoil his one remaining and trusted love. While there, Liam would curry Creena and massage his neck hoping to make travel more bearable for his mount. Every time the engine stopped for water and the wood or coal fuel needed to heat the water to steam, Liam took Creena out for exercise, sunlight and let him graze.

Liam needed to make a decision before the train arrived in Parkersburgh, Ohio. Would he disembark and travel on horseback on to St. Louis, or consider a stage coach or train? He decided to stay the night and make some inquiries in hopes of finding the trail that Cooper had taken.

Parkersburgh was abuzz with activity. It bordered West Virginia, separated by the mighty Ohio River. As such, the main economic drive for Parkersburgh was trade, mainly serviced by river and rail transportation. A stranger in town was routine.

Two weeks before Liam arrived in Parkersburgh, Van Cooper and his sidekick Dutch had stayed in the Grand Hotel. They both took liberal advantage of the hotel's saloon, winning a new grubstake playing poker with unwitting town folk and river workers. They were completely unaware that Liam would soon be following their trail and felt safe from the law. Van wanted to get to back to his hometown of Dallas, and Dutch had nowhere else to go and readily agreed. With their winnings, they purchased rail tickets to continue on to St. Louis with the plan to take the new St. Louis Texas railroad that branched to Dallas.

"We be needin' more money, Dutch," Van said.

"Yeah, I was thinkin' the same thing. What do you have in mind? Don't think we can milk these townies for much more without them gettin' ideas about our card shark'n'."

"I was thinking about that mercantile with that old pinhead owner and his pretty young daughter. They seem to do a fair bit of business and I saw him putting a stack of cash in the small safe beside his desk. How about you and me payin' them a visit just before closing time the night before we leave?"

Grinning, showing stained teeth, Dutch said, "Yeah, maybe have a bit of fun after we get that money out of the safe."

Disembarking and entering the Parkersburgh train station, Liam, stepped off the train, stretched his stiff limbs, and walked to the counter to ask the stationmaster to recommend the best hotel in town.

"Well sir, seeing how's you look like a man of means, I would suggest the Grand Hotel. It is clean and has the best dining room in the city. If you wish, I will have your luggage sent over."

"I have my horse and saddle in the baggage car and would want him well cared for as well."

"The Grand has its own stable. Mr. Pritchet runs the stable and is a good man. He will take good care of your mount. I'll arrange for that as well."

"Thank you Mr...."

"Mr. Woodsom."

Handing him a silver dollar, Liam said, "You have been most helpful, Mr. Woodsom. Thank you."

Offering his hand, he said, "I am Liam deBláca. One more question, when does the next train leave for St. Louis?"

"That'll be tomorrow. It arrives this evening and leaves at first light. Would you like to book passage?"

"Possibly. I need to make some inquiries first."

"Excuse me for prying, Mr. deBláca, I noticed your badge. Are you a U.S. Marshal?"

"Yes, I am and I am looking for a person that may have come through here. His name is Van Cooper, although he may not be using that name. About five feet ten inches, handlebar mustache, chiseled, with a tanned face. Perhaps you have seen him several weeks ago?"

Removing a folded piece of paper from his inside pocket and unfolding it, Liam said, "This is what he looks like."

Squinting his eyes in a frown that suggested he was thinking deeply, "Gee Marshal, I see so many people coming and going through here, it is hard to remember. Let me think on it and if I remember anything that might be helpful, I will contact you at the Grand. It is on the opposite side of the main street, just two streets to the south."

"I would be much obliged, Mr. Woodsom."

As a matter of courtesy, Liam walked into the town sheriff's office while on the way to the Grand Hotel. The sheriff was seated at a beat-up blond oak desk. His feet were resting on an open desk drawer and was holding a newspaper open, covering his face. As the door closed, he put the paper down on the desk and asked, "What can I do for you, sir?"

"I am Chief Inspector deBláca, of the U.S. Marshals Service. Mind if I ask a few questions?"

"Sheriff Kobb. Sure, have a seat." He drew his feet from the desk and motioned to the chair facing the desk. Kobb looked to be in his fifties, a few pounds' overweight, with a wrinkled face and alert gray eyes. He gave off the impression of realizing he was a bit past his prime but still had some years left.

"I am looking for a man named Van Cooper. About five feet ten inches tall, strong upper body, brown hair, handlebar mustache, slightly graying. He may have come through here within the past few weeks. He is wanted for multiple counts of murder and arson." He showed the same drawing that was made by the U.S. Marshals' artist before he left Washington.

"Warrants?"

"Several."

The sheriff got up and walked to a potbelly stove on which lay a well-used coffee pot. "Coffee?"

"That would be quite welcome."

Kobb handed Liam a cup and then pouring the steamy rich black coffee that looked to have been cooking all day. "It has been pretty quiet here over the last few weeks. And I like quiet, Marshal, like it a lot. The only real incident we have had recently was the murder of the mercantile owner and the assault of his young daughter. That happened three nights ago. I haven't found a single lead, just assumed the persons involved lit out that night for yonder."

"The daughter was assaulted but not killed? Is she still here in town?"

"Yes, sir. Molly Wicks. And she is pretty broken up about it, as you can imagine. You can find her at the mercantile at the south end of this street. But remember Marshal, I am the law in this town, not you."

"Sheriff Kobb, I understand and respect your authority. However, I may not have been clear. I am the Chief Inspector of the United States Marshals Service, not a District Marshal, and am not bound by town, city, county, or state jurisdictions. My authority comes from the President of the United States, personally and directly."

The sheriff, somewhat taken aback, stammered, "Ah, um, then you have my full support, Chief Inspector."

Extending his hand in friendship, Liam said, "Thank you, Sheriff. Would you care to join me?"

As they walked south toward the mercantile, Liam took in the character of Parkersburgh. It was a large town, but not like a city at all. The streets were crude dirt pathways with deep ruts where the rainwater flowed. The long and broad wooden boards piled neatly by the stairs to shops were likely used as a bridge above the mud during heavy rain. People were pointing at him, probably, he surmised, because he was walking with Sheriff Kobb and was obviously new in town. There were small and large rigs moving people and goods in all directions. Odors of dust, horse apples, and axel grease assaulted his nose.

"This here is the mercantile, Marshal."

A bell rang when Liam opened the glass windowed door to the mercantile. The woman behind the counter looked up and smiled briefly at Liam. The smile disappeared when she noticed the sheriff behind Liam's large frame. She had shoulder-length hair the color of corn silk. Her sky blue eyes were alert yet soft and spoke of sadness. Liam sensed this was not the real Molly Wicks but rather the store clerk Molly Wicks, the businesswoman persona that she likely used as her protective shield.

"Molly. This is Chief Inspector deBláca of the U.S. Marshals Service. Would you mind if he asked you a few questions?" the sheriff asked.

Extending her hand to Liam, Molly responded, "It is a pleasure to meet you Mr. deBláca. Have you come from Washington?"

Liam assessed Molly as a poised and educated young woman, perhaps twenty-two or twenty-three years old. There was a bruise on her left cheek that was carefully covered by a light-colored powder. "Yes, I have just arrived on the train. To be direct Miss Wicks, I am hunting a man that may have come through this town in the last few days or weeks. He is wanted for arson and the murder of twenty people."

"I see. And you think the man that robbed and murdered my father might be that same man?"

"It is possible Miss Wicks, and we don't wish to leave any potential lead unanalyzed."

Molly paused considering their presence, before continuing, "Mr. deBláca, may I offer you coffee or tea? Sheriff?"

"That is quite kind of you, Miss Wicks. Tea would be splendid."

"Nothing for me", the sheriff added.

They all sat at a table in the center of the store that appeared to be used for laying out samples. Liam was enjoying the mercantile's rich aroma of leather goods, mixed with the natural smell of oats, tomatoes, bolts of cloth, dried apples, and hard candy. There were no patrons in the store when Molly got up, closed the door, and turned the hanging sign in the window to reflect that the store was closed. No one talked as Liam and Molly sipped their tea.

"Mr. deBláca, your last name is Irish for 'black' if I remember my studies correctly."

"Why, indeed it is. Not many Americans know that. I am very impressed."

"My mother was born in Ireland. Perhaps you have heard of the area, County Kildare."

"Miss Wicks, I know the area well. I was born there myself. How uncanny!"

"Her maiden name was O'Connell."

"There are many, many O'Connell's in County Kildare. It seems we have something in common, Miss Wicks." He didn't pry about the absence of her mother, but privately wondered.

"Mr. deBláca, you are a most unusual man. We both know what you would like to ask me, and we both are aware of how uncomfortable it will be for me. Yet, you have been patient and unusually polite for a man in these parts. Thank you for your sensitivity."

She sighed looking down into her teacup, now being held almost steadily warming both hands, and began her story. "The two men arrived just after my father and I began closing the store about eight o'clock. We were tallying the sales for the day when they knocked on the door. It was locked at that point. They said they were leaving town and needed supplies. My father placed the cash in the safe behind the counter beside his desk, closed and spun the dial, and then went to the door. As soon as he opened the door, the man drew his gun and told my father to back away. They both entered and closed and locked the door. The other man pulled the door shade and curtains over the windows."

Her hands trembled as she took a small sip of her tea, spilling a small bit. "The first man seemed to be in charge. He demanded my father open the safe. My father refused and the man pistol-whipped him across his face. He repeated the demand and my father again refused. He pistol-whipped him again, opening a large gash on his right cheek. My father fell to the floor and I thought it might have knocked him unconscious. He wasn't a large or strong man, but he used the counter to pull himself back to his feet. The second man just stood there laughing with his gun pointing at me. The first man again told my father to open the safe and if he refused this time it would be me they would hit. It was then that I could see resignation in my father's eyes as he staggered around the counter toward the safe. Just as he opened the safe, the first man hit my father on the back of the head with his pistol butt. I can't get the hollow thump and cracking noise from my memory. It crushed his skull and killed him. They both laughed loudly at the sight of my father's dead body."

"I ran to my father but was stopped by the second man. I tried to pull free but he was far too strong. I can still remember his sneer, his filthy face, tobacco-stained teeth, revolting breath. He smelled of whiskey, tobacco and unwashed body dirt. While he was restraining me, the first man tore my dress from the back. I needn't provide you more details about what happened next. You understand the rest."

The color in her face blotched red and then bleached white, displaying the effort needed to control her emotions. Fresh was the memory of a tragic night that would ever be burned in her mind. She tried to lift her teacup but placed it back on the saucer, realizing she would spill its contents with her hands shaking so terribly. Tears were pooled within her eyes and fell to her cheeks when she blinked.

"Miss Wicks, I am so very sorry for what happened to your father and you. They are despicable men and I will find them both and see that justice is served. Can you provide me any more details? You didn't mention that their faces were covered."

"They were not covered at all. It was as if they didn't care. Or maybe they had intended to kill the witnesses. I just don't know."

"Can you describe the first man?"

"He was about five feet ten inches tall, strong upper body, lined face, brown greasy hair and a brown but graying handlebar mustache. His eyes were like those of an insane man, constantly darting about. It was as if they lighted on one image too long they would burn blind. The other man was a bit smaller and thinner."

Showing the likeness on the paper from his inside coat pocket to Miss Wicks caused her to flinch and cover her mouth. Tears had begun to fill her eyes but didn't drop and her hands shook. Liam understood.

"Miss Wicks, that is the man wanted for arson and the murder of twenty people, including my father and mother."

Her hand rose, again covering her mouth in shock and surprise. "Oh, my dear Lord! I am so sorry, Mr. deBláca."

"Unfortunately, it would seem we share more than we originally thought. Miss Wicks, I am deeply sorry to have asked you to relive that horrible night. Did they say anything that might hint to where they were going?"

Molly had that faraway look, as though lost in thought. Tears were again pooling in her eyes but not falling to her cheeks. She seemed immensely sad with her grief. "I was on the floor, sobbing as they were taking the cash from the safe. The second man said something like, 'This will get us to Dallas in style, Sam' — or maybe it was Tan."

"It was Van. His name is Van Cooper. And he is one of the most despicable men I know. It won't bring my parents or your father back, but I intend to find this man, arrest him, and ensure he is hanged for murder. Miss Wicks, is there anything I can do for you?"

Molly seemed distant and exhausted from reliving that night. The sheriff remained silent.

"Mr. deBláca, I assume based on what I have told you that you will be leaving on the morning train destined for Dallas. Would you think it too forward of me to suggest we dine together this evening?"

Smiling, Liam responded, "On two conditions; one being you call me Liam and the other that you join me as my guest for supper at the Grand dining room."

"On one condition, Liam. That being you call me Molly." And she smiled warm.

Van Cooper and his pard Dutch disembarked the train in St. Louis and headed to the nearest saloon. The closest saloon was called Traders and was frequented by fur trappers and buffalo hunters. Pressing through the batwing doors they both stopped to take in the men playing poker, talking up the doves and standing at the bar. The air was filled with smoke and smelled of stale beer and body odor. They were a rough-looking lot, all armed and most unclean and unshaven. Van and Dutch felt right at home and walked directly to the polished oak bar.

Van slapped his hand on the top of the bar and yelled, "Whiskey, two glasses and leave the bottle."

The bar keep was a big man, not fat but thick and brawny with heavily muscled arms. He sported a bushy head of gray hair with mutton chops of the same color. As he placed the two glasses and a bottle of whiskey, he said, "I am the owner of this fine establishment. The name is Kyle. Haven't seen you hear before... just in off the train?"

"Don't recognize the accent."

"Eye, I am from the hills of Scotland. There is no finer place in the world."

"That is your opinion friend, but there is no better place than Texas."

"So, Texans be ya."

"That's right, friend," Van said as he downed his first whiskey in one swallow.

"You must be headin' back to join the Confederate army, then."

"What the hell makes you say that?" Van showed his displeasure at being roped into a conversation when he wanted to drink, not talk.

"Well, with the war soon breaking out and Texas supporting your southern states, they be conscripting every able-bodied man into the army. Haven't you fellas heard?"

The look of surprise and concern was easy for Kyle to see on Van's face, but he regrouped clumsily saying, "Yeah, we are on our way to sign up. We'll kick those Yanks' asses!"

Van then looked at Dutch and they shared a look of fear. Both realized that they couldn't go to Texas. They wanted no part of the Army. Army pay would be miserly and the chances of living through that war would be mighty slim. They needed a new plan that would get them to their next grubstake.

Kyle had moved to the other end of the bar and was saying a long goodbye to two rough-looking characters standing at the bar. He was wishing them luck with their digging and asked them to come back at any time. When Van heard "digging" he turned and asked another man standing at the bar where they were off to. He learned that there was a massive silver strike in Virginia City, Nevada. They called it the Comstock Load.

Later that evening, Van told Dutch that where there were gold or silver mines there would be miners with metal in their saddlebags, and miners were not gunmen. Their new grubstake plans were sealed.

The Grand Hotel was a four-story building of stone foundation and first floor, and wood construction on the second and higher floors. There was a casino featuring faro, poker and roulette with a bar to the right of the main entrance and a formal restaurant to the left. Oriental carpets covered the polished wood floors and the oil lamp sconces added to the refined atmosphere.

Liam was waiting in the lobby, just outside the sliding double walnut doors that framed the entrance to the hotel's formal dining room. The hotel butler was stationed by the main door to the hotel to be prompt in opening the door and greeting the guests.

The door opened with a rush of cold air, and the lighted entrance way framed Molly exquisitely. She was dressed in black, in mourning for her father. Her blond hair radiated an aura of innocence, yet her demeanor radiated an aura of confidence and refinement. She paused at the door, her gentle smile confirmed an evening to remember. Liam moved to greet her while the butler offered to take her black cloak.

"Good evening Molly. You look lovely. I will be the envy of every man in the dining room." Liam, dressed in a black broadcloth freshly brushed suit offered Molly his arm and began to escort her to the dining room. Many of the white linen covered tables were occupied by well-dressed couples, a few with small gatherings of men. The large stone fireplace was responsible for maintaining the diners' comfort and added to the dining experience.

"Thank you, Liam." She smiled warmly.

Molly was appraising Liam after they were seated. His black wavy hair was neatly trimmed and he was clean-shaven, his green eyes soft and inviting while subtly intense. His tailored broadcloth suit with matching vest was obviously made of imported fabric. A man of taste and means, she thought. His white shirt was starched and pressed perfectly, and she wondered privately how a traveling man could keep things so tidy.

"Liam, I noticed that you don't have your six-guns on this evening. I would think a man in your profession wouldn't ever be in public unarmed."

"I agree with you, Molly", Liam said as he opened the left side of his suit coat to allow Molly to see his holstered .38. "I think a bit of discretion would be appropriate for this evening, don't you?"

They talked freely over a sumptuous meal of vegetable soup, thick cut steaks with green beans, and popovers, complete with English gravy. They shared a bottle of French Burgundy which was a special treat for Molly.

Molly searched Liam's eyes as if they were the gateway to his younger life. "Liam, tell me of your home in Ireland

and what brought you and your family to America… that is, if I am not prying and the wounds aren't too fresh?"

As was Liam's habit, he organized his thoughts carefully before responding. "Not at all Molly, I would enjoy sharing some of my memories with you, if you would do the same."

"Let's see, you know I am from County Kildare. My father, Shaun, was a noted gunsmith and my mother, Grace, an accomplished teacher. We owned a cattle ranch as well and ran several hundred head of prized beef. As a boy, my main responsibility was to watch over the herd and move them to new graze. It was a difficult job, especially while being homeschooled. The famine affected everyone and father would willingly slaughter cattle to keep friends and neighbors from hunger. The British army would help themselves if they found the herd, so I was always on the lookout for well-hidden graze."

Liam paused a moment and sipped his Burgundy before continuing. "My constant companion and friend was Creena, my horse. He stood nearly eighteen hands, black as midnight coal and trail wise. He would warn me when there were wolves about, and especially the British. You see, the British passed a law that required Irelanders to assist any British army soldier in need. The British law was referring to a wounded soldier, but the local soldiers twisted the law to their own means and needs. They knew we had a herd but they couldn't confiscate what they could not find."

"That must have been harrowing and dangerous work, and, all alone!"

Thoughtfully, Liam responded, "Yes, it was especially in the cold snowy winter months where the tracks of the herd were easier to pick up and follow, and where graze was sparse. One night three British stumbled onto our trail and followed it to my hidden shelter. Creena alerted me with his suddenly erect ears, so I was ready. The fire was still burning and the coals from supper glowed crimson but did not throw off enough light for them to assess the camp occupants. I had moved from the shelter into the brush with my rifle and awaited their move. There was no call to the camp so I knew they were up to no good. One soldier moved slowly toward the fire, his rifle at the ready, and behind him came two more."

"Liam, how old were you when this happened?"

"I was eleven years old. I knew if the British confiscated our herd, dozens if not hundreds of friends and family members would go hungry. The three soldiers began to ransack the camp when a calf bawling for his mama caught their ears; they had found the herd and sighted Creena picketed in the scrub. Well, in the deepest man voice I could muster, I told them to get out of my camp, throwing my voice off the nearby rock ledge. Their response was three shots almost in unison into the scrub where they thought I was hiding."

"Oh my God, you're here so you must have got away, but how?"

"I shot the three British soldiers and buried them early the next morning in an area unlikely to be visited by more soldiers. I then broke camp and left the area as it was before I arrived. Of course, I moved the herd to the small, hidden box canyon with plenty of graze and water, sealed off the entrance and headed for home."

The sadness had returned Molly's eyes as she came to understand the full impact of Liam's experience at such a young age.

"I told father what had happened, but not mother. It was over supper a night later that my father made the decision to leave Ireland. We were enjoying a pleasant albeit sparse meal when we were interrupted by loud banging on our door. My father opened the door to reveal a British captain with eight soldiers in formation behind him. He pushed my father aside and strode into our home, his longsword unsheathed and in his right hand. He said not a word while eyeing me first and then lingering on mother. He walked around the table where our meal was resting and with his left hand took mother's chin and lifted her head to face him. Looking at her eyes he sneered, 'Very beautiful.' Then turning to my father, he said, 'She will be of assistance to me. I know you have a herd secreted somewhere, and I mean to have it. Now, you can turn it over to me or I will take that assistance whenever and however often I please.' Then he exited our home. Even at my young age, I understood. Mother remained outwardly calm but her eyes betrayed her. We left Ireland the very next night with all that we could carry."

So recently Molly had finally understood the brutality in this world. The shocking stories of Liam's childhood — no, at eleven, then, it was young manhood — actually made her feel a closeness to Liam, a bonding of sorts. To have lived his life and rise to the head of the U.S. Marshals service was an incredible accomplishment by what she was coming to realize was an incredibly accomplished man.

As they were enjoying their coffee, there was a commotion near the double doors of the dining room entrance. Turning, Liam noticed it was Mr. Woodsom, the stationmaster, being stopped by the butler. He was trying to get Liam's attention. Liam motioned for the hotel butler to allow him entrance.

"Mr. deBláca, I am sorry to intrude like this, but I am sure you will want to know what I have found out," Woodsom said as he nervously held a note in his hand.

"Absolutely, Mr. Woodson. You have done the right thing. I presume you know Miss Wicks?"

"Yes, good evenin' Miss Wicks and I'm beggin' your pardon ma'am." Looking back to Liam, "I remembered a man that fits the description you gave me leaving the station the morning after Molly's, excuse me please, Miss Wicks', father was killed. He and his pard purchased tickets to St. Louis and then on to Dallas. So, I cabled the station manager in St. Louis and he 'membered them as well. Want to know why?"

"Yes, of course Mr. Woodsom. Why?"

"They changed their tickets, not going to Dallas. They are going to Virginia City. That's in Nevada Territory. They left St. Louis today."

"Mr. Woodsom, that is excellent information. I am in your debt. You have done well." Liam reached into his watch pocket and removed a gold double eagle and pressed it into Mr. Woodsom's hand.

"Thank you, sir! I assume you wish to have passage to Virginia City on the train leaving tomorrow morning? I will arrange for your horse and saddle as well."

Liam nodded and remained deep in thought for several minutes after the stationmaster left the dining room. Molly respected his silence and sipped her coffee while watching his thoughts take shape. After a several minutes, Liam broke the silence.

"This makes perfect sense, Molly. They were on their way to Dallas but must have discovered that, with the war close at hand, and Texas supporting the south, they are conscripting all able-bodied men. These men are cowards and loyal to no one. They would avoid Texas as sure as a posse."

"I can understand that", Molly offered. "But why Virginia City? Nevada is quite a distance from St. Louis."

"They likely haven't worked an honest day in their life. They take, rob and murder for a living. There was a large silver strike in Virginia City recently, reported to be the largest strike ever. It is called the Comstock Lode, named after Henry T. P. Comstock. Miners are easy prey and typically hold their metal instead of securing it in a bank. It would appear that Van Cooper plans to rob and murder, yet again. I plan on stopping him."

"Molly, it has been a delightful evening, one I will remember always. Thank you for help and your company. Let me escort you home and then I have planning to do. I also need to send a wire to the Attorney General with an update."

As they walked through the streets, Molly was startled when gunfire shattered the calm evening. Liam intuitively sensed it came from several streets away and posed no risk to them. Still, he pressed his left arm into his side to reassure himself that his .38 was secure in his shoulder holster.

"I really don't understand why men need to do that, Liam."

"Well, men who can't control their use of liquor typically can't control their judgment with a firearm as well."

They were nearing the end of the street and as they turned onto the street where Molly lived, two men appeared from the shadows, slowly walking toward them. There was the light from the half moon and little else, but Liam's pupils had already had time to adjust to the darkness. Liam noticed their gate was slightly unstable, probably influenced by whiskey. He took the liberty to place his left arm around Molly's back to guide her away from the unknown men. As they passed to his right, Liam met their eyes and knew instantly there would be trouble. They passed a few steps and he listened intently to the men's footfalls. They stopped so Liam also stopped and turned, facing the men while at the same time guiding Molly behind him, shielding her from harm. Liam stood facing the two men, both of whom had their Colts drawn, but Liam had not heard the hammers being cocked. Knowing they were double-action pistols meant he would have an edge. They were careless.

They stood facing each other, sizing each other up. The men resembled each other, perhaps brothers. They were both just shy of six feet tall, with worn out boots, dirty Levi's, wool shirts, one red and the other blue, and tattered derby hats. They had work gloves tucked into their belts. Ranch hands, no doubt. Both needed a trip to the barber for a shave and haircut, and a bath. Their Colts were not steady, but at this range they didn't need to be.

"Lookie what we have here, a dandy and his misses," blue shirt said with a bit of a slur, spittle falling from the right corner of his mouth. "Now dandy, this here is what we call a stickup and I'll be taking your money and the misses' bag, and I'll have that pocket watch, too!"

Liam hadn't said a word. He remained completely still with Molly behind him. With their Colts not cocked, he judged he had time to make a move if needed.

"Mister, you hard a hearin' or somethin'? Maybe we need to sweet talk the misses," red shirt added.

"Molly, may I have your purse please," Liam asked in a calm voice. Molly then passed the purse from behind Liam to his left hand, remembering that he had his pistol in tucked in his left shoulder and therefore needing his right hand free. Liam was impressed with her clear thinking and steel. Holding the purse out in his left hand, Liam walked toward blue shirt.

"Here, we don't want any trouble," Liam said as he came to within feet of blue shirt. Then, he dropped the purse, using it as a distraction, and in a single blistering-fast fluid motion, grabbed blue shirt's Colt, bringing it up by the barrel and slamming its butt into the head of blue shirt. Blue shirt dropped to the ground, and when red shirt looked up he was facing the Colt in Liam's hand pointing directly between his eyes. It was deadly steady. And the hammer was cocked.

"Drop your gun, now! I won't ask again."

Red shirt's panicked red-rimmed eyes darted to Liam's cold-steeled face and then refocused on the .44 Colt just inches from the bridge of his nose. Its dark iron was ready to unleash his death. Perspiration began building on his forehead and he was incapable of decision and ultimately, within seconds, instinctive reflex took over where reason had failed him. Red shirt panicked and wouldn't live to regret his decision to pull his trigger.

Liam didn't hesitate. The bullet entered red shirt's forehead, just above the bridge of his nose with the muzzle flash burning his flesh and exiting along with a large piece of his scalp, torn bloody, and bits of brain matter. Liam had taken a life before, but the hesitation in pulling the trigger to kill Van Cooper meant he would never hesitate again. Later, as he reflected upon this incident, he will conclude that red shirt provided no other option and that it was red shirt that had taken his own life based on his own foolish actions.

The shot alerted Sheriff Kobb who came running around the corner, pistol in hand.

"My apologies, Sheriff, we didn't have much choice. They came at us, pistols in hand, with the intention of robbing Molly and me. I gave red shirt there the option of dropping his Colt but he decided to use it instead."

"Sheriff Kobb that is exactly how it happened, it was terrifying," Molly added with her voice shaking, the inhumanity and violence bringing her father's death freshly to mind.

"I know of these men, Marshal, local hands and not the best of characters. I'll take care of this one and send the coroner to deal with his brother," the sheriff said in a fatigued voice.

"If you don't mind, Sheriff, I will escort Molly safely home and stop by your office for any official inquiries you would like to make."

Seeing Molly safely home and now standing at her front door, Liam said, "Molly means 'star of the sea' but you appear to be landlocked. Perhaps I will be fortunate enough to hear the story of your life over supper sometime soon." Smiling, Liam then added, "Molly, your company this evening..." Words simply failed him and his voice trailed off.

"Liam, I feel the very same way," Molly said as she placed her hand lovingly on his cheek, her eyes radiating the connection that Liam also felt. "Good night Liam. This has been a most wonderful and surprising evening."

CHAPTER FOUR

1861

The Civil War began on April 12, 1861, when Confederate forces fired upon Fort Sumter, held by Union troops in South Carolina.

Queen Victoria of the United Kingdom issues a "proclamation of neutrality" which recognizes the breakaway southern states as having belligerent rights, presumably to protect the needed importation of cotton.

The Nevada Territory separated from the Utah Territory and adopted its current name, shortened from Sierra Nevada (Spanish for "snowy range").

Virginia City was a study of contrasts; rough, dirty and wild but with areas that were cultured, elegant and beautiful. The city boasted forty-two saloons, forty-two stores, six restaurants and three hotels — all that supporting thousands of full time and transient residents. Van Cooper naturally blended with the rough, dirty and wild surroundings, as did his pard, Dutch. They had arrived in the city two days ago with their funds dangerously low. The safe in the mercantile had only about $400 and they had drunk heavily and gambled poorly while traveling to Virginia City; a bad combination.

Van and Dutch had tried their hand at poker in several saloons and soon learned they were not up to the level of the local talent, leaving them down to only a few days of food and liquor. They began to walk the streets looking for easy prey.

"Van, look at the size of that house! I bet they have some easy cash available."

"It is a good thing that I do the thinkin' in this outfit. Dutch, you are an idiot! That is the Savage Mining Company property. The superintendent lives there," Van replied in disgust.

"Yeah, so what?"

"You really are an idiot. That house is better protected than the bank and probably has a lot more silver and cash too. Let's get a whiskey and let me think."

They entered the nearest saloon, seduced by the piano music and off-tune singing of happy whiskey-infused miners. Pushing through the double doors, they stood letting their eyes adjust to the brighter light while looking over the crowd. This was obviously a miner's bar based on the clientele. Most of the characters looked as if they came straight from the mines to wash their throat dust down with beer and whiskey. They were filthy, bearded and generally happy. The dress was uniformly Levi's and derby hats — both soiled — and not many were wearing guns. There were about fifty or so miners and several well used doves working the crowd. The drink of preference seemed to be beer. The intense smoke in the air was from pipes and cigars but few hand-rolled cigarettes.

Van motioned to Dutch to follow him to the bar. He elbowed a small window to get the barkeep's attention and motioned for two beers. The barkeep drew the beers and slid them deftly to Van who paid in coin. The barkeep gave Van an odd look, pocketed the money, and then moved to his next customer. Standing at the bar, Van noticed that the miners were paying for their beer with what looked like rocks. Upon closer observation he realized they were paying with raw silver. So, the miners were paid by the Savage Mining Company in silver, he concluded. And that fact solved his grubstake problem.

It was nearing midnight and the bar was thinning out when Van motioned to Dutch that they should leave as well. Once outside the bar, he began walking in the opposite direction of their flop house.

"Van, our place is this way. Where you goin'? You drunk?"

"Dutch, you ain't got a brain in that fat head. I'm for getting some of that silver, and I mean right now, tonight. Let's foller those two miners. They be drunk and their carryin' silver."

They watched carefully from a distance as two miners walked unsteadily down the street to a more remote shack residence. Pretending that they, too, were drunk miners heading to their shack, they picked up their pace. As they neared the miners, Van motioned to Dutch to pull the bandana over his face. Once secure they wouldn't be recognized, Van called out, "Friend, got a lucifer for my pipe?"

The two miners stopped abruptly, unsteadily, almost falling and responded, "Sure friend."

Van pulled his pistol and demanded, "Give me your silver and cash. Every bit or you will be dead in three seconds."

They responded with zeal, emptying their pockets on the ground between them. "Mister, don't shoot, I have a wife and two boys to care for. You got my money, now let us go," one miner said, clearly shaking in his Brogan boots.

"Turn around," Cooper demanded.

Before they were completely turned around, Dutch lost his bandana, exposing his face. Even in the dark of night they would be able to recognize him. While Dutch was pocketing the silver and cash, Van hit both with the butt of his pistol and then, one after the other, strangled them both preventing any possibility of being fingered for their deaths. "You do a stupid thing like that again Dutch, and we're done. I don't mind killin', but this just makes the local law get more interested."

Back in their flop house, Van laid the silver and cash on the bunk — over $200 in cash and easily that in silver. "That was the easiest pay day we've ever had, Dutch!" Let's git out of this here flop house and move to better digs."

Mount Davidson, a peak in the Virginia Range of Nevada Territory, gave Virginia City its notoriety with the discovery of silver in 1858, although the mining rush didn't begin in earnest until almost two years later when the Comstock Lode was widely reported in the eastern newspapers. It is said that the city was named after a man named James Finney who was nicknamed "Old Virginy". His real name was James Fennimore and was credited with discovering the Comstock Lode. He fled his home state of Virginia after killing John Bishop, known as "Big French John", and today was a wanted man, but it was unknown to his business associates and the local Virginia City authorities.

The Comstock Lode was located on the eastern slope of Mt. Davidson and largely owned by the Savage Mining Company. Early in the strike, the ore was extracted with surface diggings — easy and fast money. But surface ore was quickly exhausted because it was so easy to extract, and the miners then had to tunnel underground to reach more and richer ore. The Comstock Lode evidenced in discrete but dense masses that were, at times, hundreds of feet thick. The ore was so soft it could be removed by shovel, requiring very little blasting, sometimes even able to be scooped up by hand. The ease of excavating the ore came with the danger from the weakness of the surrounding rock and earth that resulted in frequent and very deadly tunnel shaft cave-ins. The excavations were carried to depths of more than 3,000 feet, which required timbers to be set in a cube every six feet within the tunnel shaft as the ore was extracted.

The danger to miners' lives and owners' profits didn't stop with shaft cave-ins. As the shafts became deeper, the mountain's ice-cold water became the next serious problem and required pumps in constant operation. The deeper shafts passed the cold water and then ran into the next serious problem, the complete opposite: hot water, so hot the miners boiled eggs for their noon meal. Fans were then needed to move the cooler outside air into the shafts to keep the temperatures bearable for the hard-working miners. The miners all knew the risks and willingly accepted them for a share in the profits, or simply the best wage available in the west.

Clinton Weeks, the Savage Mining Company superintendent, was uncommonly focused on the miners' safety and would never press his employees into a shaft that was not ruled as safe by his foremen, and the foreman took seriously the advice of the mining engineers. His company was never short of personnel as a result. He and his daughter, Susanna, lived in the large white Victorian house set on the city's edge known simply as "The Mansion". Weeks, at 51 years of age, was still a dashing and fit man with gray crowding his mahogany hair. While in the office of his business, he would be seen in a well-tailored charcoal suit over a pressed white shirt, sporting a string tie and immaculately polished black boots mostly covered by the gray wool pant legs. But, when he was in the mines of his business, he was frequently indistinguishable from the miners with dirty Levi's, Brogan boots, wool plaid shirt, and flat brimmed soiled hat, working just as hard as the foremen.

Weeks had been a widower for over a year, having lost his wife when a team of horses pulling a carriage were spooked by a drunk's errant pistol fire and ran uncontrolled through the main street in front of The Mansion, crushing her beneath their legs. Susanna, at twenty years of age, was entering that stage where she and mom were best friends, became deeply depressed over her mother's death.

"Susanna, we had two of our miners robbed and killed last night. This city is becoming more and more dangerous. I swear, where there is money there are bandits and outlaws a plenty. You need to be extra careful, and I would ask that whenever you leave The Mansion you have Clive at your side. It would ease my mind daughter quite considerably," Weeks said over the breakfast table.

Clive added as he brought the coffee cup to his lips, "Mr. Weeks is right. It has always been a wild town Miss Weeks, but it is the wild, wild west out there now."

Susanna had long and flowing chestnut hair that contrasted her porcelain complexion and pale green eyes. However, unlike other young women of means that were seen only in dresses of the latest fashion, Susanna wore riding britches, usually tucked into knee-high polished leather boots with simple stud spurs. She could ride as well as any man, perhaps better than most, and was the most comfortable when on horseback. Unlike many of the Virginia City upper class young women that rode sidesaddle, Susanna rode astride a beautifully tooled western saddle. Susanna was a supremely confident young woman, well-educated and very bright.

"Father, I will be more careful. I have watched this city grow. And with the growth of wealth, the undesirables have increased as well. You know that I always carry my pistol and can take care of myself. So, please don't worry." Susanna almost kept hidden the frustration in her tone of being treated like a child. She considered herself a grown woman and so did the many suitors that kept calling, although none of them were of interest to her. To Susanna, they were boys and she was a woman.

Clinton Weeks just shook his head and resolved that his daughter, very much like her mother, had a mind of her own. He looked over at Clive and Clive looked back, giving a wink. He knew that Clive, as his head of security, would follow Susanna discretely and was her best chance for safety.

Weeks lifted the gold pocket watch from his vest pocket and flipped open the cover to note the time. "Susanna, I will be going to my office this morning. We have hit another vein and the mineralogists are determining its richness. Care to join me?"

"I will see you mid to late morning father. I want to take Star to have a shoe refitted and you know I won't leave her with that smith." Susanna raised Star from a colt, actually from birth as she was there to assist in the breech birth nearly five years ago. She loved her mare and they were quite a sight riding in the city. Star was just over fifteen hands, the same chestnut brown as Susanna's hair, with one white stocking on the right foreleg.

"Alright, but please, please be careful," Weeks begged as he briefly looked over at Clive. The worry in Weeks' tone was very real and even more appropriate. Virginia City was wild, tamed in some areas and completely raw in others.

The Mansion was reasonably secure, located high atop a hill looking down on the city with high stone walls and two of Clive's roving security people patrolling the perimeter around the clock. The robberies hadn't touched the Weeks' lives directly, and Clinton Weeks wanted to keep it that way. Clive Ackerman had once been a railroad detective and was as capable a man as could be found. Honest and loyal as well. His one weakness was his love for Susanna that was unknown to her but not to Clinton Weeks. Clive was ten years her senior and Clinton wanted more for his daughter than a former railroad detective. Although Clive had been brutal when circumstances required, he was also a gentleman capable of sensitivity and tenderness.

Susanna rode as if the flames of hell were at her heels. She and Star liked it that way and those that were acquainted with Susanna knew to give her a wide birth. She slowed to a trot as she spotted the blacksmith near the end of B Street on the south side of Virginia City. The day was bright and clear but cold, with both Star and Susanna's breaths visible in the air from their ride. She wrapped the reins around the hitching post and entered the smith's shop.

"Mr. Edelman, Star needs a shoe refitted. Are you able to accommodate while I wait?"

Mr. Edelman was a large, barrel-chested man, perpetually dirty and sweaty. It was hot inside the shop from the furnace that he was stoking with the air bellows. "For you Miss Weeks, I will stop what I am doing and see to it right away. Which shoe is it?"

"The white stocking, right foreleg."

As Mr. Edelman was working the shoe in the furnace, Susanna stood outside the smith's shop in the cooler air, watching the hustle and bustle of Virginia City, Nevada Territory. She was pondering the mix of people — miners dressed in Levi's, women in the latest French fashion, men in broadcloth suits, and rough cowboys in buckskins — when two lowlifes walked out of the hotel across the street and headed to the saloon on her side of the street. What made them stand out she wasn't sure? Perhaps it was the one with the graying handlebar mustache that was staring at her with the menacing crazy and wanton eyes. She needed to peel her eyes away as if ripping a board off a fence, and a chill went up her spine.

"Dutch, now that is a woman if ever there was one. Did you see that dove in riding britches and the long brown hair? I gotta have some of that before we blow this town. That's for damn sure," Van Cooper choked out lustfully.

"I saw her and she is way out of ya class, Van. You got no chance in hell."

"Yeah. You probably thought that store clerk's daughter was outa my class. But, we had some kinda' fun with her, now didn't we!"

As they entered the saloon, Van took one last look toward the smith's but Susanna had gone inside and couldn't be seen. Bellying up to the near empty bar, Van ordered two beers. "What da ya got to eat?"

The bartender replied, "Only thing today is a beef stew. Been cooking since early mornin'. Two bits a bowl and it comes with bread baked yesterday."

"Good, two bowls." Van dropped a few coins on the bar as he and Dutch moved to a vacant table.

There was a small ruckus outside the saloon. Turning, Van watched the woman of his newly-minted dreams galloping up B Street like she was chasing a train. "Hellfire, who the hell was that?"

"Oh," the barkeep said with a chuckle, "You must be new in Virginia City. That there is Clinton Weeks' daughter Susanna and she is quite the young woman. Mr. Weeks is the Savage Mining Company's Superintendent. They live in The Mansion, over yonder on that hill." Then he turned to fetch the bowls of beef stew.

Then another rider galloped by, this time it was a man dressed in black and he looked to be following the young woman. There was a no-nonsense look about him, someone to stay clear of, Van thought privately.

Van pondered the scene that had unfolded before him while Dutch was shoveling in the hot beef stew making a mess of his face and the table.

Liam had finally arrived in the far western edge of the Nevada Territory in Carson City, which lay a few days ride southwest of Virginia City, Nevada. The stage service to southern California and then due north to Carson was determined the fastest route and method. It was a long an arduous journey, but Liam decided to acquire the provisions needed for the last leg on horseback without a night in Carson as he and Creena were busting with energy.

Liam tied Creena to the hitching rail outside the general store, patted his neck and took his saddlebags with him.

"Howdy, what can I do fir ya mister?" the shopkeeper asked.

"Provisions for three days; beans, bacon, coffee, canned peaches if you have them, maybe some beef jerky. I will also need two blankets and a ground tarp, coffee pot and frying pan," Liam requested.

"Sounds like you lost your outfit, Marshal," the shopkeeper stated and then added, "Saw your badge, didn't mean nothin' by it."

"No harm done."

"Guess you be headed to Virginia City. They surely are havin' some trouble there." The shopkeeper was a talkative man while organizing the provisions. "Still, you best watch your back-trail. Lots a bushwhackin' between here and there."

"I thank you kindly for the provisions and for the advice," Liam said as he was paying the bill.

Liam guessed there was still four hours of solid daylight and kept at cantor for most of them, staying on the northeast trail toward Virginia City. Creena seemed happy to be on solid ground and away from the train's vibrations, squeals and soot. Liam felt the same. Judging that sundown was about an hour away, he began looking for a suitable camp away from the trail for the night.

Several times Liam left the trail in search for a camp only to be disappointed, but at last, with some long fingers of sunlight, he found a suitable camp well off the trail and hidden. The eastern rock cliff as a backdrop would both protect him from ambush and act as a reflector to keep him warm. It had an escarpment that would shield the wind and there was a slowly running stream of fresh water coming from the cliff, as well as an adequate patch of rich graze for Creena. Tall fir and cedar surrounded him with plenty of dry kindling for a smokeless fire.

After removing the saddle and rubbing down Creena, he picketed him on the lush graze near the brook. Then Liam went about making a small fire for coffee and to fry beans and bacon for his meal. While the coffee was heating, he took in the area with a practiced eye, remembering the advice of the shopkeeper about bushwhackers.

Approach to his camp from the north would be noisy and foolhardy as the hill was steep with loose rock under foot — he ruled that out. The southern approach was a bit easier, but up a steep grade and in the dark it would be dangerous — he ruled that out as well. The western approach, the one he himself had used to locate the camp, would be the one to use, if one was used at all.

Liam had watched his back-trail and saw no one following. As he enjoyed the warmth of his after-supper coffee, he breathed deeply of the cool fresh mountain air and relished the sweet scent of the moss, pine and cedar. He was reminded fondly of the many days and weeks he had spent on the range as a boy alone with his horse and small herd of cattle in Ireland, and then his thoughts drifted to his father and mother.

Creena was now picketed closer to the camp and the fire was out, leaving only the red coals to be reflected by the cliff. Liam had spread dried poplar leaves and cedar twigs over the western approach to the camp before wrapping in his blankets for the night with his modified Henry leaning on the cliff and two .44's within an easy hands reach. Creena was already three legged and his sleep came quickly and deeply.

It was the call from a hawk flying its morning hunt that alerted Liam of the new day. The sun had risen but blocked by the cliff. Liam could see his breath but cold as it was he felt invigorated, rested and looking to Creena he sensed his horse was of similar body and mind.

Liam was nooning just off the trail, and after cleaning and checking the action of both .44's began enjoying a cold piece of jerky while Creena grazed, when two strangers suddenly appeared from the north, didn't "halloo the camp", just walked in with Winchesters in hand, pointed low. "That's a nice animal you have there, friend," the taller of the two said. He was string-bean thin, wiry with a single Colt holstered on his right thigh. His bushy black beard hid most of his face but his dark brown red-rimmed eyes looked menacing.

"Had him since he dropped," Liam responded flatly, happy that he had checked both .44's and left the thongs off.

"Are you gunna ask us iffin we want some coffee?" The shorter one asked. He was rounded in the belly and sported a Colt tucked under his belt and had positioned himself a half step behind tall man.

"Don't have coffee and you didn't ask to come into my camp. I'd say that was plain rude," Liam responded, moving his coat aside exposing his badge, knowing that there was gunplay ahead as soon as they worked up their nerve. He judged he had an edge by the way they held their rifles. In the past their victims probably caved, being caught off guard and at the sight of two rifles, but he would not, he would wait for the "tell".

"Now, that ain't neighborly even if you be a law man, so we will just take what we want, includen ya hoss!" But, no one moved. They were waiting for Liam to cave and Liam was waiting to the telltale sign, and he judged it would come from tall man. Every man has a tell and it is usually in the eyes or shoulders. A U.S. Marshal must await that sign so that they are reacting to a threat and not initiating a gunfight that could be seen as murder. Therefore, a U.S. Marshal must be lightning fast on the draw and deadly accurate to stay alive, and Liam was just that.

And then the tell came from the tall man's left shoulder as he started to bring the Winchester up to fire. But neither even got a shot off. At this range, maybe less than 10 yards, Liam could have shot their wool shirt buttons, one at a time. He drew and fired twice, placed both rounds in their foreheads above the nose, both bushwhackers dead before they dropped to the frozen ground. Liam shucked the two spent shells and reloaded as the black smoke drifted from the warm barrel.

Cautiously, Liam looked for their horses. He didn't know if there might be another man, but seeing just the two mounts grazing he holstered his .44. Checking the saddlebags, he found wanted posters for them both that they must be keeping as bragging papers over whiskey with their outlaw friends. Well, he thought they won't be bragging any longer.

***

Virginia City wasn't what Liam had expected. It appeared to be carved into the side of the mountain. There were very few trees and lots of mud with houses, buildings and tents scattered about, organized in the cities center and haphazard in the outlying areas. It was a scene that lacked any planning or forethought. The city was larger than he had assumed and there were far more people than he was led to believe, which to his disappointment will make finding Van Copper and his pard more difficult.

His first stop would be the sheriff's office to make inquiries, then the telegraph office to send an update to Jeremiah, and then a hotel and a much-needed hot bath. A miner was helpful in pointing out the sheriff's office where he tied Creena and the two horses, carrying the dead bushwhackers across their saddles, to the hitching post.

The sheriff's office was a good-sized two-story stone building with iron bars set on all the windows. Liam was privately impressed with the apparent security it represented. He stepped up the stairs and then knocked on the door and immediately entered. The sheriff was cleaning an old Navy .44 revolver.

"What can I do for ya mister?"

"Hello, Sheriff. The name is Liam deBláca, Chief Inspector of the United States Marshals Service."

"Hmm. Chief Inspector you say. Don't rightly know what that is. Heard of District U.S. Marshals though."

"All the District Marshalls across the United States report to me."

"I see. That would make you a mighty important lawman, I 'spect."

"That would be correct, Sheriff…?"

"Sorry Marshal, Sheriff Donny. Actually, it is Donavan, but people here bouts just call me Sheriff Donny." The

Sheriff looked formidable and experienced. He was near Liam's height, a little heavier and older with broad shoulders, muscled arms and sharp pale gray eyes. The full head of graying hair was neatly trimmed and the gray broadcloth vest matched his trousers. He had an easy way about him, confidence exuded naturally, and the Navy .44 looked as if it seen considerable action.

Extending his hand to the sheriff, who rose to his feet to accept it, "Pleased to meet you, Sheriff."

"What brings you to these parts, Marshal?"

"Murder. The murder of twenty-one people that I know of, rape and arson." His mind paused at twenty-one; the eighteen employees of the Black Arms Company, Molly's father, and his mother and father. He felt his jaw grind tight, the muscles flexing.

"Sounds like a really bad one you got there."

"Mind if I ask a few questions, Sheriff?"

"I'll help ifin I can, Marshal."

"I am looking for a man named Van Cooper, five feet ten, chiseled face, heavily lined, handlebar mustache, graying a bit. He may be with his partner, named Dutch. Don't know the last name or a solid description. Does that fit anyone you've seen lately?" He showed Sheriff Donny the likeness he carried.

"Marshal, we have more than ten thousand people in these parts, half of them in the city proper. That description and likeness could match hundreds of 'em. Sorry."

"I was afraid of that. Have there been any robberies, assaults or murders in the last few weeks?"

"Marshal, we have assaults multiple times a day. Murders are right popular with all this silver floating around. Same with robberies. Why just last night two miners from the Savage Mining Company were killed and robbed right at the end of B Street. I have a staff of twenty-six deputies just tryin' to keep some type of law and order in this city. It ain't easy. Even my deputies patrol in twos with scatterguns for their safety."

The sheriff's office door behind them suddenly burst open and a man half running in, winded, he screamed, "Sheriff, there are three men squaring off right outside. They're wanting to take Jenkins' wife and he won't let 'em. Someone gonna get dead if you don't stop it, but fast!"

"See what I mean, Marshal? Jenkins owns the general store cross the street and is surely no gunman," Sheriff Donny said as he was reaching for his double-barreled scattergun, checking the loads and then reaching into a box of shells pocketing a few. He headed to the door when Liam asked, "Mind if I join you Sheriff? With three men, two lawmen would be better odds."

"Much obliged, Marshal."

Liam took in the scene in a glance. Three tough-looking men stood facing the store owner across the street from them. They were on the street grouped together, looking up at Mr. and Mrs. Jenkins who stood on the top stair by the store entrance half embracing one another. The shop owner was yelling at the three men to leave his wife alone and never to come into his store again. He had a gun tucked in his belt. It was clear that Jenkins was not proficient with firearms by the way the revolver was tucked into his pants. The three men, all of whom appeared to have been drinking and were laughing, had tied down Colts. They were a rough bunch that had the look of hardened men.

The street that was busy with people, wagons, carriages and horses when Liam entered the sheriff's office was now empty, still, quiet. Shop doors were closed or being closed and presumably being locked. A gentle brisk breeze hinted at his back. The only sound was a dog barking from some back alley. Sheriff Donny walking up about thirty feet behind the men so they easily heard the hammers of his double-barreled scattergun being pulled back. "Now boys, if you want to live to enjoy your supper, get on your horses, ride out and don't come back. Your kind is not welcomed in Virginia City."

The men were experienced. As they turned to meet the sheriff's eyes, they spread out so that the scattergun could only challenge one man. Little puffs of dust rose at their feet and blew down the street as they spread out. Liam recognized the strategy and walked about ten feet to the left side of the sheriff. Stopping, he removed the thongs from the hammers of his holstered .44 pistols and pulled his jacket to the side, exposing his badge. The sheriff knew that if the men pulled iron, he would take the man on the right and Liam would take the one on the left, but they would both take the center man first.

The tough in the center spit a long wet wad of chew onto the dirt and toward the sheriff and left a dribble down his chin. "Old man, if you want to see your fat old lady for supper, alive that is, you best turn and hightail back to where's you came from. And I mean now!" He then focused on Liam. "What's your piece of this mister? Ain't seen you round these parts before."

Liam appraised each man carefully and determined that left and right would wait on the play from the talker in the middle. He slurred his words, obviously liquored a bit, but how much he didn't know. They were all unclean and unshaven, sweat stains leaked through their hatbands. Probably not miners. They carried their guns low and tied down, so probably not punchers either.

"I asked you a question Mister, and I ain't the type ta ask again!"

"U.S. Marshal. You've done enough and you should take the sheriff's suggestion to fork your broncs and ride. And, take this from me as a warning: if you don't, he will arrest you and I will assist him if he needs it, and if you try to pull iron you'll all be dead before you clear leather. That is a promise. And I won't tell you again." His authority and seriousness was clear to all within hearing distance. This was a law man to give a wide birth. But it was his complete lack of fear that worried the three toughs in front of him most.

Liam watched their eyes for the tell-tale flinch that would precede a draw. The eyes and the shoulders were the best tells. The man in the center gave the telltale and started his draw. Were there three shots or just one with an echo? The scattergun never fired. The three hard cases lay on their backs in the dirt, and each tough had a hole in the center of his forehead just above the bridge of his nose. The man in the middle was still clutching the unfired Colt that hadn't cleared leather completely. Jenkins, the store owner, just stood with his mouth agape. The dust from the three men falling hard on their backs in the middle of the street had yet to settle, caught in a gentle breeze mixing with Liam's powder smoke and drifting down the main street.

Never again would Liam hesitate. If he drew his .44, he would fire it. If he hadn't hesitated, his mother and father, Molly's father, and eighteen men of the Black Arms Company would be alive today.

The sheriff turned to his left to see Liam shucking the spent shells and reloading. He then realized that he would have been killed had Liam not been at his side. He simply nodded his thanks as his eyes smiled.

Liam returned the smile and asked, "Sheriff, can you recommend a hotel and a livery to care for my horse? And, where would the telegraph office be?" It was asked as if he had just finished breakfast as opposed to staring down and out drawing three toughs. "Oh, almost forgot, here are the dodgers I found in the saddlebags of those two bushwhackers tied across their saddles there, that tried to relieve me of my horse and outfit while on the trail here. They won't be troubling anyone anymore," Liam said as a matter of fact. "Would you notify the other local law men?"

Clinton Weeks preferred a formal meal and would never dine with those who preferred beans, biscuits and gravy. It isn't that Weeks had never dined in that style, but rather now being a man of means he could afford to dine in the way that he most enjoyed. This evening Clinton, his daughter, Susanna, and his head of security, Clive, would enjoy roasted venison, proper English popovers, steamed vegetables and French red wine. The table could seat ten people easily, so Clinton sat at the head with Clive and Susanna flanking him right and left at the table's end creating a more intimate gathering.

"Mr. Weeks, there was a shooting today in the city. Three men wanted to take Jenkins' wife. Jenkins faced them with his pistol in his belt. He sure is a fool for doing so, but not a coward. The sheriff was called and arrived there with his scattergun."

"Ah, so Sheriff Donny earned his pay again today. Good for him," Clinton replied while cutting a piece of venison. "He is a good man."

"Well, not really. Oh, I'm told he did face the three men. But, a Federal U.S. Marshal sided him. When one of the men drew, the marshal drew and shot all three men before Donny raised the scattergun, let alone even pulling the trigger."

"That is a bit unusual, seems unrealistic. I suspect that people are embellishing the story, Clive. Wouldn't you agree?"

"No sir, it's exactly how it went down. I took the time to validate the story with the sheriff, Jenkins and several eyewitnesses. That is exactly how it happened. The sheriff said he had never seen or even heard of such speed and accuracy. The marshal, his name by the way is Liam deBláca, is actually the Chief Inspector of the U.S. Marshals Service. He reports directly to the U.S. Attorney General and is here hunting two men. I plan on meeting him tomorrow."

"He might be the man I saw riding into town from the west this morning. I passed him as I was riding home after the smith replaced Star's shoe," Susanna added. "He was a big man riding a huge black with four white stockings; a beautiful animal."

Weeks was not sure which Susanna was referring to the horse or its rider, or both. But, based on the passion in her voice, there was obviously something there to consider.

"Sheriff Donny said he is staying at the Palace Hotel and I have left a message with the hotel that I would enjoy his company over breakfast tomorrow," Clive said. "Would you like to join me, Mr. Weeks?"

"Yes, yes I believe I would indeed."

That same night, Van and Dutch arrived late at another saloon and were enjoying whiskey now that their pockets were full. Van was keeping a careful watch on the miners, looking for their next mark while trying hard not to appear obvious. This saloon had a mix of patrons, both miners and locals. The locals were paying with coin and most miners paying for their beer with silver dust or small rocks of silver. The barkeep kept a scale at the end of the bar and appeared to be honest and fair with the weights and valuation. Van decided to be cautious and never pay for his whiskey with coin and then at the same saloon use silver, as it would raise questions.

He took an immediate interest in a middle-aged well-dressed man that was winning at the poker table. He was dressed in a pale gray broadcloth suit trimmed in black, string tie, and white high-collared shirt. By the way he was sitting at the poker table Van could not see if he was armed, but assumed he was, but with what? His derby hat was placed neatly beside his winnings on the table. A half full glass of whiskey rested beside the derby.

Van, having heard the man stating that this would be his last game, motioned to Dutch to drink up. He wanted to be out of the saloon before the gambler left so as to not be connected to the robbery soon to happen. Outside the saloon, they secreted themselves in an alleyway shadow, awaiting the gambler's exit while checking their pistols and knives. Van was keeping a careful eye out for the deputies that patrolled the streets in twos, both with Colts and double-barreled scatterguns. They were a very real concern and seemed to vary their patrol timing and locations.

Finally, the gambler pushed through the double doors and stepped onto the saloon's boardwalk. He waited in the shadows for his eyes to become accustomed to the darkness and scanned the street. Feeling comfortable that no threats were about, he turned left, away from Van and Dutch and began walking away, presumably to home.

Van and Dutch hurried through the rear alley to get behind the saloon and ran three blocks ahead, and turned into the alley that the gambler would pass in a minute or two. They could hear the gambler's footfalls on the boardwalk and waited for him to pass. Van motioned to Dutch to pull his bandana over his face and made a threatening face that meant, "Don't screw up this time."

They waited until he had passed them and neared the end of the alley crossroad, then jumping out behind him, Van pushed the barrel of his gun into the small of the gambler's back and pulled him into the shadows, saying, "No sudden moves and you will live to see ya family, try anything and the last thing you will feel a bullet tearin' up your back. Now, hand over the money in your vest pocket and don't turn around!"

"Okay, okay!" The gambler was obviously concerned for his life.

"Now, keep your right hand at your side and use your left hand to pass the money to me. Very slowly!" Van pushed the pistol barrel hard into the gambler's back as a reminder.

The gambler had a derringer, and while pretending he was reaching for the money carefully lifted it from his vest pocket and placed it in his grip. Then he reached for the paper money and presented it to his right side with the derringer hidden by the vest wallet. When Dutch reached for the wallet the gambler pulled the trigger but missed Dutch due to the bad angle and the wallet fell to the ground. An instant later, Van pulled his trigger and the bullet severed the gambler's spinal cord, dropping him like a sack of flour, falling on top of his wallet. The gunshot would certainly alert the deputies and they would be here in minutes.

"Dutch, get the money. Quick. We got to get away from here fast!" Dutch rolled the gambler over, grabbed the wallet, then emptied it of the cash and dropped the wallet. Van kicked the gambler in the ribs and head to relieve his anger and they ran back down the alley, then entered another saloon casually and ordered whiskey.

Later, back in their hotel, they counted out the money and were pleased that it totaled more than six hundred dollars. Laughing due to nervous energy and happy for their luck, they didn't think twice about another killing. They were becoming greedy and more confident.

***

Clinton Weeks and Clive, his chief of security, rose early and rode into Virginia City to breakfast with Liam deBláca at the Palace Hotel. It was another cool, crisp morning and the sun had not yet burned off the mist blanketing the shallows. Workers lined the hard mud streets, moving somberly in the direction of the mines, facing yet another long day of labor in the caverns of the mountain. Some miners tipped their hats when Weeks trotted by, others plodded by without the slightest recognition.

Weeks and Clive reined up as they approached the Palace Hotel, then dismounted and looped their reins over the hitching rail fronting the boardwalk. Liam watched through the lobby window as they climbed the stairs and approached the hotel's front door, noting the alert eyes and determined and easy gait of the larger man as well as the tied-down Colt on his right hip. He surmised quickly and correctly that he was a man to reckon with.

Meeting the pair at the door and extending his hand, Liam greeted them, "Good morning, gentlemen. I assume you are Mr. Weeks."

"Yes, and this is Clive Ackerman, my Chief of Security."

"Liam deBláca, Chief Inspector, United States Marshals Service," Liam said, as he extended his hand now to Clive.

Seated at a round table in the Palace Hotel's restaurant, having ordered their breakfast, they began a light conversation over rich, steaming black coffee. "Mr. deBláca, I have not encountered the title of Chief Inspector before," Weeks said as more of a question than a statement.

"Well, Mr. Weeks, most people have not. I report directly to the U.S. Attorney General and am under orders directly from the President. My reports go directly to both. The important distinction is that I have jurisdiction everywhere within the United States and its territories, and all Deputy U.S. Marshals report to me. I am not bound by state, county, city or town law, but rather by federal law. By simple example, murders, rapists and robbers frequently cross a state line, commit their crime, and cross back over to their original state, or to a different state, without fear of chase. That is not the case with me."

Clive jumped in, "Mr. deBláca…"

Liam interrupted, "Please, Mr. Ackerman, call me Liam. My friends do and I hope, in time, we will become friends."

"Thank you Liam. And it is Clive." He said with a genuine smile. "Your responsibility seems enormous! The United States and its territories is a mighty big piece of geography for a single man to police."

"It is Clive. That is why I am focused on the worst of humanity and have the help of the deputy marshals when needed."

Weeks joined the discussion as breakfast was being served. "I assume your visit to Virginia City is official?"

"Mr. Weeks, you are keenly observant. Yes, I am trailing a man who has murdered twenty-one people, including my father and mother. I have been following this man all the way from Washington and suspect he and his pard are here in Virginia City. He is brutal, scum, sent directly from hell, and I will bring him in. Here is a likeness of him. Have there been any robberies or killings here recently?"

Before Weeks could respond, Sheriff Donny approached the table, "Mornin', Weeks. Clive." Then looking at Liam he said, "Another murder and robbery last night. This time a local, mostly known as a gambler. Shot at close range in the back. So close, his coat was burned from the powder. That probably muffled the shot so my deputies had difficulty locating where it came from. There were no witnesses. But, I see it as the same outlaw that has killed your miners, Weeks. Robbed and murdered in the shadows. I thought you would like to know, Liam."

After the sheriff left, the three sat in silence, pondering the situation over coffee. It was Weeks that broke the silence. "Liam, would you consider joining Clive and my daughter Susanna for supper this evening? I would like to talk more of this. Please don't misunderstand; I have complete confidence in Clive. He is a most capable and trusted man. I trust him with my life, the life of my daughter and my miners. But, you have knowledge of this outlaw that he doesn't, and we have knowledge of this city that you lack. Possibly we can help one another bring an end to this terror."

"I would be pleased to join you all. Thank you for the invitation and the offer of cooperation."

"Shall we say seven for a pre-supper whiskey?"

That afternoon Van sat at a table in in the saloon deep in thought, a whiskey in his right hand's fingers, twirling the glass from the top rim. Dutch was sleeping in the hotel, preparing for another late evening of spotting and robbing their next mark. Van could not stop thinking about Susanna's fire and beauty. Actually, he didn't want to stop thinking of her. He wanted to experience her. It was how and when that occupied his devious mind. His pockets were full so there was no need for immediate action. But, his loins were protesting and pushed for action, soon.

Pipe smoke choked the air of the saloon. The piano played marginally off key. The vapors of stale beer, the arguments at the faro tables and the clinks of beer mugs were all oblivious to Van.

And then it came to him. He sneered which was a smile in his mind. Lifting the whiskey-filled glass to his lips, he drained it so roughly whiskey dripped from his graying handlebar mustache. He slammed the glass down on the table so hard it shattered. He had his plan.

***

Liam approached The Mansion's iron gate in the post sundown darkness, identified himself to the guard who was obviously expecting him. He scanned the security around The Mansion; ten-foot high stone walls surrounding the mansion and roving well-armed guards, and a guard tower on the wall to the right of the gate. Impressive, he thought privately. He concluded that this must be where the silver is stored before shipping.

He was met at the door by a servant that took Creena to the stables and was told that his horse would be curried, watered and grain fed, and would be ready for his return trip to town this evening. Before approaching the stairs leading to the door, he took in The Mansion. It was a huge rock and timber two-story structure. Stone was, of course, readily available but timber less so. The first floor was above a man's height, making it difficult to scale and enter from the ground. The front door was of solid oak boasting large black-forged iron hinges and door locks with a small, barred leaded-glass viewing pane about head high. Nodding, he concluded that Weeks and Clive take their security seriously.

Liam's thoughts were interrupted by a slight squeak from the hinge as the door opened. He was temporarily stunned by the woman profiled by the lighting from within The Mansion. He couldn't yet see the face, but he was struck by the grace and beauty that radiated from her body. Her stance was that of a very confident woman, older than her years.

"Welcome to our home Mr. deBláca. Her voice was melodic, firm, cultured, sultry but yet mischievous. "Are you going to come in or should we plan to serve supper out here," she adding a little chuckle for Liam's benefit.

As he approached the door where the woman was standing and removing his black, flat-crowned hat, he offered his hand, "Liam deBláca, ma'am." She took his hand softly in hers, covering his hand with her left hand and said, "Susanna Weeks." She smiled warmly, and Liam's knees buckled slightly.

"Ahhh, there you are Liam! Welcome! I see that you have met my daughter, Susanna. Come, join us for a whiskey," Weeks said as he moved to the table where several crystal decanters rested, all filled to various amounts with golden liquids. "What is your pleasure Liam? Whiskey, American that is, scotch, or tequila? Or perhaps your tastes run more to Irish whiskey straight from your homeland, or a Kentucky bourbon?"

"Father, a scotch for me please and if I am a judge of a man, I would say American whisky for Mr. deBláca."

"You are a good judge ma'am; whiskey would be my choice. Thank you."

"Mr. deBláca, I would prefer if you addressed me as Susanna. And, would it be too presumptuous of me to address you as Liam?"

Smiling at a woman of uncommon beauty, with confidence, poise and intelligence radiating from within, Liam said, "I would be honored, Susanna."

They were soon seated with Weeks at the head of the enormous table, Clive and Susanna in flanking positions, and Liam sitting beside Susanna. Up until now, the conversation had been casual with talk of the town and the mines and the recent new vein discovery. With a meal of roasted meats, vegetables and breads served, Weeks began the more serious discussion by asking Liam to describe more about Van Cooper.

"Weeks, he is the worst of human kind, completely devoid of remorse and totally focused on his own needs and pleasures. He kills not only without the slightest care; it almost seems a pleasure. He is evil, pure evil, and poison mean. He is a calculating man, driven to acquire another man's wealth and his own carnal pleasure. Make no mistake however, he is a creative and thinking man, all a bad combination for those law abiding people around him."

"That I know of, twenty-one deaths are credited to his hand. Perhaps your robberies will make it twenty-four if proven. And at least one... molestation. I first encountered him in Washington when I was Director of the U.S. Marshals Service. I resigned my position to hunt him down and, believe me when I say; I will find him and bring some amount of justice to those twenty-one people. It is my best guess that he is in this city because he prays on the innocent and unsuspecting. And women are fair game, if not better game. Miners with silver in their pockets and gamblers with bills in their wallets are easy pickings for him and his partner Dutch. I have no proof that he, and his partner Dutch, are responsible for the deaths of your miners. It could be a simple coincidence. But, I do not like coincidences."

Clive asked, "How will you find this man?"

"I have had a personal encounter with him and I will never, never ever, forget his face. I'll look for him, discretely, of course, because he has seen my face as well. That is why I have left the black beard disguising my normally clean-shaven face. It may give me an edge. My guess is he will frequent the bars and, forgive me Susanna, the brothels."

"How can we be of help?"

"I am happy you asked Clive. I suggest you alert your miners and tell them that groups of four would likely scare Van and Dutch away. That should prevent any additional loss of life in your miners' ranks. Your security here is good, quite good. Therefore, I wouldn't expect a direct assault. Susanna, I would suggest you stay close to home until this is over. This man is brutal, to man or woman."

"You need not worry yourself over me, Liam. I travel armed and I know how to use a gun and I am not afraid of using it!" She was a bit more vocal and seemed upset that Liam thought she might not be able to take care of herself.

"Susanna, I was not implying that you could not protect yourself. You seem quite capable. But, a man like Van Cooper is a back shooter and a dry gulcher, and no one is immune to such ugly tactics. Not me, Clive or your father. And... not you. Give me time to catch this scum, please!" Liam said with concern.

Plates having been cleared, they now sat quietly with coffee thinking about what Liam had described and suggested. Weeks ended the evening by saying, "You seem a very capable young man, Liam, and we will take your suggestions. If I or Clive can be of help, in any way, I expect you will come calling. Susanna, would you walk Liam to the door, please?"

Susanna and Liam talked quietly as a stable hand brought Creena to the front steps and alerted the guards of his departure. Now, standing a few feet apart, for a long moment they just looked into one another's eyes, communicating wordlessly, aware of their breath rate increasing, acknowledging the depth of their spark. Each sensing the other's need to part for their own private quiet reflection, extended their hands and bid good evening. Susanna smiled warmly.

The eastern sun was beginning its morning voyage over the mountain, fingering long shadows over boulders and trees. A blanket of mist floated over the low areas below approaching the town but not on the hill where Van and Dutch were secreted, watching.

"Van, I still don't know why we left the hotel for that ratty shack way yonder, southeast of town. The hotel had a saloon and it was close to the whorehouses."

"Dutch, you are one dumb hombre, you know that! I don't know why I keep you around. You couldn't find your ass with a pair of deer antlers! Now, keep watchin' that front gate and tell me when she rides out. And, don't let me catch ya lookin' at anything but that gate!"

They were well hidden in the shadows of large boulders, well above the mist. None of The Mansion's guards could see them and they were completely hidden from the town view. Waiting was an acquired skill. Wolves were born with such a skill, it having been bred into them since the beginning of time. Dutch had no such breeding. He kept fidgeting and complaining. After the first hour, Van took over as he was concerned Dutch would miss Susanna riding out. It was over an hour later when the gates opened and she trotted out on her mare. Van waited until he could be certain of her direction before he roused Dutch and mounted their horses in distant pursuit.

They left their hideout too soon to see a second rider pass through the gate, also in distant pursuit.

That same morning, as Liam left the telegraph office having updated Jeremiah, the U.S. Attorney General, regarding the status of his pursuit of Van Cooper, he was hailed by Sheriff Donny holding his scattergun in the hollow of his left arm. "Mornin' Marshal, anything new?"

"I enjoyed supper last night with Weeks and Clive. They are suggesting to their miners that groups of four would be a good deterrent until Van is found and arrested."

"I bet you enjoyed the company of Susanna as well," the sheriff said with a sly grin. "Groups of four make good sense. Let me know if I can help ya."

This morning, Liam planned to walk the city looking into the saloons and checking the hotel registries. It would consume the morning and perhaps some of the afternoon. Later in the day he would check the whorehouses.

Virginia City was alive, teeming with people on horseback and rigs raising dust everywhere. Silver had brought in the prospectors and the miners. The miners needed housing, food, and pleasure. Stores, hotels, banks, saloons, liveries, and blacksmiths all grew out of the needs of the city, and created yet a larger city. But Liam believed he didn't need to search the entire city as Van would prefer the lesser hotels. Not rooming or boarding houses, but a slightly seedy hotel with a saloon in or nearby, and, more than likely, whorehouses nearby.

That would be where he started and, with nine of the twelve hotels checked without success, Liam began to question his logic. Could Van have robbed so successfully that he would be staying in a hotel the caliber of the Palace? It was possible, but not likely as his manners and dress would cause him to stand out far too readily. No, I am on the right track, he thought. Stick to your plan, he concluded.

It was the eleventh hotel that gave him hope. Looking at the sketched likeness that Liam showed the desk clerk brought recognition to his face. "Yes, he was here and a real hard case he was; checked out this morning. Didn't say nothin'. Just paid his bill, and he and his pard left," the hotel manager said.

"How long was he here and what time did he leave, exactly?"

"Hmm, let me see now Marshal. He's been here for three or four days I reckon. They checked out before sunup."

Liam had scored on two counts. He now had conclusive evidence that Van and Dutch were in fact here in Virginia City and he had a solid description of Dutch. But, where did they go? Another hotel possibly? Virginia City may be a silver city but it was a gold mine to Van. Easy pickings. Why would they leave? Had Van seen him and decided to run? No, he thought. If Van had seen him, he would plot to kill him, which was worth consideration. He concluded that Van must have another and probably bigger scheme to line his pockets and that worried him deeply.

The chestnut mare was at full cantor with Susanna secure in the saddle, both enjoying the morning ride in the brisk mountain air. Star was a Rocky Mountain pure bred that enjoyed Susanna giving him his head. The sun had begun to soften the crisp morning air and encouraged Susanna to extend her ride deeper into the adjoining hills. Refreshing menthol from the giant fir trees lining the path flooded the air. Star's footfalls were softened by the aspen leaves and pine needles over the soft earth. She reined up as she approached the stream where she typically allowed Star to water and rest before the ride home.

Susanna loosened Star's cinch and walked her down to the stream to drink and then ground hitched the mare, allowing her to graze of the lush streamside green grass. She sat with her back against a large evergreen and watched as Star fed. Her eyes closed and she became so deep in thought about the interesting and handsome Liam she didn't notice Star lifting her head and twitching her ears. But a moment later, she became aware that the grass munching had stopped and stood abruptly.

As she turned to investigate what Star had heard, she was struck hard on the head and the world folded into blackness.

Clive had followed her on her morning rides and was aware of her typical stopping point, so he secreted himself about a hundred yards down the trail awaiting her return.

He began to worry after nearly thirty minutes had passed and decided to quietly move in for a closer look, staying well off the trail. Walking, leaving his horse ground hitched to graze, he came to the stream, but Susanna was not to be seen. He could see signs that she had been here, Star watered and grazed. Cutting a wider circle, he found signs of two other horses, and boot prints worn down at the lees, and then the prints of three horses heading further down the trail at a fast gait. Damn!

Clive ran back to his horse and pressed heels to flanks, running his horse hell bent for leather down the trail. The trail was easy to follow at first, but then the three horses went into the stream and Clive couldn't find where they exited. He looked for signs over several hours on both sides of the stream before admitting that he needed more men. It was now mid-day, and although there were several hours of daylight ahead, time was not on his side. He pressed his horse to the limits to get back to The Mansion to get more men and a fresh horse. Dread began to wash over him.

It took less than thirty minutes to reach The Mansion and as he approached, he drew and fired three quick shots in the air to alarm the guards of trouble. The guards recognized Clive and his horse before he fired and had the front gate already opened as the lathered horse and rider ran through and reined up.

"Hal, get Jose, Matt, Briggs and Spence saddled with two days of provisions ready to ride in fifteen minutes! Susanna has been abducted! Leave Walt and Billy here on guard. Oh, get me a fresh horse saddled and make sure this one is watered and fed a bag of oats. Hurry man!"

Clive took three steps at a time getting into The Mansion, only to remember that Weeks was at his office in Virginia City. Quickly, he sat at the writing table and wrote out two notes, one to Weeks and the other to Liam explaining what had happened. Then he summoned the cook and told her to deliver them both to Mr. Weeks immediately, knowing that Weeks would find Liam and then ran to meet the hands.

The six riders left at a trot, saving their animals for what could be a long ride. Reaching the stream Clive briefed the men. "I cut sign for two horses that joined Susanna's mare up this path. They carried two men based on the boot tracks. They entered the stream here in hopes of losing any trackers. This is where I lost them. Hal, you take Spence and Jose and search on the far side of the creek. Matt and Briggs, you're with me on this side. Let's do this thorough like, no mistakes, don't miss anything! Move out. Susanna's life is in our hands!"

Nearly two hours had passed as they looked for anything that would provide a hint of where Susanna and her abductors had gone. Two groups of three, on foot leading their horses, hunched over looking for a hoof scrape on a rock face, a broken twig, depressed grass and hoof print, but nothing. Hal yelled across the creek, "Clive, they couldn't have stayed in the creek for this long. This is a mountain run-off and the cold would shy their mounts. And, we've been extra careful and I know we haven't missed anything. So, that could mean only one thing. They went in the other direction, not away from town, but back toward town."

"Sumbitch! I am not thinking straight. Of course they could have. This creek runs a bit north which would have put several hundred yards between where I was waiting for Susanna to return. So, I wouldn't have heard their horses. Let's ride, boys!" Clive was furious with himself for not having thought of this himself.

The two teams of three reach the point where they had entered the creek and were now cutting sign due west. About twenty minutes later, Clive was rewarded with the clear hoof prints. "Got it men, over here!"

There they were on the side of the creek closest to the town, three horses heading straight for the path and that would be a problem. There are too many horses using that path and these three don't have anything unique about their shoes. No cracks, nicks or bent nails. Clive again began to fear for Susanna's life.

Clive began to think through the options. Back on the path, would they have been ahead of him or behind him. It was about thirty minutes before I found her missing but how long before that did they abduct her? He reasoned that Susanna would have cared for Star first, say ten minutes, then rested enough time to allow the men to approach unseen and unheard, say another ten minutes, and then five minutes for the abduction because they would have to tie and gag her. That would mean they were in the creek when I was running back to get my horse. They had to travel west. They couldn't have gone east or we would have run straight into each other.

But, Clive was thinking, he had lit a shuck back to The Mansion, following this path all the way to the tree line. If they were on the path it was likely he would have overtaken them, so they left the path between here and the tree line. Clive shared his reasoning with the boys and they all agreed. It was back to searching on both sides of the path. Daylight was their enemy.

Weeks found Liam at the Palace Hotel and quickly told him the story. "Now, Clive and five of our hands are tracking them," Weeks said, finally catching his breath. Worry had overcome him and his face was white with fear.

"I found Van Cooper and Dutch this morning, or more accurately where they were staying up until this morning. They checked out before sunup. This could be a coincidence but as I have already told you, I don't believe in coincidences. They are running short of daylight, Weeks; I am going to help."

"I am with you," Weeks said.

"No. That isn't a good idea. You are too close to this, too emotional. It could get you killed and perhaps others. If I am any judge, Clive is a good man, one to ride the river with. And, I think he cares for Susanna, not that he needs any additional motivation," Liam said in a softer tone, but no less commanding. What he didn't say, but was thinking through, was the possibility that if it was Van Cooper, Susanna might be held for ransom. Van would know that Weeks had a small fortune in silver steeled away in The Mansion, all company money, not Weeks' personal fortune, so he would be less likely to resist paying. Van is devious enough to have planned this carefully and, worse, brutal enough to leave no witnesses.

"Rider approaching, Clive," Hal said.

Clive recognized both man and horse. "It's alright boys, that's U.S. Marshal Liam deBláca, I reckon he's come to lend a hand. Good man too." All the hands continued to cut for sign, heads down, leading their horses.

Clive reined up in the path center between the men. "Got your message, Clive. Damn sorry this happened. And, I have a bit of news. Found where Van Cooper and Dutch were staying, but they checked out of the hotel before sunup this morning."

Clive looked a bit distant and refocused, asking Liam, "You thinking what I'm thinking?"

"I am. And it scares the hell out of me for that poor young woman! I know Susanna can handle herself, but these men are poison mean and brutal."

Clive was working a few more things in his head. "This path goes west to the tree line outside the city. If they checked out of the hotel, then they are likely not heading back to the city. That would mean they are in these hills, an abandoned mine or miner's shack."

"That makes sense, Clive."

"But, why Susanna? There are hundreds of women, many that would want their type of company," Clive said as he rubbed the whiskers on his chin.

"I have a theory Clive, and if proven right, may help us narrow down where they might be."

"Let's hear it man!"

"Van Cooper has never worked an honest day in his life. He has killed, robbed, and stole for his money. He is a thief, and he is good at what he does. Then he arrives in Virginia City, where miners are paying for whiskey in silver dust. He robs and kills miners, takes their hard-earned silver. He gets a taste of 'real money'. Then he learns where there is a lot of silver, The Mansion. But, he isn't as skilled a robber as would be needed to take The Mansion…"

Clive caught on quickly and interrupted Liam, "So, he kidnaps Susanna for ransom."

"That is my theory. But Clive, there are two aspects of this that I worry about. How will Van Cooper get that much silver out of Virginia City? After all, silver is heavy. Also, the ransom process could take a few days and Susanna, alone with those animals during that time — I just don't want to think about that. And she will most likely have already seen their faces…"

Clive jumped in again with a whisper, "They can't leave any witnesses."

Susanna first became aware of a strong must in the dusty air. Then, in the distance, she could make out mumbling. All was dark until she became conscious enough to realize that her eyes were closed. She remained still and began trying to put the pieces together. She could feel her hands tied about her wrists and feet tied at the ankles. Her head was pounding with every beat of her heart and every breath into her lungs. That confirmed that she was alive. It came to her in scraps, unordered and confusing. She remembered watching Star graze, then stopping her gazing, her head lift, ears twitch… then she turned, but after that nothing else came to her. Her head pounded, and she realized that she must have been struck from behind. Panic began to consume her as she organized all the pieces. She had been abducted!

Keep your breathing under control, she admonished herself. Remaining perfectly still, she dared to open one eye to a slit. The lantern light caused her pupil to dilate which caused pain to shoot through her head like bolts of lightning and explosive loud thunder. She determined that she must have a concussion. Before closing her eye again, she took in a filthy cramped room containing a potbelly stove, a round decrepit table with four chairs, some empty shelves, a filthy window, and a door. It looked like an old cabin, possible an abandoned miner's cabin.

She was better able to understand the mumbles better now. "You hit that girl too hard, Dutch! She is still out cold. You cain't do anythin' right. She may be out though this whole night."

"That don't mean ya can't have some fun, Van. Its jist like she was a sleepin'!"

"Oh no! I want me a fightin' woman; and that there is a woman with fire. She'll fight."

"You can wait then Van, but I don' care if she is awake or not, I mountin' her right now!"

"You touch that woman before me Dutch and I gut shoot you. That's a promise!"

"Alright, alright. You first."

"Glad we got that settled. Now, you take this note to that kid at the livery and tell him to deliver it to Weeks right away. Give the boy four bits. Then you git right back here. No saloons and no whorehouses. Hear? No saloons and no whorehouses!"

Billy brought the note to Weeks immediately, figuring it had something to do with Susanna. The message was short:

We have yur daughtr. $50,000 gits her back alive tomorow sundon. 2 packhorses cash, gold or silver and provisons for 2 weeks. If we ain't followed I will let her go after one week. If ya follow us, she dies gut shot. One of us will get the packhorses where we grabed her.

"Is it bad news, Mr. Weeks?" Billy asked.

"It is a ransom note Billy. They want $50,000 by sundown tomorrow. They plan on keeping Susanna for another week."

Billy thought about what that meant for Susanna and cringed.

"Clive. Who knows these hills better than anyone?"

"That would be Joe Crabtree. He's a breed. Sioux, I think. Lives in a cabin outside the southeast part of town," Clive answered. "You're right, Liam, there's just too much land to cover and with darkness setting in we will never find her. Let's go but leave the boys here cutting sign. It's a small chance they will find something, but right now that's all we have."

"Boys, Liam and I are going to fetch Joe Crabtree. We reckon he knows these hills better than anyone, and we hope he can narrow down our search area to a few spots. Keep looking and we'll be back directly." Then Liam and Clive turned west toward Virginia City at an easy trot to save their animals for a long night ahead, with the sun low on the horizon and in their face reminding them that time was running out.

The sounds of the saloon piano grabbed at Dutch but Van's orders were to return right away. But, he needed a drink of whiskey. Just one drink, quick. But then, Van would smell the whiskey on his breath and all hell would rain down on him. Dutch swore at himself, turned and mounted his horse heading east out of town.

At that same time on their way to Joe Crabtree's cabin, Liam and Clive were riding down Virginia City's main street, the very street that Dutch had just left.

"Helooo the house," Clive yelled. "Joe, its Clive Ackerman and we need your help."

The cabin door opened slowly and a man appeared, framed by the lantern light from within. He was holding a Sharps .56. "How do Clive? Coffee's hot. Come in and set."

They brought their horses to the trough and let them drink their full then looped the reins around the hitching pole. Liam needed to duck walk into the cabin as the door was only about six feet high, but inside was warm, neat and comfortable. They sat at a clean square table and waited for Joe to bring the mugs of coffee.

Joe Crabtree was stout and muscled. His black straight hair was pulled together and tied with a pigging string at the back of his neck, framing his dark complexion and bright, even white teeth. He was dressed in clean fringed deerskin. His eyes were black, alert and friendly and gave the correct impression that they didn't miss anything.

Clive started, "Joe, this is Liam deBláca, U.S. Marshal. Actually he is the top dog, the head of all U.S. Marshals." Liam and Joe nodded to each other wordlessly as Clive went on to explain why they needed his help.

Joe sat quietly for several minutes before commenting. "Susanna is a nice girl. She knows horses and cares for them. I like her. She is kind and always had time for me. Strange, you asking about an abandoned mine or vacant cabin, second time this week."

Liam jumped in, "Second time?"

"Yes sir, second time."

Liam removed the likeness from his pocket and turning it so that Joe could see it right side up, asked, "Was this man the first time?"

"Yes sir. That is surely him. Didn't like him much. Shifty guy. Bad eyes. Unclean. Treated his animal poorly." Joe responded shaking his head.

Clive urgently asked, "Joe, what did you tell them? Time is wasting!"

"Well, I told him there were three possibilities; the old Clayton mine that was played out but the company had boarded up the entrance, the Rogers and Whitney dig, and old man Riggs's cabin in the southeast hills. He kind of liked the cabin, perked up when I mentioned it. Gave me a double eagle for the advice."

"I know where that cabin is, Liam. It is well away from where the boys are now. We can get there in an hour or so, but it will be full on dark by then," Clive said with the urgency still in his voice. "Thanks Joe, you may have saved Susanna's life."

Liam and Clive watered their horses again and headed out to the southeast hills. They were thickly forested with fir, pine and cedar. The air smelled fresh and clean with a hint of syrupy pine menthol. As they rode, Clive described to Liam the cabin location and surroundings.

"There is one trail that leads directly to the cabin, it ends there. Trees all around. The cabin sits on a shelf with its back to a steep rock face. To the right, just through the trees, there is a fall off of more than one hundred feet. Same to the front. The trail comes up from the left."

"The cabin is a one-room shack, really. One window, as I recall, facing the approaching trail. Riggs died a few years back. He had himself an altercation with a grizzly that didn't work out well for him."

"Clive, this place sounds exactly like the spot Van Cooper would choose."

The trail had a number of switchbacks to get to the higher elevation and on one of them Liam thought he saw another rider ahead of them. "Clive, I think there is someone ahead of us. Watch the next switchback," Liam said in hushed tones.

"You're right. I did see him."

Liam was thinking it could be Dutch. If his theory was right, a ransom note would need to be delivered and Van would send Dutch for that. If they could catch Dutch...

"Clive, how can we get ahead of Dutch and take him out?"

"I believe on the next switchback there is an old miner's rail. You know, the kind they would use a rope and pulley to lower an ore car. It is pretty steep and will be hell on our mounts, but we might make it."

Reaching the old mining trail, Liam noticed that there were timber supports laid into the hill supporting the iron rails. "Clive, we can't take our mounts up this trail without alerting Dutch. The horse's hooves will likely click on that rail. I will go up on foot and you follow with my mount. Make sense to you?"

"I see it the same way."

Liam dismounted and handed his beloved Creena's reins to Clive. He jumped up to the first timber, steadied himself and began to climb on hands and feet. Slower at first, but then his speed increased as he learned how to achieve stealth with his footing. Several times he stumbled in the darkness but was able to right himself before sending loose rocks down the hill that would have alerted Dutch. His knees and hands were scraped and bleeding, but he continued to the top, nearing the switchback path.

He reached the top, eyes level with the path and secreted himself behind some scrub and searched down the switchback. Dutch was not yet visible. Thinking through his objective, Liam determined he needed to get to the other side of the path to a higher elevation. To be sure he took Dutch without a shot that would surely alert Van, he would need to jump Dutch. Running across the path, he looked for a place from which to jump and was rewarded with a sizable boulder at the edge of the path and made it to its top just as he heard the footfalls of Dutch's mount approaching.

Liam laid his body chest down on the rock, and positioned himself with knees bent and boot toes wedged into a crevice for pushing leverage, ready. He watched Dutch amble up the path, head down, possibly dozing. His horse's head bobbling at every step, obviously tired and not well cared for. Liam waited until Dutch was directly in front of him before jumping. Then everything happened in a lightning flash. Liam sensed his body was in mid-flight and saw Dutch lift his head to the right. Their eyes locked. Fear shown in the eyes of Dutch, determined resolve in the eyes of Liam.

Liam hit Dutch squarely with his right shoulder driving into Dutch's right side with such force that both landed on the path's opposite edge and then began rolling down the old mining rail toward the switchback path below. Liam kept his wits about him and flattened his body to stop the roll but Dutch did not and hit the path below with a thud and then lay sprawled and still. Quickly, Liam assessed his legs and arms and was relieved that nothing was broken.

Liam checked his guns and was rewarded by their touch. The thongs had done their job and held the custom .44's in their holsters. He made his way quietly down the mining track. Dutch was alive but unconscious. Liam dragged the body behind some scrub, removed his filthy coat, and tied his hands and feet with pigging strings. Then he stuffed Dutch's dirty bandana in his mouth and used another pigging string to hold it in tight. Quietly climbing back up the mining track to meet Clive he was able to retrieve both his and Dutch's hats.

Clive offered a hand up onto the path. "You all right? You look a mess!"

"Yeah, nothing broken but my pride. Dutch is out cold. I secured him behind some scrub."

"What you doing with his coat and… I see. You'll be riding up to the shack looking like Dutch. Good plan and it might give you an edge," Clive said. "Good, I have his horse. I'll back you."

The air thinned with elevation and misty clouds hung within the firs. Moonlight was scarce and thinly penetrated the mist. A slight wind whispered through the firs and rock outcroppings. A coyote sang in the distance. But for that, in mountain terms, the night was still.

Clive had ground hitched the horses within a small level and sparsely grassed meadow and was making his way afoot toward the shack, keeping to the shadows. Liam had dawned Dutch's smelly coat and hat and rode Dutch's bronc, plodding slowly toward the shack. He was trying to look sleepy and normal as he plodded up the path. The plan was to do what Dutch would have done, ride straight to the lean-to stable, remove the saddle and bridle, fork some hay into the manger and walk to the shack. Liam was taller than Dutch, so he slumped a bit as he walked to the door. There was a lantern burning inside the shack, but he couldn't risk looking into the small window as he approached for fear of being recognized.

Knocking on the weathered door, Liam disguising his voice as best he could, said. "It's me Van, don't shoot. I'm cumin' in." He waited for a response, but there was only silence.

Repeating himself, "Van, it's me. I'm a-cumin'. Don't shoot." But, again, the only sound was the screaming wind through the mountain. "Van, wake up you bastard!"

Liam had to risk it, drew his right .44 and pushed open the door.

There before him was the one-room shack with a lantern setting on the small wood table. The small flame cast shadows that danced on the roof and walls. The only thing that moved was Liam. The shack was empty.

Holstering his .44, he stepped quickly to the table to retrieve the lantern. There was a note held beneath it. Lifting the lantern and bringing the note into the light, he read:

Clive, you didint think I was a fool, did ya? Dutch was gunna get caught, fur sur. And he would sing. You want the gurl, folla the instructins I gave Weeks.

Liam grabbed the lantern and ran to the lean-to stable. Only one horse, Dutch's horse. It had been too dark when he stabled him to see the stable was empty. Moving to the other stalls, kneeling, he felt their droppings. Cold. They had been gone for hours.

Clive, watching from the shadows, was momentarily confused by Liam's behavior. But after stitching things together, holstered his Colt and walked into the lean-to. Liam handed Clive the note.

"Son of a bitch! He could be anywhere and he knows we can't track him in the dark. He will have a solid ten hours on us, Liam."

"Yes, but two things remain in our favor. One, this note is addressed to you, so he doesn't know I am here. And, two, he still wants the ransom. But I can't imagine what Susanna is going through right now."

Weeks was pacing back and forth in The Mansion's great room when Clive and Liam arrived. Clive filled Weeks in, adding that they left Dutch with the sheriff for prosecution.

Clive asked to see the ransom note.

We have yur daughtr. $50,000 gits her back alive tomorow sundon. 2 packhorses cash, gold or silver and provisons for 2 weeks. If we ain't followed I will let her go after one week. If ya follow us, she dies gut shot. One of us will get the packhorses where we grabed her.

Liam read and then reread it after Clive was finished. "The ransom is today at sundown, precisely where Susanna was abducted. Clive, you know where that is, right?"

"Yes, and it isn't good, for us. There isn't much cover. Two packhorses, provisions and only $50,000. He's smart.

The weight won't be a factor. The horses can handle it. He has all the cards!" Clive said as he slammed the ransom note on the table.

Weeks jumped in yelling, "I don't give a damn about the money! I just want Susanna back safe, unharmed. You understand, both of you! Just give him what he wants and get her back."

Both Clive and Liam knew it wasn't going to be that easy. Van was keeping Susanna for one week while he made his escape. His promise was to gut shoot her if he saw anyone on his trail. Yet, they had to trail her to be there if he made good on his other promise and release her in seven days. Both knew that he would never let Susanna go alive and the longer she was his captive, the more horrible her nightmare would be.

Liam took control, "Okay. Let's get the packhorses loaded exactly as he demanded. Clive, you will deliver the packhorses at sundown. You know it will be dangerous; he could shoot you where you stand. But, I don't think he will. He knows he has all the cards. It is a power trip for him and a big score, his biggest. He will want to see your back riding away, beaten and humiliated, to pump his ego. He knows that you will trail him, but he doesn't know of me. This is a dangerous game, Clive. Your life and Susanna's are at risk here. Stay way back, but allow him to know you are there."

"Now, here is where it gets really dangerous. I have been tracking this man across the country, all the way from Washington. I know this man. He'll dry gulch you, but he is only an average long shot. Clive, you will need to figure out when and where it is likely to reduce the odds of hitting you. No matter if you are hit or not, fall from your horse and don't move after the shot. Cooper won't come to you and he doesn't care for your horse either. He will just move on, believing he is free. I will be to your east and on his trail. And then, the edge will be ours. I will hit him that night while he camps with his guard down."

Clive was pensive, thinking the plan through. "It may work and if I keep my distance I should be alive to see Susanna home. But, he has been one step ahead of us all the way. What if he has something up his sleeve that we haven't thought of?"

"That is a possibility. I think it is Susanna that may trigger it. We don't know how she is or if she still has her .31 secreted. But, we do know that if she has a chance to escape, she will take it," Liam added.

Van Cooper rode north all night, scouting for a place to rest. Susanna was tied belly-down over her saddle, and Star was jittery knowing something was not right. She continued her ruse of being unconscious and it continued to keep Van away from her. How long she could keep this up, she didn't know, especially with the discomfort of being belly-down of Star, with her head severely pounding. She was desperately hungry and thirsty, but to get food and water would require her to gain consciousness and that she couldn't do. She needed to hold out to give Clive and Liam time to find her. She prayed that she had the resolve.

Cooper found a hollowed-out section in one of the hills. The opening was about four feet wide but it led to a small meadow with plenty of graze and a fresh pool of water fed by a mountain stream trickling from the cliff above them. He guessed he would be only a two-hour ride to where he abducted Susanna.

He went to the water first and took several long drinks, then letting his horse drink his fill. He untied the rope holding Susanna's wrists and legs from under Star and let her slide from the saddle and fall onto the ground. "We'll see if you are really bad hurt, girl." Taking his knife from its sheath and placing the blade to her throat, "How's this woman? You start pleasing me or you die."

Susanna was nearly white with fear but showed nothing; just lay as she had fallen from the horse. "Playin' a game are ya. Okay." He then pushed the point of the knife into her neck, believing if she was faking, the pain would give her away.

The pain was near unbearable but Susanna remained motionless, knowing that if she cried out or moved all would be lost and she would be at his mercy. She knew he wanted a fight while he used her, and Susanna was determined not to give him what he wanted.

"Shit woman, you better wake up soon. There ain't much time left!" Van went about setting up camp, and making a fire to heat some coffee.

The blue sky was cloudless when Clive and Liam set out late that afternoon. Clive headed for the fir tree near the stream where Susanna was abducted, and Liam to the east of that location, looking for a higher vantage point from which to observe Van Cooper's approach as, more than likely, that would be his retreat as well.

Van had chosen sundown because that is the time when eyesight begins to fade and because of the increased difficulty in tracking him through the darkness, Liam thought. Smart. But, he assumed that Clive was the only threat and that was our edge.

As Clive rounded the last curve in the trail, he saw Van Cooper for the first time, standing beside his horse leaning against the fir tree. He had an evil grin on his face amplified by his unkempt mustache. The only sounds were the footfalls of Clive's horse, the bubbling of the nearby stream, and Cooper's horse chomping the graze.

"Why if it ain't Mr. Security man," Cooper said with a chuckle. "Tie the lead rope for those pack hosses on that branch there.

Clive complied using all the self-control he could muster to not draw down on this scum. "Where is Susanna?"

"Oh, she is doing just fine. I thinks she likes me, security man. She sure is purty. So, soft. So wild. What fire she has! You should have had some of that your damn self." Van stopped talking and just looked quizzically at Clive, gaining understanding from his eyes, "Wait a minute, you be sparking her. You're sweet on her. Yeah, that's it. Well then, you need to be thanking me for breaking her in for you. Now she knows how to please a real man."

Clive reached for his gun and stopped when Cooper didn't move a muscle. He just laughed. "Think that through, security man. You kill me you won't be seeing your sweetie again. She will be wolf and bear food, and something that pretty would sure be a waste on a wolf, now ain't that right?"

Clive let the iron drop back into the holster. "You're a dead man Cooper. Never have I known a man deserving of being killed more. You're scum, the worst kind. I'll piss on you while you're dying!"

"Thank you security man. I take that as high praise. Now, you fork your bronc and hightail down that trail. And, be rememberin', ifin I see you following I will as sure as I am standing here gut shoot that girl and leave her to die. Real painful. You best be rememberin' that. Now git!"

Cooper waited almost an hour half-expecting Clive to sneak back, but he didn't show. Could he be a coward or did he have another plan? He dismissed those thoughts, knowing the trail he would use to get back to Susanna had a field of view at times of more than three miles. He would pause there to scout his back-trail, and if he was being followed he would know then. He knew he would be followed eventually, it was just a matter of knowing when and where.

Liam had already tracked Cooper's entrance to the exchange. From there he cut sign through the first long and open canyon. There he secreted himself and Creena, awaiting Cooper and the two packhorses. Creena was picketed well away from the trail to avoid nickering to the other horses, and Liam was concealed under a shaded outcropping out of the sun's burn feasting on jerky and water.

He heard the animals before he saw Cooper. Emotions vomited through his body now, for the first time, looking at the man who murdered his family. The hate that had been contained was now burning in his veins. Realizing his eyes were boring into the man, increasing the risk of alerting Cooper's senses, he had to bury his face in his hat to break the connection. Thoughts of his father and mother flooded his consciousness as he waited for Cooper to pass.

When the noise indicted that Cooper had passed him, Liam very slowly looking down over the outcropping and watched the three horses move slowly up the trail. Then Cooper stopped, dismounted and led the animals into a small crevice, and was out of sight for a moment. A few minutes later, he watched as Cooper climbed to an observation point and focused his glass on the back-trail. Privately, he hoped that Clive was being cautious, but Cooper had not taken his rifle so he concluded it was observation only.

They had left the mountain region and the terrain eased to rock cliffs averaging one hundred feet high interspersed with boulders the lower being rounded smooth by running water in the distant past mostly gray in color with spots of mustard.

Liam focused his glass on the farthest view of the back-trail. Nothing. Almost an hour had passed when he saw Cooper quickly moving down to his horses. Swinging his glass back to the back-trail, he saw a dust cloud. Clive was coming, but Cooper was leaving. What was going on? Cooper could have stayed had he had his rifle and taken Clive out. Something else was at play, but what? He decided to think on it as he moved east, almost in parallel with Cooper, out of sight without chance of raising dust.

Cooper made it back to find Susanna lying where she was when he had left to get the ransom, still unconscious, maybe in a coma. Stupid, clumsy Dutch had hit her too hard and may have killed her. Such a pity. Well, he thought, plan B. He had plenty of money now to buy the women he needed to satisfy the aches in his loins. He would need to eliminate Clive soon and then he could move on.

That evening Cooper, verified the provisions and the money and was rewarded to find it all there. He was giddy with the best score of his life. Everything had worked perfectly, well almost everything, he thought, as he looked over to Susanna. And, he wouldn't have to share with that idiot Dutch.

The morning found Cooper shouldering Susanna up the cliff side, finally placing her dangerously on a ledge with easily a fifty-foot drop should she roll forward. He cut the pigging strings, freeing her hands and feet, and then moved about one hundred yards away and waited. Susanna was clearly visible to anyone riding through the canyon, just as he had planned.

Clive soon entered the canyon and saw Susanna high above him, dangerously close to the cliff's edge. He knew it was the trap he and Liam expected and just as he began to dismount, was struck in the shoulder with the report coming seconds after. He was hurt bad, that he knew, but he remained flat on his back unmoving. His mount was well trained and didn't move. Blood had soaked through his shirt and puddled under his shoulder. An hour passed and vultures began to circle. He drifted into blackness.

He must be dreaming as he thought he felt someone attending to his wound. Opening his eyes, he saw the face of a goddess and he knew he was either dead or dreaming. But the goddess was talking to him, "I have stopped the bleeding, but you need a doctor, Clive. I think the bullet is still in there and infection could kill you." He then became fully awake and looked into Susanna's compassionate eyes, alive and well.

"Cooper is gone. We will ride double back to The Mansion. I will help you mount up." Clive went in and out of consciousness, but was held in the saddle by Susanna. When he was alert, he told Susanna the plan he and Liam were working and she told him how she had fooled Cooper by pretending to be on death's door so neither Cooper nor Dutch believed she had seen their faces.

Liam had heard the shot from his position further down the canyon and hoped Clive was not badly hurt. He knew he must keep parallel, tracking Cooper to save Susanna, and it wasn't until late that day that he sighted Cooper leading three horses. Susanna was no longer a hostage. One shot, a rifle shot, long range. She must have made her escape during that distraction and would hopefully be able to help Clive. Of course, she could be dead, her throat slit, but his instinct led him to believe she was safe and he prayed she was.

Tracking Cooper had become easier as he believed he was no longer being followed. He was still heading due east, probably to the small town called Fallon about three days' ride from where they were. Fallon was the only settlement noted on his map. Scoping what lay ahead, Liam began to worry. The cliffs ended and what appeared to be desert began. Cooper seemed to know the lay of the land, Liam did not. Liam was unaccustomed to the desert and Cooper, a born Texan, had the advantage. He knew why Cooper had taken Star; an extra horse would prove useful should a mount stumble. Also, with no cover, Liam on his back-trail will be spotted easily, if not by Creena's profile surely by a dust trail.

A broken land faced Liam now. Its change from the cliffs, rocks and canyons of the lower Trinity Range on his back-trail was abrupt. He viewed a barren and lifeless land, and as far as his eyes with the help of the glass could see, nothing lived. It was not a Sahara-type of desert, but rather what appeared to be hard-packed sand and gravel which would provide better footing, a small benefit among a host of liabilities. There was no evidence of water or grass and trees dependent on it for life, just intermittent scrub.

Liam reasoned he had two choices. One, he could take Cooper this very night while he slept before he ventured too far into the desert, which should not be difficult as he believed there was no follower. Or two, he could distance himself and make his way to Fallon and take him while he rested in town, unaware. He chose to distance himself and take Cooper in the town. It was the conservative choice and the safest, since Cooper was most likely skilled in the way of the desert and he was a tenderfoot. And, with Susanna out of Coopers grasp, time was on his side.

He decided that he must learn the way of the desert since, as Chief Inspector of the U.S. Marshals Service, he would likely spend a lot of time in the west where deserts are plentiful and varied. For now, Liam would need to be both teacher and student, leveraging the logic of his legal skills and the physics of his engineering skills. He knew that his mind was a weapon always, but never more than at present.

To prepare, he rested Creena for the balance of the day near a clear-running stream with plenty of rich graze and shade. Creena would need the rest and water to take on what would be a grueling ride through blistering heat by day, chilling cold by night, and dry desert. He had two canteens and both would be filled before leaving, but he worried that they would be inadequate for what he concluded would be a three-day trek. He eyed his saddlebags full with provisions and had an idea. The bags were tightly double-stitched, and after removing the provisions he placed the empty bags into the stream, holding them down with a large stone to swell the leather. He carefully considered the provisions, wrapping what he could in his blanket. He then went about cutting as much grass as he could with his Bowie knife, filling his slicker. If he was unable to find graze on the trail, it would at least be enough for one full meal for Creena. He could do no more.

Before leaving camp at dawn he watered Creena again, filled the canteens and saddlebags — which had swelled tight overnight — with water. After he had saddled Creena, he checked his weapons for their loads and satisfied, he swung into the saddle and headed east about a full day behind Cooper.

"Well doc, how is Clive?" Weeks asked the aged doctor. Weeks was noticeably relieved to have Susanna home and unharmed, busting with pride over how she had handled Cooper.

"He has lost a lot of blood and the bullet was logged deeply in his shoulder muscle, but there was no bone damage, thank God. I was able to get it out but unfortunately I needed to cut more of the muscle than I typically would.

That will delay his recovery a bit. Infection is our worry now, but my guess is he will pull through. I was able to clean the wound and the dressing will need to be changed twice each day after cleaning the wound with hot water. I will be back tomorrow to look in on him."

Then the doc looking only at Susanna, added, "Susanna, he is a very lucky man for if you hadn't brought him home when you did, he would surely be dead now. Here is some salve for your wrists and ankles and that cut on your neck. It will help the healing and prevent infection."

Weeks thanked the doc for all his help and suggested that Susanna some get some badly-needed rest. "Father, I will as soon as I eat. I am half starved! But first, I want to see Clive."

"I will join you," Weeks said.

Susanna knocked lightly on the bedroom door. It wasn't a permission knock rather a warning that she was about to enter. Clive lay on his back with pillows stuffed under his upper back and head, and a navy blue wool blanket pulled to his chin. He looked frail and week which was quite the contrast to the virile, strong and determined man she admired. Susanna was the first to speak softly and passionately, "The doc said you will make a full recovery, Clive. I can't begin to thank you for coming for me."

"I am… so sorry that animal… abducted you in the first place," Clive said, clearly in pain. "I was charged with the responsibility of keeping you safe. I… let you down, as well Weeks."

"Clive, you couldn't be everywhere all the time, and Susanna is home and safe. And she played possum, so she is completely unharmed."

"Possum?"

"I was hit from behind Clive, out cold. I just pretended to be in a coma the entire time and was left untouched."

"Oh, thank God!" Clive asked for some water, and after drinking his fill asked, "Any word from Liam?"

"None at all," Weeks replied. "I would think it will be seven to eight days. We looked at the maps, and assuming Cooper kept his easterly heading, Fallon would be the likely destination. That is a good three days' ride, a hard ride through the desert. If I am any judge of the man, he will wait and take Cooper in Fallon."

Susanna could see the fatigue building on Clive's face and said, "I will ask the cook to bring you some beef stew, you must be hungry. Then rest… and Clive, thank you." Susanna placed her hand on the side of Clive's face, tenderly, and smiled into his eyes.

Weeks saw the concern evident on Susanna's face and added, "Liam will be just fine. If I am any judge of the man, you will be seeing him in a little over a week at most. I know you are missing Star, but we will find another horse for you when you are ready."

The desert was a foreign environment for both Liam and Creena. There would be no breeze, and then suddenly a large gust of wind would bring bits of lava rock, sand, and alkali-laden dust into their face and eyes and lungs and mouths. The salt and alkali attacked their eyes and nostrils with a vengeance. The sand and gravel upon which they walked reflected the sun's rays, increasing the burn on the bodies and dehydration. Heat rays swirled from the ground in the distance, distorting the vista into drunken, dancing images. There were few markers to guide their easterly direction and no trail existed. It was a land that regularly took life, but both horse and man were determined it would not take theirs.

Liam stopped every few hours and allowed Creena sips of water from the saddlebags and wetted his kerchief to wipe the sand and dust from Creena's eyes, nose, and mouth. He took only small sips from the canteen, respecting and rationing the life-sustaining liquid. He walked, leading Creena, every few hours to relieve him of his weight. So far, they both remain strong.

As dusk approached, Liam became watchful for a place to stay the night but there was little in the way of shelter. Finally, a large solitary boulder provided a shelter from the intermittent wind, and if he could find fuel, a place to shelter a fire from any observer east of him. He reasoned that Cooper could double back to check his back-trail, but doubted he would do so in the darkness of night.

Here he found some dry scrub and sagebrush that would provide a small fire for coffee but there was no graze. He cooked a small portion of bacon and beans and coffee. Before he sat to eat, he rolled out the slicker for Creena to feed on the grass he had cut last evening, saving a little for the following day. Creena shied, having never foraged for a meal like this, but hunger got the best of him. Watering Creena with the remains of one saddlebag was the last thing he did before rolling into his blanket for the night.

Liam sat in his blankets facing west with his back against the large boulder, cleaning his guns of the sand and grit that invaded during the day and then checking the action. He was entranced with the crimson, rose and tangerine sunset that appeared as fire falling into the mountain peaks that he had breakfasted in that morning. The desert was a conflict of beauty and hardship. Creena was already three legged and as he drifted close to sleep, he could hear the distant cry of a coyote.

The night proved uneventful but startlingly cold, a reminder that there is little within the desert to hold the suffocating daytime heat. Before pulling his boots on, he was sure to check for scorpions that may have found it a warm place for the evening. He reheated a meal of leftover bacon, beans and coffee for breakfast, and watered Creena with a portion of the one remaining full saddlebag. The little grass remaining in the slicker would wait for evening. Then he swung into the saddle and headed east once again, knowing he would need to make at least thirty miles.

Liam rode directly into the fireball with his hat low upon his brow, shielding the sun's effect on his eyes. The desert was awash in silence and the monotony of Creena's footfalls was interrupted only by Liam's encouragement and patting of his withers. Suddenly Creena shied violently, jumping to the left nearly throwing Liam from the saddle. It was a close call as a diamondback rattler that blended with the sand, thick as Liam's arm and nearly six feet in length, slithered by. Glancing to its left with a look that conveyed, "This is my home you are invading." Another learned experience, and another way to die in the desert.

The second day in the desert was much like the first, but both man and horse were beginning to show their fatigue. Liam began talking to Creena, providing soft words of encouragement, and in a way, keeping them both company. As dusk drifted toward them again, Liam watched for a suitable camp for the night but was not rewarded immediately. Thinking the fatigue evident in his eyes might be misleading him, he decided to trust his eyes and moved on another mile. There he was rewarded with a slight crevasse, not deep enough to be called an arroyo, but that would prove a suitable shelter from the wind for the night.

Seeing to Creena's comfort first, he stripped the saddle, rubbed him down, shedding as much of the salt and alkali as possible. He then let Creena drink heartedly, using most of the water from the last saddlebag. He had picked up anything that would burn while walking Creena during the day, providing for a reasonable fire hidden from sight within the crevasse. As bacon, beans and coffee were heating, he gave Creena the last of the grass from the slicker. It was little and inadequate but Creena wasn't a complainer.

The night was devoid of sound and still, with a blanket of black sky salted with twinkling stars and a half moon. Rolled in his blankets with his head resting on the saddle, the vista above brought him back to the voyage from Ireland where he would spend countless nights on deck relishing the fresh sea air. The black ceiling… Tears began to fill his eyes as he visited with the memories of his father and mother. Those memories were assaulted by the vision of the burned-out husk of the Black Arms Company. He renewed his vow to bring Cooper to justice.

He wondered how Martha and Joel were faring in Washington and decided he would telegraph them when he reached the settlement.

He thought about Cooper — how does a man become so dehumanized? How does someone live without a conscience? Are they born to it or is there a mental deficiency? Was it a weakness in a person's character or is one completely devoid of character altogether? Can greed and lust create an animal like Cooper? Is death the only cure? Surely the devil must own his soul and must continually look for him to prove his worthiness. Liam resolved that the answers to these questions were beyond his grasp and drifted to sleep.

Morning arrived with a terror of wind. There was no fuel left and the coals had long since died. Cold beans, bacon and coffee sufficed but Creena had no food, only the last of the water from the second and last saddlebag. It would be a long day but he reasoned they should reach Fallon tonight where hot food and water were aplenty.

Stopping to rest at noon, Liam poured most of the last canteen into his hat for Creena, keeping a few sips for himself and enough to clean Creena's eyes, nose and lips. He could make out what could be the settlement in the far distance but was unable, yet, to accurately gauge distances over such a flat expanse. He prayed they would make Fallon tonight. There was a spire, or what looked to be a spire, that could be a church steeple or high rock outcropping, but it was his desired direction and he kept it between Creena's ears as a guiding beacon.

It was full dark when they entered the town and stopping at the first water trough, letting Creena drink his full. Then Liam immediately headed for the livery and, reining up outside, was greeted by the liveries owner.

"Howdy stranger. What can we do fir ya?" The old hostler asked, rolling his wad from the left to the right cheek.

"I will be here for a few days and my mount needs to be rubbed down, watered well, and double portions of oats each day."

"We can do that. It be two bits a day extry for the oats."

"Any other strangers come in? Possibly yesterday, with three horses on a lead rope?"

"Yes sir. This being the only livery and all. Said he be here for several days I believe."

"Thanks. Good to know. Can you point me to the best hotel, perhaps with a café?"

"Sure can. He asked the same question by the way. There is only one hotel in town. It's straight down this street. Not far from the sheriff's office, seeing you are wearing a badge 'n' all."

Liam took five silver dollars from his vest pocket and placed them into the owner's hands, "I would appreciate you not mentioning this to anyone. Can I count on you?"

With a smile that showed a few broken and a few missing teeth he said, "Names Porter, Josh Porter, and you can count on me, Marshal."

"Thank you Mr. Porter. Liam deBláca, U.S. Marshals Service," Liam said, shaking Porters hand.

Liam hugged Creena softly, talking with him and scratching his chin and ears and then whispered, "It was you, my friend, that made it through that desert and I will be forever thankful."

Liam took his empty bags, light with the few remaining provisions and change of clothing, and threw them over his shoulder while carrying his customized Henry rifle in his left hand. Walking down the street, he decided to stop at the sheriff's office before going on to the hotel. The off-tune piano music and laughter filled the street reinforcing Fallon as the oasis it was.

"I will see that and raise you ten dollars," Cooper said slurring his words. "Well, what's it gunna be, mister?" His half-full bottle of whiskey was standing beside an empty glass.

Throwing in his cards, the young cowboy said, "You have more luck than a rich man in a whorehouse."

"You sayin' I'm a-cheaten', mister?" Cooper said more as a threat than a question.

"No sir. I'm saying I should find another way to spend my time. I'm out." The cowboy got up and walked from the saloon.

The piano was way out of tune and if it were not for the whiskey, it would be more than annoying. Yet, the cowboys and miners in the Sheep's Head Saloon seemed unaffected. Smoke filled the air. The odor of stale beer and unwashed bodies assaulted the senses. The senses seemed to have a way of adjusting the longer one stayed within the foul air the less revolting it became.

Cooper was in his element. He had never scored as well and was free, a rich man. Nothing occupied his thoughts except whiskey, poker and women.

Fallon was recently settled, Liam concluded. Small, maybe a hundred or two hundred residents, one main street, a few side streets, and several houses and shacks on the periphery. There were a few shops, a mercantile, saddle shop, bank and several saloons. It looked like a town that had prospects, not that it would become a Denver, Carson City or a Chicago, but a small town for where a man could scrape out a satisfactory existence and raise a family.

Light spilled from the sheriff's office. Night was the busy time for all peacekeepers. Liam knocked as he entered saying, "Good evening, Sheriff."

The sheriff was standing in front of a potbelly stove pouring coffee from a battered pot. "Evenin'. What can I do for ya mister?" He hadn't lifted his eyes from the cup to take in the measure of the man entering his office, obviously relaxed, not the sort of behavior one expects from a sheriff, especially at night.

Liam delayed his reply until the sheriff eyed him. "I am just checking in with you, Sheriff; name's Liam deBláca, Chief Inspector, U.S. Marshals Service." He studied the sheriff, a man nearing fifty, short and stout, balding with a gray handlebar mustache and quiet gray eyes.

"Checkin' in, what fir? I'm the law in this town."

Liam sensed that there would be little cooperation but still needed to set the record straight. "Yes, you are, but so am I and my authority exceeds yours, Sheriff. I am the top law officer in all of the U.S. and its territories, under orders directly from the President and the Attorney General and here to arrest a man. Will I have your assistance?"

"Never heard of such a thing and the President done nothing for Fallon. You break my law and I be arresting you!" The sheriff said belligerently.

"Sheriff, it has been a real pleasure meeting you. I'm sure you are a comfort to all the Fallon citizens. Just stay out of my way and you won't get hurt."

"You threatenin' me, Marshal?"

"Not at all, just providing you with some obviously much-needed advice. Good evening." Liam then turned and walked out the door, not waiting for the sheriff's response and leaving the door opened to the street.

As he walked the street toward the hotel pondering the odd interchange with the town sheriff, he concluded the sheriff might walk both sides of the law, or he could just be incompetent or lazy. Clearly, a U.S. Marshal being in Fallon was not welcome, so something unlawful either is happening or about to happen, he thought.

Registering at the hotel, he arranged for a bath but not a shave. Keeping several weeks of black beard might offer some disguise and give him an edge with Cooper. The bath refreshed him considerably and the hardy meal in the café of beef and potatoes placed before him by a pleasant young lady set him nicely for a desperately needed quiet night's sleep.

Shortly after Liam left the sheriff's office, the portly sheriff left in a rush for the bank across the street. "I need to see him, now," he demanded of the tall guard standing beside the door.

"Settle down, Bosworth. What's this all about." The tall man with two tied-down Colts asked.

"That's between the boss and me, now git outa my way, Ross!"

Ross chuckled, "You wait here and I see if he has time for the likes of you," and pushed Bosworth back so that he could open the door. Several minutes elapsed before the door reopened, "Mr. Carter will give you three minutes and he said it better be good."

Bosworth walked into the bank and then all the way to the rear office. The door was open and Mr. Carter sat behind his massive mahogany desk, a cigar in his hand. Carter sat looking over Bosworth, neither spoke, and Bosworth was not greeted nor offered a chair. Carter was a big man who filled his leather swivel chair completely, not a heavy man but rather tall and fit. Drawing heavily on the cigar, and seeing the Bosworth was suitably intimidated, said, "What is this about, Sheriff?"

"We have trouble, Mr. Carter. A U.S. Marshal just rode *in*."

"So what, why would that be trouble?"

"He said he was hunting a man but that could be his story. He might know somethin'."

"He has no authority in town, I, as Mayor of this fine town, have given you that authority as Sheriff."

"Not what he says Mr. Carter. He is Chief Inspector of the U.S. Marshals Service; says he is under orders direct from the President and Attorney General of the United States."

"Interesting. But he is only one man and a long way from Washington. If you can't handle him, Ross will. I will plan to meet this Marshal tomorrow, as Mayor of Fallon. Now, I have work to do." Carter turned away from Bosworth indicating the interview was terminated.

Ross entered soon after the portly sheriff left. He was a capable man and functioned as Carter's muscle. Ross was known around town as a man of self-importance, quick to anger and blazingly fast with a six-gun. "What was that about, boss?"

"It would appear we have a new man in town, a U.S. Marshal here from Washington. He states that he is the head of the entire U.S. Marshals Service and is hunting a man believed to be in Fallon. It could be a ruse, or could be the truth and just a coincidence. I'll meet him tomorrow as Mayor to learn more."

The day broke crisp and clean under a bright blue sky. Liam was dressed in freshly brushed black broadcloth suit, feeling renewed after three days in the desert. He had cleaned and checked his .44s and wore both tied down and now he headed to the café for breakfast.

"Good morning Marshal, coffee?" She was the same pleasant woman that served him the evening before.

"Yes please, and four eggs, bacon and bread if you have it."

"Yes, sir, coming right up."

The café door opened and a tall well-dressed man entered with another a few steps behind him. The woman shied but said coolly, "Good morning, Mr. Carter," but didn't address the other man. The well-dressed man was near forty and carried himself with a sense of importance. He looked fit and capable. The other had two Remington's, tied down, a gunslinger. He had the eyes of a cat on the prowl in conflict with a perpetual wise-ass grin.

The well-dressed man walked to where Liam was sitting and said in a cultured voice, "May I join you, Marshal?"

Liam motioned to the chair with his left hand holding the mug of coffee, his right hand on his lap, free. As a precaution, he had already taken the thong off his .44, in case he ran into Cooper, though he doubted the man would be up this early.

"I am Quinton Carter, Mayor of Fallon. Sheriff Bosworth mentioned that you rode in last night. Consider me the welcoming committee. Welcome to our humble town, Marshal."

Liam noticed that the other man just stood leaning on the wall by the café door, obviously the Mayor's protection, but protection from what? Why would a Mayor of a small town need a gunslinger? Caution filled him.

The pleasant woman placed his eggs, bacon and bread on the table and then refilled his coffee. She did not address the Mayor. She seemed afraid of him and clearly didn't like him. I will need to learn more about that, Liam thought.

"What can I do for you, Mayor?"

"I was told that you were hunting a man; may I be of help to you? Who do you hunt, Marshal?" Carter asked while seated leaning back in the armless wood chair, hands folded in his lap as if he owned the place.

"Just your garden variety murderer; nothing I can't handle, alone," Liam said while enjoying his breakfast. "Who is your sidekick over there?" again motioning with his coffee mug.

"Just an associate of mine. I also own the bank. He is my... shall we say, security."

Pieces were falling into place for Liam. Mayor and bank owner; Carter owns the town and, based on the reception he received in the café, was not well liked or respected. That would also mean the sheriff was owned by Carter as well. He was determined to find out why before leaving the town of Fallon. But, the primary business was the arrest of Van Cooper.

Carter realized he was getting nowhere with the marshal, "I will let you finish your breakfast in peace, but please call on me if I can be of service. My office is at the bank across the street from the sheriff's."

When Carter walked out the door, the security man Ross paused and eyeballed Liam with that smirk on his lips. Giving Liam a two-finger salute to his hat, he turned and left. It was clear to Liam that the two would face each other, the only unknown was when.

The pleasant woman returned, refilled his mug and said, "Marshal, my name is Patty and my father owns this café. If don't mind me saying, Mr. Carter is not a man to be underestimated. Neither is his gunslick Ross. He is poison mean and has killed three farmers who owned property east of town. They say all three fights were straight up fair, but I doubt it. Are you here to help us?"

"Thank you Patty. I'm Liam deBláca, and I am here on other business but will look into this matter. Who can I trust?"

"You can trust me and…," She was interrupted from a voice back in the kitchen area yelling, "Patty, see to the other diners and quit your gabbin'!"

Patty did an abrupt about face and quickly went to the kitchen counter, picking up plates and coffee mugs, hurrying to other tables.

Liam paid his bill and walked to the telegraph office. There he sent Jeremiah an update indicating he intended to arrest Cooper today. He sent separate telegram inquiring about Fallon and Quinton Carter, indicating he need information quickly. Then he started for the saloons determined to find his quarry, Van Cooper.

It was no surprise that the saloons were lightly frequented in the morning. Cowboys were at work on their ranch and miners busy at their trade looking for metal. He stopped at the livery to visit with Creena, giving him an apple he got from the café, and was pleased to see he was well cared for. Cooper's horses and Star were still stabled. Seeing Porter, he said, "Thank you for caring for my horse, Mr. Porter."

"Marshal, I love horses more than people. They be more dependable too! And I respect a man who loves his horse. And, I respect you fir it."

"Mr. Porter, who is this man Carter?"

Porter let out a long whistle and replied, "Didn't take ya long, Marshal. He be the big man in this town, him and his gunslick Ross. He has five others on the payroll but they be the ones out collecting on loans. Owns jist bout everthin' in the town but the hotel and this livery, and he ain't getting my livery!" Then letting out a long spit of tobacco he added, "Owns the sheriff, too."

"Seems he is not well liked, why is that Mr. Porter?"

"Well, he owns the bank. Hear tell he has been calling some loans on the ranches east of here, causin' some ruckus. Don't have the details though."

"Thanks Mr. Porter. You have been helpful. You'll let me know if those horses leave?"

"Sure thing Marshal. Ain't seen his hide since I stabled them."

Reaching into his vest pocket for three more silver dollars and handing them to Porter, he said, "That mare with the single white stocking belongs to a lovely woman, a friend of mine. Would you see to it she is rubbed down and given double oats for me?"

"Pleasure Marshal, as always."

Liam left the livery and noticed that Ross was standing across the street watching him, making no attempt to hide, and still wearing the smirk. Liam concluded that Ross would challenge him soon and was determined to use caution. He judged that Ross would not shoot a man in the back, but would work the courage for stand-up play, or so he hoped.

The doc walked down the stairs with a concerned face toward Weeks and his daughter Susanna. "Well, infection has set in. The good news it isn't as severe as it might have been. I have cleaned and disinfected the wound as best I could, and changed his bandages again. His fever is high and when it clears he'll break out in a cold sweat. I have left my nurse with him and she will keep cold compresses on his forehead. Weeks, if you can spare some whiskey and get it into him, it will help. A good half bottle if he can handle it. He may hate you through the worst hangover but it will help the body fight the infection."

"Susanna, how are your wrists and ankles?"

"Thanks to that salve you provided, they are already healing."

"I am pleased to hear that. The cut on your neck looks like it is healing as well."

Weekes added, "Would you stay for coffee, doctor?"

Cooper rose late in the morning, suffering from an excess of whiskey and a lack of sleep. He determined that food would be the cure and maybe a whiskey or two, hair of the dog. The bright of day assaulted his red-rimmed eyes as he walked out of the hotel front door. Liam was ready and waited for him to walk onto the street. He had purposely positioned himself with the sun to his back and therefore in the weary and tired eyes of Cooper.

Liam watched as Cooper stumbled but using the rail, righted himself on the hotel stairs and felt the emotion flooding his body. Here was the man that killed his father and mother, the man that had killed twenty other people, possibly more, the man who raped and robbed, a vile man without conscience, scum. Here was his purpose, to bring to justice a man he had been tracking for months and thousands of miles, but what would he now do, arrest or kill? The question haunted him.

The street was washed with small shadows of a mid-morning sun, and dust devils appeared and disappeared in the cross streets where the wind became confused. Shop owners were greeting customers, placing goods on their porches and lettering advertising messages with chalk-on-slate billboards to attract more. Dogs were barking. Horses were tied at the rails, a wagon lumbered by under heavy load raising a low dust trail, and Liam used it as cover to enter the street's center.

"Van Cooper," Liam shouted menacingly, "you are under arrest for murder, robbery and rape. Stand where you are, drop your holster using your left hand. If you pull that gun, you will die. Make no mistake about that. I will not repeat myself. This is Chief Inspector Liam deBláca of the U.S. Marshals Service. Do it, now!"

Cooper halted mid-stride, almost facing Liam in the middle of the street. Activity all around him seemed to evaporate, the boardwalks suddenly empty of people, the wind stilled. It was beyond his comprehension how this man found him thousands of miles from Washington, yet he was here, and this was life and death. He could not talk his way out of this, there was nowhere to run and no one was siding him. His breathing was ineffectual, unable to deliver desperately needed oxygen into his lungs. The cobwebs in his brain clearing slowly left him with the realization of his options; draw and hope to live, or give up and wait for a time to make his play.

A sly grin suddenly appeared on Cooper's face and he said, "I would never have believed it, Marshal. You cumin' all this way to git me. Well, you did. I allow that much. All right, I'll be dropping my holster so don't you go an' git trigger happy. You hearing me, Marshal?"

Cooper's words were lost on Liam. He was concentrating only on Cooper's actions, for he knew better than to trust this snake. Never let your guard down and never, ever hesitate were rules deeply engrained in his mind.

Cooper began to unbuckle his holster and began let it fall. Then, Cooper's right hand instinctively reached for his Remington. He was fast, but neither fast enough nor accurate enough, assuming he got a shot off. Liam had fired before Cooper cleared leather and immediately began walking toward Cooper, with his .44 still in hand, shucking the spent cartridge and replacing it, watching Cooper fall to his knees and then topple onto his back while clutching his right shoulder. Blood the color of old port wine leaked onto his shirt and into the road dirt.

Liam kicked Cooper's gun away, holstered his weapon and bent down, opening Cooper's vest to assess the wound. "Thank you, God," was all Liam could say.

"Thank God fir what, you son of a bitch!" Cooper screamed, the pain from his wound lining his face.

"I thanked God for giving me the restraint and courage not to slaughter you like the pig you are, but to bring you to justice. You are the worst scum on earth and I hate the air you breathe and you will indeed experience the justice you deserve!" Liam replied as he jerked Cooper from the ground by the back of his shirt collar and half-walked, half-dragged him to the sheriff's office.

"Sheriff Bosworth, I intend to use one of your jail cells for this piece of shit and don't you try to give me any attitude about it or I will put you in the other one. Go fetch the doc, now!" Bosworth didn't hesitate and nearly ran from the office.

While the sheriff was fetching the doc, Liam retrieved his handcuffs and shackles, and when the doc arrived he found Cooper's legs shackled to the cell's iron bars and his hands cuffed. "Just a shoulder wound, he will recover in a week or two, Marshal. No bones hit and it was an in and out the rear of the shoulder."

"When will he be fit to ride, doc?"

"I'd say in about three days' time the wound will have healed adequately to allow riding."

"Bosworth, where are the keys to that cell?" Liam said as he pointed to the jail cell occupied by Cooper.

"That hook by da desk."

Liam tested the keys to both jail cells and found that the keys were unique, one individual key per cell. "Where is the other key to this cell?"

"Ain't no other key, just the one."

"I will hold on to this key then, just for a few days. And listen carefully… Sheriff, this prisoner is to have no visitors short of you delivering his meals and take out the slop bucket, and the doc to check that wound. Got that, no one else?" Liam's eyes were electric, penetrating and fierce and in them Bosworth saw no fear only ruthless determination.

"Yes, sir."

Liam left the sheriff's office to check on his telegrams and made a mental note to go through Cooper's room and retrieve the ransom money, or what was left of it. The town was back to normal with the excitement of a gun fight now over. People gave him a wide birth as he strolled down the boardwalk, women with flirtatious grins to which he tipped his hat and men, some who showed fear, some respect.

He asked the young wire operator if he had a reply to his earlier telegrams and was pleased to be handed two sealed envelopes. Liam paid the teller and stood opening the first, and in doing so noticed a small tear on the envelope seam giving evidence it was previously opened. "Son, do you know that wire tampering carries a three to five-year jail term and a one thousand dollars fine?"

"No sir, I surely didn't," the teller replied, nervously fidgeting in his chair.

"I will see to it that you serve that time if you don't tell me who opened these envelopes," Liam said as he opened his coat wider so that both his badge and guns were adding to the intimidation.

The blood loss evident in the young teller's bland face assured Liam that the next words from his mouth would be the truth. "It was Mr. Carter; he owns the telegraph station and says he has the right to look at all telegraphs. But, he wasn't happy with those, I can tell you that for sure, Marshal."

"Thank you, son. In the future you should know he does not have that right and you need to report that to the law immediately… that is as soon as I am able to find the law in this town."

Turning from the teller, Liam read the first message:

GOOD WORK FINDING COOPER STOP GOOD WILL BE ARRESTED STOP ASSUME HEADED TO VIRGINIA CITY FOR PROSECUTION STOP ADVISE

The second message was a bit cryptic:

NOTHING KNOWN ABOUT NEW SUSPECT STOP SECOND MAN WANTED FOR MURDER STOP TRENT MASTERS IN FALLON TOMORROW WITH DETAILS

Liam could arrest both Carter and Ross, Carter for wire tampering, which was weak, and Ross for murder but he didn't have the details yet. At the café over a luncheon of sandwiches and coffee, Liam considered the situation. It was clear that Carter, owning the bank, was calling in loans from ranchers on the east side of town. Ranchers couldn't make the payments, perhaps due to outrageous interest? He, as yet didn't know or why, and why now…

Liam pushed his sandwich plate away and was surprised to find a note under the plate. He palmed the note and discretely placed it in the inside pocket of his suit while reaching for his vest pocket, paid his bill, and left the café heading for the hotel.

Once in his room Liam opened the note, from the waitress Patty as he had guessed. *Meet me behind the café at ten PM, be very careful. Patty.* Liam set the note afire, let it drop into the washbowl and then set about catching up on his reading by starting with the pile of old newspapers collected from the hotel lobby earlier.

Liam decided to distance himself from the café for Patty's sake and took a late supper in the Cattlemen's Saloon located well down the street. It was an upscale establishment that featured a bar separated from its restaurant, softer and in-tune piano music filled the air. The evening's special was lamb chops, in conflict with the establishment's name, and they were large and delicious and the red Burgundy suggested was a perfect compliment. The grandfather clock announced with a single gong that it had just reached nine thirty; he paid the bill and strolled out the front door very casually.

Liam took Patty's *please be very careful* seriously, and exiting the Cattlemen's Saloon turned right heading away from the café to watch for a tail. Stopping intermittently gave him the opportunity to look back and across the street without being obvious. There was no one following or observing his actions that he could see, so he crossed the street and went into the alley that would eventually lead him to the rear of the café.

In his black broadcloth suit, black boots, and black hat, Liam blended with the night and Patty jumped when he whispered hello. "Oh, I didn't see or hear you coming. I was startled. Let's walk to the river. I have much to share."

Liam, ever the gentleman, took her arm and they walked away from the café toward the river about one hundred yards away. There were no words exchanged until they both sat upon a large cottonwood that had fallen years ago, parallel to the river. Crickets filled their ears with their chirping. The river bubbled and bats darted about eating insects but there were no other sounds.

"Marshal, you mustn't tell anyone about our meeting here tonight or what I am about to share with you. It could get my father, me, and even you killed," Patty started in hushed tones, knowing that sounds travel further at night.

"Patty, I will agree to keep our conversation confidential as long as what you tell me doesn't need to be retold in a court of law. Is that enough for you?" Liam replied whispering.

Patty hesitated, "It will have to be. Marshal, this town is scared and being bled dry by Carter and his bullies. They have put three ranches east of here in foreclosure and then Carter buys the property for pennies. If the ranchers try to prevent it, they are braced and killed, supposedly in a fair fight, or burned out. The law, Bosworth, is no help. He's Carter's lap dog. That gunslinger Ross has been eyeing me and he makes my flesh crawl."

"How has Carter been able to force the foreclosure?" Liam asked.

"I heard tell that there is a very complicated payment clause in the loan documents where a late payment, even a single day, causes the interest to increase substantially, so much so that it becomes impossible for the rancher to pay and the loan can be called by the bank; Carter's bank. I also heard tell that some cattle have been missing from some of the ranches. Don't know for certain, though."

"Patty, why are you taking such a risk in telling me all of this?"

"I could tell from the first time I laid eyes on you that you were a capable man and, if I am any judge, an honest man. We need help Liam, and you are in a position to help. Will you be able to help this town survive, Liam? We have nowhere else to turn to."

"A Deputy U.S. Marshal will arrive tomorrow. He is a very good man and is carrying a warrant to arrest Ross. That will be our start. I have an idea of what is happening with the ranches but need to telegraph Washington. Are the three foreclosed ranch owners still around?"

"Use the telegraph office carefully. Carter owns it. Yes, some of the hands are dead, but the owners are hiding out with other ranchers for the present."

"Get word to them that I may be able to have their ranch returned to them... may be able, Patty, no guarantees. Ask them to stay local. Now we better be getting back before people notice we are gone. And Patty, thank you for your confidence in me. I hope to prove you a good judge of men."

"Mr. Weeks, Mr. Weeks, the fever has broken!" the nurse exclaimed to Weeks and Susanna as they were eating their breakfast. Both pushed back from the dining room table and hurried to Clive's bedside.

The bed sheets under Clive were as wet as if they were just taken from the wash tub. "Well Clive, you look hard ridden and put away soaking wet", Week said with a chuckle. "Looks like I don't need to look for a new head of security. Right appreciate you coming back from the dead."

Susanna was beaming behind her father.

"Any word from Liam?" Clive asked in a raspy whisper.

"Got a telegram yesterday as a matter of fact. He has arrested Van Cooper. Seems Cooper pulled iron on Liam when the arrest was initiated, and Liam shot him in the right shoulder and will be ready to ride in another few days. Yes, he is bringing Cooper here for trial. What do you think about that?" Weeks exclaimed, unable to hide his excitement.

"Well I'll be a horse's apple if that don't beat all. Knowing what Cooper did to his family, for him not to shoot to kill… That is some kind of man to ride the river with," Clive whispered, relieved that this affair would soon be behind them all.

Quinten Carter sat behind his big oak desk savoring a cigar with his whiskey; his feet crossed and perched upon the right desk corner, and deep in thought. He was so close, with at worst only a few weeks before the announcement would be made. Those last two ranches must be in his control in the next few days to help ward off suspicion, so he would need to accelerate his plan with more aggressive action. "Ross, come in here!" Carter screamed.

"Yeah boss, what can I do for you?"

"I have it on good authority that another marshal will be coming to town, arriving tomorrow. He mustn't be allowed to arrive to help this deBláca fellow."

"I can handle that," he said as he was getting up to leave.

"Sit, there is more. You might be interested to know he will likely be arriving from the west. Now, we need to accelerate the acquisition of those last two ranches. Get your men to put more pressure on them, a lot more. I will give each man a one-hundred-dollar bonus if they are in my hands in less than three days, and you double that." Carter was nearly screaming as he finished his speech, emphasizing his point by stabbing the air with his cigar. Obviously Carter was becoming nervous.

"There may be blood shed over this, boss," Ross added.

"I know that. You make sure that the ranchers start it; your boys defending themselves can finish it. That way we are clean. Bosworth won't get in the way. Understood?"

"Understood, boss," Ross said and waited a moment and added, "When the time comes I want the marshal myself."

Carter studied Ross and wondered if he was up to the task. The marshal seemed a right curly character. In the end, with Ross out of the picture, it would save giving him his cut. If it went the other way and the marshal was out of the picture, it would be one less complication. Either way, he resolved, it works out. "I figured as much. Same goes for you, make it clean."

The telegraph was answered in a matter of two hours and it proved Liam's suspicions accurate. The railroad was coming westward through Fallon and then on through the range down to Carson City and then to Sacramento. That would mean the eastern parcels of Fallon would be worth a great deal more compared to only cattle range. Somehow Carter had been tipped off and was securing the land for himself and would soon be making an enormous profit in the process. Not only would Carter gain from the sale of the land to the railroad, but with a railroad stop in Fallon, the town would grow tenfold, and right now Carter owned most of the town. Wealth and power, two of the most common motivators for criminal activity, he thought privately.

Liam's thoughts drifted in a new direction. What hard evidence do I have? Rumors of cattle rustling, unethical loan contracts — but likely not illegal — wire tampering, yes, and I can arrest Ross for murder when Deputy Marshal Trent Masters arrives with the warrants. I think I will ride out to those ranches and have a talk. Creena will enjoy the ride as well after being stabled for a few days, he concluded.

He cantered heading due west to elude anyone that may be watching, and once over the rise turned south and then east toward the ranches. Creena was anxious to run, having been stabled over the last days and Liam let him have his head. Creena with his head and in full trot allowed Liam to survey the country. He surmised quickly that it was excellent cattle country; lush green grasses, streams and rivers aplenty, and several ponds with a few sizable enough to be lakes. It was open range and no wire to be seen. The path intersected with a trail wide enough for a wagon that he rightly assumed to be the main thoroughfare used by the ranches to and from Fallon. He turned left, heading north, and soon began to see cattle grazing to his right and soon thereafter a complex with a ranch house, large barn, a smoke house, a bunk house, corrals and several out buildings.

It was a tranquil and beautiful sight, looking down upon the ranch and watching the horses play within the corrals under the cloudless blue sky. This was a great deal more than a ranch. It was a home and the man and woman who built it should be right proud of their accomplishment. Liam put heals to Creena's flanks and headed down to the house.

Slowing to a walk about fifty yards from the house, Liam helloed the house. Two men appeared on the large porch. Both had rifles. "State your business, mister!"

"I mean no harm. I am U.S. Marshal Liam deBláca, hoping to ask a few questions if you have some time. Been hearing you and other ranchers have had a bit of trouble lately," Liam replied in an easy and nonthreatening tone.

The men conversed privately and quietly for a bit and then the taller of the two said, "Heard of you, Marshal. I'm Jake Smithers and this is my son Miles. Miles will water your horse. Come on in and set, coffee's hot."

As Liam stepped up to the porch, Jake offered his strong right hand and they shook with eyes locked and respect exchanged wordlessly. As they entered Jake's home, he was introduced to Martha who offered the men coffee in the well-appointed great room. It was Jake that started the conversation.

"Marshal, I am fifty-one years old and I started the 'JS' thirty years ago with a Herford bull and forty-two cows, and today we run more than nine thousand head, all natural expansion. This land is deeded to me free and clean. Miles, he has grown up on this ranch and will soon take over so that Martha and I can take it a bit easier. He's a good man and a top hand and he loves this ranch like Martha and I do."

Liam let him unburden himself and took in his surroundings as Jake talked. The great room was large, but not overly so, and comfortable. There were several leather easy chairs that had seen their use, evidenced by the polished seats and arms. The tables were original rough-cut oak but sanded and polished smooth and a large stone fireplace was the room's centerpiece. Everything confirmed his first instinct that this was not just a ranch house but a loving home built by caring and dedicated people.

"Of course we have had our ups and downs, Marshal, with rustlers, Indians and bandits. Good hands helped us keep what are rightfully ours, and God willing, we will keep it still. The 'JS' spanned thirty-eight thousand acres up to six months ago when we purchased a parcel that been foreclosed on and is adjacent to the southern range. We borrowed ten thousand dollars from Carter's bank. And that, Marshal, was my biggest mistake. Well, perhaps not the actual borrowing, but not having an independent lawyer review the loan document."

Martha came in with the coffee pot held with a thick towel to prevent being burned and refreshed their coffee, then sat in the chair facing Liam after placing the pot on flagstone on the adjacent table. "Now Jake, don't be shooting your foot about that. We will get through it."

It was time that Liam asked the key question, "Jake, what was it specifically that put this beautiful home and ranch at risk?"

"Well," Jake took a deep breath and whistled it out, "the loan document has a payment penalty for late payment that was written in a way that surely misled me. The lawyers at the loan closing explained it to me and I was satisfied with their explanation. But, the independent lawyer I hired recently explained it as it is written. The lawyers at the closing were the bank's lawyers, Carter's lawyers. Nuff said about that. If I miss a payment date, even by a day, the loan can be called and the interest increases tenfold retroactive to the first day of the loan. I don't keep that kind of cash on hand. My assets are the ranch and stock," Jake said, his head down and near tears.

Liam asked, "Couldn't you sell some stock for the cash you need?"

Jake laughed, not a funny laugh but sarcastic, and replied, "Of course, that is exactly what I tried to do but every time the hands completed a gather, the herd was stampeded. So, we couldn't get the herd to market in time to turn it into cash."

"I suppose your hands tracked the boys responsible for the stampede," Liam replied.

"Yeah, but they rode with the stampeding herd and their tracks were wiped out. But, we all know they were Carter's boys, just can't prove it. So, we are in trouble, Marshal. Same thing happened with the Rogers, Clayman, and Bucks' spreads. There are only three of us left. My lawyers are trying to save us but they have all but given up now."

Liam sat quietly contemplating the situation. It was likely, based on what Patty had told him and Jake substantiated, that he would hear the same story from all the ranchers. A suggestion of a plan was forming in his thoughts and he needed Jake's help to get the evidence needed to put Carter behind bars. And there was an outside chance he could get the foreclosed-upon ranches back to their rightful owners.

"Jake, Martha, I have an idea but will need your help. Are you up to it? It might be dangerous."

"If you can help save our life's work, we will give you all the help we can, Marshal. What do you have in mind?"

"I suspect you are right about Carter's gang stampeding your gather. We can connect them to Carter and void the loan documents if we can catch them in the act. I would like you to start another gather immediately. It doesn't need to be a real gather, just look like one, but keep it secret. I'll tip that the gather is in process in town so that Carter finds out. Then I will stay hidden near the gather in hopes of catching them in the act." Liam didn't tell them he had found out Carter's plan to sell to the railroads. That would come later.

"Sure, we can simulate a full gather, some two thousand head in a day. We already have much of it done to move a herd to new graze. I'll do it tomorrow. And, Martha and I thank you mightily, Marshal," Jake said in a more positive tone than was evident when they met. Having a plan and having help provides hope and optimism, and Liam silently hoped he let wouldn't them down.

Liam took the same route back to town that he took reaching the ranch. Going south and when intersecting the path, turned west. When he reached the northern path, he headed back toward town. A single rifle shot from further west of town caused him to rein up. It could be a hunter, but his instinct suggested he should investigate.

Turning west he decided to veer off the path and work his way through the cover of brush and trees in the hills, nearly paralleling the path. Creena, sensing the need for stealth, moved sure-footedly through the brush with hooves muffled by the pine needles. He heard the footfalls of a horse on the path and dismounted quickly, crawling to a vantage point that gave him a view of the path below. There he watched Ross ride east toward Fallon, a rifle in the saddle boot.

He waited some minutes for Ross to get well down the path before leading Creena back to the path and continuing west. Soon he saw a rider-less horse and a body lying on the path, and he stopped well back to survey the scene. It looked like the scene of ambush; likely the shooter was Ross, for why else would he be fleeing and not investigating the shot? The ideal location for ambush would be to the right on that rise where a good line of sight existed as well as hidden picketing for his horse.

Liam moved in slowly, dismounted and walked to the face down body. The man's horse shied, but with a few pats on the neck and soothing words, settled down. The man was tall, easily six feet, dressed in clean Levi's and a sheepskin coat. His chestnut curly hair was clean and recently cut. Liam began to turn the body face-up when it abruptly turned on its own in a fraction of a second, a pistol pointing to the center of his chest.

"Don't move a finger, dry gulcher, you are under arrest for attempted murder!"

Under arrest? "Hold on there pard, you must be Trent Masters. And if you are, then you know my name as well."

"Liam deBláca. Hello, boss. What in tarnation is going on here?" Trent said, trying to hide the pain while holstering his six-gun.

"Let's take a look at that wound first." Liam opened Trent's coat and blood began to spill, gut shot. That murdering coyote shot Trent in the stomach and left him here to die an awful death, slow, inevitable and painful. Looking at the wound carefully he surmised that the bullet didn't go through and therefore must be lodged in his stomach.

"I'll need to unbuckle your holster to get at this wound." The buckle was troublesome. It wouldn't unlatch. It was then that he saw that the bullet had hit the iron buckle post and had been deflected left into the holster strap where the leather was double-layered and hard-stitched. The bullet was half lodged in the leather, with half penetrating Trent's stomach.

"Well Trent, as they say in my former country, 'you've the luck of the Irish'. The bullet hit your holster strap and that took the steam out of it, only half penetrating your gut. I suspect you will have quite a bruise around that hole for a bit and some sore muscles, but you'll be arresting criminal's tomorrow. Let me get a bandage on the hole to slow the bleeding." Liam then helped Trent up on his horse and they headed to Fallon together.

Trent could sit a horse better than most anyone. He was a tall, straight-backed Texan, brought up in Apache country. At six feet, one hundred seventy pounds, with broad shoulders, a slim waist, and arms of iron he was an imposing man. His curly, chestnut hair blended with his deep brown eyes, and a dark-tanned face conveyed a friendly easygoing cowboy, which contrasted sharply with the face Liam had been confronted with when turning Trent's body over.

As they rode side by side toward Fallon, Trent said, "Here is the warrant for Ross. His last name is Tewksbury. He's wanted for murder in Denver and Wichita, and now, attempted murder of a Deputy U.S. Marshal. I suspect you want to handle him so I will stay out of the way and side you."

It was late afternoon when Liam and Trent rode into town. "The livery owner is Porter, good man. Hotel is down the street and is the only one in town. The doc should look at the gunshot wound, just to make sure it doesn't get infected.

The saddle shop on the other end of town should be able to care for your holster. I am going to talk with our friend Ross."

The sun was low in the western sky, casting long shadows from the false-fronted buildings on the western side of the street but it would be another hour or so before it set. The streets and boardwalks were less populated than mid-day. Liam listened to the off-tune piano music playing a somber arrangement that he couldn't place as he walked down the street's center toward the bank. Ross was in his usual place to the left of the bank's main entrance, twisted grin affixed to his face.

As Liam approached he lifted the thongs from the hammers of both .44s and Ross acknowledged in kind while walking down the bank's steps into the street. They were no more than forty feet from one another when they stopped their approach and moved to center street.

"Ross Tewksbury, you are under arrest for murders in Denver and Wichita and the attempted murder of a Deputy U.S. Marshal just outside of Fallon this afternoon. With your left hand, unbuckle and let your holster fall. One move toward your guns and you'll die right here in this street. I will not repeat myself." Liam had chosen the direction to approach the bank so that the setting sun was more facing Ross than him. The street and boardwalks would normally be without people as a gunfight approached but in this case the opposite was apparent, everyone hoping to see the town bully fall.

Ross stood still and contemplated his options, yet he had been waiting for this, hoping and anticipating this public display of his speed and prowess. "Marshal, you have no right to brace me like this. I've done nothing wrong, broken no laws, and you have no authority here. You'll die here trying to take my guns, so I suggest you turn and hightail it out of this town while you're still upright," Ross replied in a sarcastic tone.

Liam knew it would be this way, as did Ross, and he watched for the 'tell' in the eyes or shoulders knowing it would come momentarily. And then it happened, the almost invisible but very real flinch as Ross drew. Ross had cleared leather but had not brought his gun up when the hole just above the bridge of his nose began to trickle with blood. His Remington was slipping from his right hand when he died still standing, before the body crumbled to the dusty street. The dust was still airborne as Liam walked to Ross's body while shucking and reloading his .44 and then, as a cautionary habit, he kicked away the gun that rested in the dirt near Ross's right hand, turned and walked away. Noticing Sheriff Bosworth as he walked to the telegraph office he said, "Clean up your mess, Sheriff."

What Liam did not see was Carter watching the entire affair from the corner of the bank's front window.

The sun was peaking over the mines in the eastern hills of Virginia City, suggesting another warm day under a cloudless sky. The miners stumbling from their homes and shacks preferred the sun to the rain, but would prefer cooler weather altogether.

The Virginia City Gazette had published the story of Susanna's abduction and Clive's rescue, and the editor wanted a follow up, arriving at The Mansion in the early morning warmth.

"Mr. Weeks, thank you for the update," Standish Johansson, the Gazette's editor said. "May I have a brief word with Mr. Ackerman now?"

"Yes, but keep it brief. His fever broke just yesterday and he needs his rest. I'll show you to his room."

Entering Clive's room, Weeks was surprised to see Susanna sitting bedside, holding Clive's hand. "Clive, you know Mr. Johansson of the Gazette. Mr. Johansson, you of course know my daughter Susanna."

"A pleasure to see you again, Miss Weeks and you as well, Mr. Ackerman. I'll keep you both only a moment for a few questions to include in the follow-up piece. You, of course know that Van Cooper's partner in crime, Dutch, has made a full confession and it confirms that the deaths and robberies of the miners and the gambler were committed by Van Cooper. Dutch was present and is facing a life of imprisonment, Van Cooper likely facing death by hanging. Do either of you have a comment?"

Clive's voice, that had returned from a whisper only a day ago, said simply, "I will attend the hanging." Susanna uttered not a word but thought back to how close she was to never seeing her home, her father… and Clive. Her life was forever altered by these events, both for the bad and the good and she chose now to dwell on the good and on the man who knowingly rode into the rifle shot, risking his life to save her. His love and devotion had been proven beyond all doubt.

Over breakfast in the café, Liam filled Trent in and laid out the plan for the day and evening. He had asked Porter to mention the gather in the Sheep's Head Saloon while having a beer so that he could be overheard, but do it carefully so as not to be obvious. Trent and Liam would conceal themselves on opposite sides of the gathered herd and wait out the day and night for Carter's men to stampede the herd. Their plan was to capture one or two of the men and force them to talk and get, first hand, the evidence they needed to convict Carter and return the ranches to their rightful owners.

Before going to the livery, Liam stopped at the sheriff's office to check on Cooper. Seeing Liam, Cooper began yelling, "You son of a bitch; let me out of these shackles. I can't even take a proper piss, you bastard!"

"Good to know you are feeling better, Cooper. We will be riding soon. Oh, you may not have heard, Dutch has made a complete confession to Sheriff Donny yonder in Virginia City. My guess is you'll hang," Liam said with a straight and determined face. "What, no wise cracks or demands now, Cooper?" Then turning to Bosworth, "You got a problem?"

"None sir, none at all."

As he walked toward the livery, Liam sensed there was more energy in Fallon, a lighter atmosphere with laughter in the streets, and he liked it. Fallon was a town becoming what it wanted to become, a home for families. Stopping at the telegraph office he was pleased to receive a telegram from Martha in Washington. She and Joel were doing well and missed him terribly, and they wondered when he would return. Their home was fine but there was increasing tension in Washington resulting from the southern states' succession.

"Good morning Porter. Thank you for saddling Creena. Keep this quiet but I suspect I'll be leaving tomorrow or the next day. Those four horses will need to be on double rations as well. In case we don't see each other, here is something extra for all your help."

"Marshal, this be a double eagle, it's too much!"

"No, Mr. Porter, in my opinion it isn't enough. You're a good man and this town needs good men. Good day."

Liam and Trent left Fallon at different times and from opposite ends of town. They planned to circle and meet just north of where Trent was ambushed by Ross the day before. Trent's abdomen was quite tender and badly bruised, as every step his dun took reminded him. The plan was to meet at the JS ranch and ride out to the gather with some hands to blend in. Once at the gather, they'd slip away, secret themselves, and wait.

Trent had chosen the south side of the range and Liam the north, because the herd's position suggested a stampede, if there was to be one, would most likely come from the west pushing the herd east and it would be the best way keep them both out of harm's way. They had provisions for luncheon and supper, and full canteens. Their horses were picketed close to them, cinched tight, for a quick chase or getaway. The hands were to add a few hundred cattle to the gather and then head back to the bunkhouse. It was up to Liam and Trent from then onward.

Carter was more than annoyed that he had to personally meet with his hands now that Ross was killed. The bright side was he would keep Ross's share. That was something, not much in the full scheme of things, but something, he thought as he rode to their shack north of Fallon. He reached the shack sooner than expected and was met by Old Reed, the ramrod of this outfit. "Odd to see ya, Mr. Carter. Where's Ross at?"

"Well Reed, he picked a fight with someone that was faster and tougher, bad judgment on his part. But, he won't be making that mistake again, will he?" Carter was speaking from horseback, reins wrapped in his hands as the lay on the pommel.

"No, I would say that there surely is a case of bad judgment." Reed was a big bruiser of a man with bushy black hair and beard, wearing a greasy buckskin jacket. Anyone that laid eyes on the man would use caution. Four other men looked on from outside the shack's door.

"I hear there has been another gather on the JS and I want it broken up… today. The time of day or night is up to you Reed, just get it done. There will be something extra in it for you."

"That is right easily done, Mr. Carter. I will take care of it fir ya but there may be bloodshed."

"You come on into town when it's done, meet me at the bank." Then Carter pulled the reins, turning, and rode back toward town.

Trent was a born and raised Texan and therefore he knew cattle and stampedes. He had cautioned Liam that a rustler stampede would come out of nowhere, swift and dangerous. One moment the beeves would be grazing with some lying down, and the next moment they would be in the height of terror running en masse in any direction, but usually as a herd, sometimes as a few groups. Guns would be firing in the air, riders pushing the cattle in their selected direction. There would be nothing that he or Liam could do to stop the stampede, once started it must run its course on its own. It would be like changing the course of a twister. It's going to do what it's going to do. The riders wouldn't hear them over the thunderous roar of thousands of cow hooves pounding into the earth, and visibility would be poor if it occurred at night, so the plan was to approach from the rear of the stampede and try to take one or two riders and squirrel them away quickly. In all likelihood they wouldn't be missed until they all met at their hideout and that should give Trent and Liam a few hours to encourage them to talk.

The wait continued through the day and now into the dark of night, as Trent suggested would be the most likely time of attack. The drovers who created the gather had returned to the bunkhouse as planned, and were no doubt well fed by now. Liam could not see Trent, nor Trent Liam and that was as encouraging as it was a concern. They trusted each other as marshals, always having each other's back, but right now they couldn't have the back of someone they couldn't see.

The first shot in total darkness came from the west as Trent had guessed it would. It was obviously the signal to start the stampede, as it was a full minute or two before multiple shots rang out. The stampede direction was confirmed as toward the east, and Liam ran to Creena and swung into the saddle assuming that Trent had done the same. Shots continued and the sound of panicked bawling cattle running was thunderous.

Liam picked out the rustler closest to him and quickly gained on him, knowing the panicked herd prevented the rider from hearing his approach. He was no hand with a rope so he drew his modified Henry from the saddle boot then grabbed it by the barrel and rode swiftly behind the rider, swinging the stock and hitting the rider squarely at the back of his head. He connected just above the rider's neck, spilling him to the ground. Grabbing the rider's horse's reins, he turned abruptly before the rider could recover. The rider was out cold so Liam quickly tied his hands and feet and gagged him before tying him belly-down across his saddle. He then headed to the rendezvous location to meet Trent, leading the rustler's horse by the reins.

Trent was equally swift and successful but lassoed the rider, pulling him off the horse, and captured the rustler as he lay stunned on the grass with the rope tight around his arms and torso. He arrived at the rendezvous just after Liam with his rider tied forked on his horse and gagged.

They were in a box canyon, the entrance of which was so well hidden Jake, owner of the JS, said he was the only one that knew of it. There was a tank of spring-fed water and plenty of graze for the animals. Liam was starting the fire as they had planned. Both captives were disarmed of Colts and knives and tied together, sitting back to back. They waited until the coffee was a boil before addressing the captives.

"You are sure in a world of trouble mister. I am Trent Masters, Deputy U.S. Marshal, and I have you for rustling, which is a hanging offense, and probably murder. But no matter, you will hang. Ever see a hanging? It's a nasty way to die. Now, lucky for you that your friend there is still unconscious so you have an opportunity and I will give it to you only one time. Do you hear me, one time? Nod if you understand."

The conscious rustler nodded. It was a vigorous nod and it was clear he was scared, and he should be.

"You're smarter than you look. Now, you know that my partner has killed Ross and we will arrest Carter in the morning. He is going to swing, no doubt about it. So, here is your one and only one chance; you will tell us what you and your pards have done to these ranchers, who gave the orders, and yours and your pards' names. I am going to take the gag out and my partner will write down everything you say, word for word, and then you are going to sign it. If we believe you, I will cut your bindings and let you go. If we don't believe you, your one chance is gone and you will hang. I will personally see to it. Understand?"

The conscious rustler nodded, again.

Liam took the gag out and said, "Talk." His tone was menacing and all business.

"You serious, you'll let me go?"

"Serious. Now, last chance, talk," Trent said.

"Okay. I am called 'Frenchie' as I come from Canada. My real name bein' Jean Baptiste. The other guy here is Chase. Mostly we got da orders from Ross. Ross, he got 'em from Mr. Carter. Mr. Carter, he give us orders to. Jist did this mornin'. We rustled cows from all de ranches east of Fallon and sold em. We git a share of that. We was to prevent da ranchers from sellin' so they cain't pay Mr. Carter's loans…"

Liam documented the confession for Frenchie to sign, then the document was witnessed by both Trent and Liam. That done, Trent cut Frenchie's bindings and said, "Get on your horse and light a shuck. If we see you again, you will die. Now git!"

"What about my guns?"

"I said, git!" Trent's face showed controlled anger as he watched Frenchie running to his horse.

It was nearly midnight when Old Reed entered Mr. Carter's bank office. "Have a seat Reed," Carter said. "Would you like a whiskey?" as Carter handed Reed a glass. Normally Reed would drink directly from the bottle but he had enough awareness about him to use the glass.

"Sure would wash the dust down, Mr. Carter, thanky. We got the job done but we may have lost two men, Frenchie and Chase. They didn't show at the hideout after the stampede. It was purty dark and they may have been trampled."

"They can't be traced to us and we are almost done, so that shouldn't be a problem. You will get their share. Good job, Reed. Here is a little something extra as promised," Carter said as he handed Old Reed ten double eagles. "Tomorrow, I will take over the JS legally and with that the last two ranches will cave."

By the time Chase had come around, Frenchie was long gone. Chase was never aware that Frenchie had been captured. Trent replayed out the "one chance" routine with one change: if needed, he also had to testify in court that his confession was given without undo duress. It was approaching midnight and Chase was now occupying the one empty cell in the sheriff's office and wondering who was manacled to the bars in the other cell. Liam and Trent had retired to the hotel, committing to meet in the café for breakfast at sunup.

Dawn broke eerily still as if the earth was not yet aware of the new day. Liam was seated in the café with Patty pouring him steaming coffee when Trent entered. "This is my partner, Patty, Deputy U.S. Marshal Trent Waters. Trent, this is Patty and she has been a big help in this whole process."

"Nice to meet you Marshal, I'll be back with a mug of coffee for you," Patty said with a smile as she turned and headed to the kitchen area.

"Okay Liam, how do we play this with Carter today?"

"I received another wire last night, delivered to the hotel. Jeremiah thinks Quinten Carter may actually be Quint Brooks," Liam said.

"Brooks, the gun fighter? Hmmm, that might change things a little. He's killed over twenty men, supposedly in standup gun fights. He's likely to be hellfire with a gun," Trent said with obvious concern in his tone and on his face.

"Trent, I intend to brace him before he enters the bank. He normally arrives at about eight and I will be waiting. I'll make a proper arrest, but if it really is Brooks, he'll likely want to pull iron. Just watch my back in case he has replaced Ross."

Patty served them both plates of eggs, bacon and fried potatoes with lots of rich black coffee. Liam told Patty in confidence what had transpired last night and his plan for this morning. He asked if she could arrange for him to meet with her, and Jake and Martha from the JS ranch later that morning. Having finished their coffee, Liam and Trent left the café and took positions near the bank to wait for Carter.

Trent position himself on the bank side of the street in the alley's shadows by the mercantile, looking outward toward the street. Liam waited in the street leaning on a hitching rail across from the bank with the sun warming his back. He had taken his jacket off to allow free access to his

.44's and removed both thongs. The town was alive with energy, unaware of what the next few minutes might bring.

An apparent stranger entered Fallon from the west and kept riding up the street, stopping in front of the bank, his back to Liam, hitching his horse. He was dressed in Levi's, gray vest, white shirt and a gray flat brimmed hat but it was the double tied-down Colts that had Liam's attention. It took Liam a few moments to realize that this is Carter!

Liam moved into the street immediately to prevent Carter from reaching the bank. "Quinton Carter, or if you prefer, Quint Brooks," Liam shouted, "You are under arrest for murder, conspiracy to commit murder, and fraud. I am Chief Inspector Liam deBláca of the U.S. Marshals Service. Now, with your left hand, unbuckle your gun belt and let it fall into the street. This is the only warning you will get," Liam half yelled and there was no mistaking his authority and resolve. Trent was witness to the proper arrest if needed later.

Carter turned very slowly, making no move toward his guns. Around him all activity ceased and the street stopped in time. "So, you know my name, how clever of you, Marshal. But, my work is done here and you won't get in my way," Carter — Brooks — said as he casually moved to a better position in the street while Liam tracked him by his eyes. It was clear that Brooks had experience in gun fighting. He was calm and calculating.

"I watched you take down Ross from the bank window. Impressive, but you will need to be far more impressive with me, Marshal. You know my name so you know that I am no tenderfoot. Now, you don't need to die hear this morning, just turn slowly and walk away."

Liam just watched Brooks' eyes. He had said his piece and knew that now it was to the death. Only one of them would be alive in the next minute and there was a real possibility neither would live. It was Brooks that needed to make the play, and Brooks knew that a Marshal couldn't so he was biding his time, waiting for the edge that was not going to come.

"Last chance, Marshal. I have business to attend to. I know that a U.S. Marshal can't draw until he has been drawn upon; can't be murder on your part, only self-defense. What will you do if I don't draw, Marshal? You'll look rather foolish, won't you?"

Liam knew Brooks was just trying to get an edge so he waited for the 'tell' and determined that a chest shot would be safest since Brooks had witnessed the head shot to Ross. Seconds seemed like hours, the air still, a horse stomped its hoof, a wagon wheel brake squealed, a stray dog barked, as they stared at one another locked eye to eye, waiting. To be distracted was to die. Then the slight twitch of the right eyelid and hands blurred.

Both shots rang out as one. Liam placed priority in accuracy before speed, Brooks priority was speed before accuracy and died from his error in judgment. Brooks round-burned Liam's left shoulder going for a heart shot, but Liam's round hit left of chest center, straight into Brooks' heart. Brooks had died before the dust from his body hitting the ground had settled on his face. Trent approached Liam, both with guns drawn, Liam shucking his spent shell and reloaded, but there was no other fire. It was over.

Brooks was the third man Liam was forced to kill on his quest to bring Cooper to justice. He wondered why he felt indifferent about their deaths. He had taken their lives, snuffed them out in an instant, yet his conscience was clean. It was they who made the decision to give their lives, not him and to Liam, that was the difference and he was of clear conscience.

Later that morning, Liam and Trent met Patty, Jake and Martha at the café. Over coffee he told them the entire story. "Now, the loan documents will have the interest acceleration removed retroactively, for everyone, so no ranches are owned by the bank as a result of foreclosure. The Attorney General will be sending the new documents. So, get the word out to everyone. You'll need a new banker and a new sheriff. Trent will stay on here for a few days to help you get this all sorted out. There are three of Carter's boys left, but we suspect they will have ridden out hearing of this morning's affair, but Trent will check that out as well."

Liam paused for a moment and it was Patty that stepped in, "Marshal, why was Carter, or I should say Brooks, after those ranches… surely it wasn't for the money alone?"

Taking a breath, Liam responded, "Good question Patty, and it gets to the heart of the matter. This town is going to change some over the next year and you are going to need a good mayor, someone with solid business sense. You see, the railroad is heading for Fallon, coming from the east and straight through your ranchland, Jake, and the other ranches east of town. Now, it may sound bad at first, but there is no good reason your cattle can't walk over those iron rails to graze on the other side. What I am suggesting is, the railroad will pay dearly for what's called a 'right of way easement'. It means you still own the land but they have access to lay the iron rails and run their train into Fallon."

"Well I'll be a pretty smellin' skunk," Jake said ending with a whistle. "How did Carter find out?"

"My guess is he paid off the surveying team but we'll never know for sure."

"There is a bit more. The train will stop here but it will be a major line going from here to Carson City and then on to Sacramento. Fallon is going to grow, a lot!" Liam added, noting the smile that Martha had in her eyes while looking at Jake. "It will be a lot easier and faster to bring your cattle to market as well."

Looking at Patty, Jake and Martha, Liam continued, "I want to thank you all for your help. Trent and I couldn't have cleared this up if it weren't for you. You have helped your town and should be recognized for the risks you took in helping the U.S. Marshals Service." Then he shook Jake's hand, hugged Martha and then a longer embrace with Patty. "I will be leaving at first light."

Over supper that evening with Trent, they shared marshal stories and relaxed. Trent heard the full story of Cooper, the attempted robbery and the abduction of Susanna, and Liam was pleased to hear about Trent's life as a U.S. Deputy Marshal. Trent also talked about the deserts and Indians in the south and west, providing Liam with knowledge that he would need in future travels. In parting that evening Trent shook Liam's hand saying, "Boss, you are someone to ride the river with! Anytime, anywhere you need me, I'll be there to cover your back."

Van Cooper remained shackled, hands cuffed at the wrists and feet looped under his mount. Not that there was anywhere he could go with his horse on a lead rope behind the two packhorses and Star. The sun suggested it was nearing high noon on their second day riding west toward Virginia City, Nevada Territory, and Liam decided to stop and water the animals. On one of the packhorses were two kegs of water for the horses, Cooper had two canteens as did Liam.

Liam unlocked one side of Coopers shackle to allow him to dismount. "Marshal, those damn shackles are cuttin' into my legs. It ain't right!" Once he had dismounted he was forced to lay face down on the desert floor while his legs were safely re-shackled without comment. After watering the animals and a cold luncheon of beef jerky, they continued westward.

"We will walk the animals for an hour or so. They need the relief," Liam said as he attached a lead rope to Cooper's handcuffs.

"Damn it Marshal; you treat your animals better than me! At least let me walk ahead of the hosses. I'm eatin their dust."

Liam grabbed Cooper by the throat and was squeezing the life out of him when, after a deep sigh, he let him go saying, "Keep complaining Cooper, it warms my heart. You're worse than the dung from those animals!" Liam replied with a laugh.

The knot of horses with a prisoner, led by Marshal Liam deBláca, entered Virginia City just after sundown and reined up in front of the sheriff's office. Liam released the right shackle cuff to allow Cooper to dismount, pulled him down roughly, and pushed him up the stairs toward the office door, one side of the shackle dragging and clanging behind.

"Well I'll be a busted bronc if it isn't Marshal deBláca! Looks like you had a productive trip, Marshal. I assume this is the skunk that's been a-killin' people," Sheriff Donny said as he rose from his desk and welcomed Liam back to Virginia City. "You look like you been through hell and back, son. Almost didn't recognize you with the black beard shaved off."

"Nice to be back, Sheriff. Got a cage free for this pond scum?"

"Sure do and we have a rope ready and waiting for him as well. Got your wire and the Judge is sittin' tomorrow afternoon in a special session just for him. You staying in town tonight Liam? I'd like to buy you a steak and hear the whole story. I can fill you in on Dutch as well."

"I will meet you here after I clean the dust off me and get into a fresh change of clothes. I'd like that, Sheriff. Oh, and keep him away from Dutch." Sheriff Donny motioned to one of the deputies to lock up Cooper.

Liam took a long look at Van Cooper while handing the handcuff keys to the sheriff's deputy, eyes locked. The once crazed and snake like eyes had dimmed a bit, clouded with defeat and the realization that all was lost.

The trial commenced the following afternoon and was a cut-and-dried affair with both Dutch and Liam's testimony bolstered by the federal warrant issued by the U.S. Attorney General. Dutch was sentenced to a minimum of twenty years in prison as an accessory to murder. Cooper was sentenced to hang by the neck until dead, which many in the courtroom thought was far too quick a death for such an animal.

That same afternoon Liam rode out to The Mansion with Star on a lead rope and the ransom money over her back. Star had renewed energy as she recognized her environment, home. He was waived in along with hellos and applause from the gate guards. Susanna met them at the door and, upon seeing Star, ran down the steps and hugged her horse around the neck, scratching her chin and talking softly. Star responded, happy to be home with her mistress.

Liam had dismounted Creena and stood to the side watching, his heart warming. Susanna turned slowly and walked to Liam. They paused a few feet apart, looking into one another's eyes, and then she stepped in to him with a caring embrace. Liam sensed something had changed; it was caring not loving. Of course she would have changed, having been through the horrors of captivity and near death.

"Liam, I cannot thank you adequately for saving my life and saving Star for me. She means the world to me.

Come in, Clive is in the living room and anxious to talk with you. He isn't fully recovered yet, but on his way."

"Recovered?"

"Come in and we'll share stories over coffee," she said with a warm and happy smile. "We are engaged to be married."

Liam attended the hanging of Van Cooper; it was his first hanging, but would likely not be the last. It was a gruesome affair made more so by the spectacle the onlookers created. Husbands, wives, and children crowded around eating popped corn, sweets, and with the men drinking beer. It was a macabre carnival celebrating a human being's death with roaring cheers when the trap door lever was pulled by the hangman. Perhaps it would be a caution to any onlookers thinking of riding the outlaw trail.

Cooper said nothing when asked if he had any final words, rather his eyes bored into Liam with hate and the resolution that all was lost. He was offered a hood which was declined. The hangman tightened the noose and awaited the judge to give the nod to pull the trap door lever. The nod was given and the trap door opened with a loud whoosh. Cooper plunged straight down until the rope was played out, and his neck cracked with an abrupt jerk. His pants were soiled, tongue protruded, face dark red from trapped blood, and eyes bulging but now quiet. Van Cooper would hurt no longer.

For Liam, it was closure of the worst chapter of his life. Yet it was also the beginning of a new life, one that he had become to believe was his purpose, his calling. A feeling of directionless flooded through him as his quest had ended. Alone in a vast country with no family and few friends, the road on which he would now travel offered no relief. He resolved that the U.S. Marshals Service was now his family, the marshals his new friends.

Before returning to the hotel, Liam went to the telegraph office to update Jeremiah. He sent a wire also to Molly Wicks, who had been molested and whose father had been killed by Cooper and Dutch, hoping that she could gain some closure as well.

Molly had touched him more deeply than he was aware. Yes, he thought, she is beautiful, but it was her poise, sensitivity, intelligence and confidence, and her smile that now dominated his remembrance. He had been so focused on bringing Cooper to justice that Molly had unintentionally been pushed to the background of his thoughts. Now, alone, with his quest completed, she became ever present in his thoughts and he resolved to write regularly and visit as soon as he could manage it.

Settled into the hotel, Liam began to catch up on the country. The hotel's newspapers were a week old, but their content was news for him. He was shocked to read of the attack on Fort Sumter by Confederate forces hoping to acquire food, guns and powder, and fortunately no one on either side was killed. He read of the riots in Maryland that could block Union supply routes from the north and the potential succession from the Union, and President Lincoln's clever use of the Writ of Habeas Corpus that was overruled in Maryland but upheld by Jeremiah Black, the Attorney General, which squelched the trouble. Liam was disheartened by what was happening to his adopted country, thinking it was a body being pulled apart by its own arms.

A knock on the door interrupted his thinking. "Marshal," the wire operator said, "I have a wire for you from Washington. I thought it was important and brought it right over."

"You did well, son," Liam said as he placed a silver dollar in the wire operator's hand.

The wire read:

Well done son Stop There is trouble in Sacramento California Stop Wire when you arrive Stop

CHAPTER FIVE

1861

The Union burned its ships that were at the Norfolk Navy Yard to prevent their capture by the Confederates.

Union soldiers stationed in the western territories were recalled to the east to fight in the Civil War and largely replaced with civilians.

It was a perfect morning, intense azure sky with cotton ball clouds, crisp clean air with a slight chill and the sun warming one's face. It was the type of morning that stimulates the soul with fresh energy and excitement, where you feel happy to be alive, invigorated, and closer to nature. The birds frolicked and darted about seemingly enjoying the morning as well and even the colorful fall leaves in the trees happily danced to the ground and then off again with the soft easterly breeze.

The main road southwest to Sacramento was teeming with farm wagons, buggies, men and women on horseback all dressed in their Sunday's best and all choking on the dust from wheels and hooves. The wagons held pigs, chickens, goats, pumpkins and squash cradled in fresh hay, some with cows tethered to the wagon rear. Men, women and children, ambivalent to the dust, were smiling, laughing, with some even singing songs. There was frolic and excitement in the air.

Liam, riding his beloved horse Creena, overtook one family's wagon and slowed asking the man with the reins pinched between his fingers, "Howdy friend. What is this all about? Where is everyone going?"

The driver laughed and shook his head, his hat brim flopping in the breeze, and said, "Friend, you must not be from these parts or you'd fir sure know. We all headed to the Sac-re-mento city fair. It's a big deal to us folks that work our farms year round. Prizes and lots of em. Six thousand dollars in prizes. You should enter that horse, mista, mighty fine animal."

"Thanks friend, I may just do that. And, good luck to you!" Liam then galloped ahead hoping to get in front of the human and animal created dust storm and into Sacramento in time for a bath and a good meal.

Liam had left Virginia City, Nevada, several days earlier following the conviction and hanging of Van Cooper and the imprisonment of his pard Dutch. Cooper had killed twenty-four people, including Liam's mother and father and eighteen of his father's employees at The Black Arms Company. That number also included the father of Molly Wicks in Ohio, a woman that Liam was quite taken with and longs to visit with again soon.

The telegram Liam had received a few days back in Virginia City from Jeremiah Black, Attorney General and Liam's boss, simply stated:

WELL DONE SON STOP TROUBLE IN SACRAMENTO STOP WIRE WHEN YOU ARRIVE

The city of Sacramento lay on the southern border and at the intersection of the Sacramento and American rivers. Both rivers brought the mountain's spring melt where, in the past, there had been significant flooding within the city, so much so, there had been boats seen floating down the main streets of Sacramento. Man dug arroyos and small ditches to help direct the rivers overflow as well as earth embankments and levees, all common protection measures to save the city.

Liam was advised to approach the city from the northern banks of the American river and ride westward until he came to the Auburn Road Bridge. There he could cross the American river and head directly into the city's inner district.

Approaching the bridge, Liam noticed a wagon stopped off to the right near a large aspen tree and then heard a woman scream. He put heels to Creena's flanks and galloped across the meadow to the wagon to lend assistance. He could see several people in the wagon, a large man and the head of a smaller person standing on the opposite side of the wagon. Reaching the wagon, he confirmed that there were two young men and a girl in the rear wagon bed and an older woman on the front wagon bench, assuming mother, sons and daughters. He concluded that the father and another daughter were standing on the opposite side, both facing the wagon.

"Hello the wagon," Liam yelled as he began reining up. "I heard a woman scream. Can I be of assistance?"

"Mind your own business, mista. Mosey along," The man said belligerently.

Liam could see the buggy whip in his hand and the girl, maybe ten or eleven years old, with tears flowing down her cheeks and fright in her eyes. "What is going on here?" Liam demanded. He could see the fear on the mother's face as well as on the faces of the boys and girls in the back.

"I told you to git, now git or I will use this on you!" the father demanded, raising the buggy whip.

"Mister, put that whip away and do it right now!"

When the father raised the whip and struck the girl again, Liam swung his left leg over the saddle horn and dropped to the ground on Creena's right side, instantly running to the other side of the wagon where he saw the young girl's dress raised, her bottom exposed and bloody from the welts. The father then swung the whip, intending to hit Liam's face. Liam was prepared and grabbed it mid-air and held it firmly. The father wasn't prepared for this and Liam pulled it abruptly, causing the father to lose his balance and fall face first to the ground.

"Miss, are you able to get back in the wagon?" Nodding toward the mother, he added, "Would you please help her?"

"You got no business interferin', mista, this is family business!" the father said as he began to stand.

"U.S. Marshals Service, sir, and I have every right! What you did is despicable and you should be ashamed of yourself!" Memories of the abuse his fellow Irelanders endured at British hands spilled from his mind.

"She is my daughter and how I teach her is my business!"

"What I just witnessed is assault, sir, and I can arrest you right here and now. It carries a two to five-year prison sentence. Did you know that?"

The father, beginning to realize he might be in serious trouble began to backtrack, saying, "No sir, I didn't."

"I am going to give you two options. How many times did you whip that young girl?"

"I don't know." But the mother said in anger, "He whipped her four times, Marshal!"

Appalled, Liam shaking his head said, "Disgusting, here are your two options; I arrest you right now for assault, you will be convicted and serve your time in prison or you drop your pants here and now and I whip you four times so you realize the pain and humiliation you caused your beautiful and helpless young daughter."

"You cain't do that, Marshal. It ain't right."

"No. I can do it and I can't think of a better way to teach you a lesson. What is your choice, sir?"

"I am a deacon at our church, Marshal," the father said lowering his head in humiliation.

"Then you should be even more ashamed sir. What will it be?"

The father began unbuckling his belt, his decision made with the realization that being arrested would likely be more humiliating and could cause the possible loss of his ranch. He then turned and leaned on the wagon, facing his family.

Liam delivered four hard whacks, each bringing a loud scream from father, the third and fourth bringing tears to his eyes. His wife, sons and daughters restrained their smiles and swallowed their laughter.

"Alright, pull your up trousers and listen to me very carefully. You are to apologize to each person, individually, in this wagon that you have ever abused in this way. And, as a deacon, you are to solemnly promise that you will never, ever again, raise a whip or your hand to your family. Do you understand me?"

Wiping the tears from his eyes and in a meek voice responded, "Yes, sir." And then, he apologized to every person in the wagon and promised to never abuse them again. Liam believed he appeared to be sincere.

"Now, I will be in Sacramento for some time and will check on you periodically and if I believe you have broken that promise, you will be arrested and I will guarantee a conviction. Understand me?"

"Yes sir."

Liam watched as the father unsteadily walked to the driver's side of the wagon, hoping he learned something here. Then addressed the mother, "I have no doubt that your husband loves you and the children very much and was doing what he thought was best. But, fathers are people and all people make mistakes. I hope you can find it in your hearts to forgive him because he now knows how severe and unwarranted his discipline has been. If you ever need me, check in at the Sacramento police office. Have a good day." Then tipping his hat, Liam turned and stepped into the saddle.

The mother said, "Thank you, Marshal, God bless you!"

The young girl mouthed without speaking, "Thank you."

He was one of the few riders heading into the city, with the majority of the citizens heading north out across the river to the city fair. Creena was his one true love and drew most of the attention from the citizenry with his massive size and coloring, standing seventeen hands, midnight black with four white stockings, and head held proud and high. Liam had helped deliver Creena years ago in Washington and trained him from a foal. They were as if brothers, inseparable and of one thought.

Taking in the view while paused just outside the city, Liam was amazed with the earthen levees which at some points seemed to be easily twelve feet high and encircled the city. He concluded they were protection for river overflows. He also noticed an unusually organized network of streets and the buildings along them which stood in stark contrast to Virginia City, Nevada where they were haphazardly placed. The city proper was much larger as well.

After crossing the bridge, riding down Auburn Road into Sacramento Liam noticed that each east to west street was identified by a letter, while the north-south streets were named. He asked a young man where he could find the law office, "Well, that would be the police department. It is straight ahead, six streets down on the right side."

Arriving at the building, Liam loosely wrapped Creena's reins to the hitching post and climbed the eight steps to the porch and then opened the door to the police office.

He walked directly to a counter-type wooden desk with a uniformed officer standing behind and said, "Good morning, officer."

"Good morning to you, sir. How may we be of service?" The officer's uniform resembled the U.S. Army officer's style, blue wool with brass buttons and a holstered Navy Colt belted high on his right hip.

Liam extended his right hand to the officer saying, "Liam deBláca, Chief Inspector of the U.S. Marshals Service."

The officer took Liam's extended hand and shook it in earnest, "Officer Campbell. I assume you would like to speak with the Police Chief and if you would wait here one moment, I will inquire as to his availability." Then before Liam could acknowledge, the officer turned and briskly walked into the hidden-from-view office area with his footfalls on the wooded floor being the only evidence of activity.

Moments later, a large imposing man obviously muscled and fit with a shock of gray hair and matching walrus mustache, turned the corner. His booming voice echoed off the field stone walls, "Chief Inspector, I have been expecting you! Welcome," and then extending his hand to Liam, "Chief of Police Samuel Oaks. Come on back to my office."

"Marshal, I was just about to pour coffee, but I have tea as well. What's your pleasure?"

Liam took in the spacious and well-appointed office, thinking that it reminded him of Jeremiah Black's Washington office. There was a large dark wood desk, probably mahogany, flanked by supple chocolate leather chairs, a compact cast iron stove vented to the side wall in the corner upon which the coffee pot was resting. Behind the desk was a large map of Sacramento with several notations in ink and pencil. Newspapers were piled on the desk along with several papers and envelopes and parcels. This was a busy and serious man, Liam concluded.

"Coffee would be welcome, Chief Oaks."

Police Chief Samuel Oaks exuded capability and confidence. He was indeed a man comfortable being in charge, but was not in uniform — rather he was dressed in a gray pinstriped broadcloth well-fitted suit and vest, white pressed shirt and gray string tie. There was no weapon visible so Liam assumed a shoulder-holstered pistol.

Handing Liam a porcelain mug of steaming coffee he asked, "No trouble on your trip from Virginia City?"

Taking a careful sip of the hot coffee and then replying, "None at all and it was a welcome departure from the last several months. May I call you Sam?"

"Absolutely, Liam." Both nodded acceptance.

"Sam, you said that I was expected?"

"Jeremiah and I are old school chums. He sent me a letter with another letter attached for you. In it he asked if I would do some investigating prior to your arrival to help you get a head start on your next assignment," Sam said. Then he added, "He didn't explain what the role of Chief Inspector was, however, so perhaps we could start there?"

Liam enjoyed another sip of the steaming black coffee while organizing his thoughts and then responded, "That is as good a place as any. I was the Director of the U.S.

Marshals Service when a son of the devil, Van Cooper, placed a valise of dynamite in our family business, The Black Arms Company. It took the lives of twenty people, including my mother and father. Jeremiah, knowing that I needed to bring that animal to justice, activated the Chief Inspector position within the U.S. Marshals Service, for which I am forever in his debt."

Staring into the depths of his coffee, lost in memory for a moment, he went on, "As Chief Inspector I focus on the more serious crimes, especially those that breach state and territory borders. You know of the gangs that commit a crime in one state and then escape the law by entering another state where the local sheriff and marshals end pursuit as their geographic authority ends. I have no such restrictions because I represent federal law and am not bound by state, county, city or town law. All of the U.S. Marshals report to me and can be deployed, therefore, at my discretion."

Sam, now sitting behind his massive desk where his elbows rested, fingers forming a steeple, face pensive, said, "Well now, that is quite a responsibility. Jeremiah must think very highly of you, and therefore, I do as well."

They both sat in silence for a moment enjoying the rich black coffee before Sam added, "That helps explain what Jeremiah asked me to investigate."

"What was that, Sam?"

"The Pony Express, the very same that delivered the letters from Washington, has been robbed each of the last four months and multiple times within the month. The Pony Express riders were not killed but merely knocked unconscious. It is unclear what was taken. The robbers attacked in Nevada, which is well outside of my authority, so my investigation was limited to interviewing the riders when they arrived here in Sacramento. Each rider is required to report any mishap to me when they arrive and all reported still having their pouch but the locks were removed. Odd, wouldn't you say?"

"Yes, quite odd. You say they were knocked unconscious. Did they not see the robber?"

"No, and each of rider's reports are exactly the same. They were riding through Paiute Pass, which is a dangerous stretch, and the next thing they remember is coming to, lying on the path with a killer headache. Their horses are well trained, so when ground hitched they won't stray. They all report the mochila, that is the mail pouch, was still on the saddle but the locks were gone. Some riders speculate it was a Paiute raiding party, and that could be, but why would the Paiutes break the mochila locks? More, why were the riders not killed and the horses taken? After all, they were in Paiute lands."

Liam was deep in thought and had forgotten about the mug of coffee in his left hand that had tipped to the point of nearly spilling its contents.

"Liam, mind the coffee."

Smiling and coming out of his trance-like state, he replied, "Oh, sorry Sam, but no harm done, after all, the coffee is too good to waste. How far is Paiute Pass from here?"

"Well, that would be about two hundred miles west and slightly north. They all report it happening just after Castle Rock station, that's twenty Pony Express stations west of here."

Again, they both sat sipping their coffee in silence, thinking through the mystery. Riders were robbed several times each month over the last four months, but little or nothing taken. Was it a robbery? If nothing was taken could it have been an assault or a Paiute territorial warning?

Liam then came alive. "Sam, you said there was little or nothing taken. What does 'little' refer to?"

"Ahh, good point Liam. As you may know, the Pony Express mochila contains a maximum of twenty pounds to spare the horse on such a grueling ride. Letters, post cards, contracts, official government documents, money, and sometimes small jewelry items are included. It is expensive. By 'little' I mean we couldn't detect anything missing."

Liam pondering that asked, "I assume the contents of the mochila are weighed before leaving St. Joseph, Kansas to be sure it isn't overweight. Are they weighed again upon arrival in Sacramento?"

Sam replied with a chuckle, "I see why Jeremiah is so fond of you Liam. That is a very good thought. No, the contents are not weighed again. There was no need because the mochila is locked and the riders do not have a key. The master key is located in the Pony Express office here in Sacramento. So, I assume your point is, we really don't know if anything was indeed taken — and a valid point at that!"

"Yes. But, we also don't know if anything was added to the mochila."

"Good point. But why would someone want to add something? Not to save a few dollars on postage."

"I'll need to think on that. Regardless, the Pony Express is under contract to the U.S. Post Office and, by extension, subject to the same federal laws and tampering with the U.S. Mail can have very stiff penalties. You mentioned there was a letter awaiting my arrival from Jeremiah."

Sam reached into a leather valise and removed a wax-sealed beige-colored envelope addressed to Liam, penned in Jeremiah's own hand, and handed it to Liam.

"Thank you Sam, for your help and support. It will make solving this mystery much easier. Can you direct me to the telegraph office and recommend a good hotel?"

"That will be easy, Liam. The telegraph office is the very next building south. You can enter their office without leaving our raised wood porch. The hotel I would recommend is the Marin Hotel, just a few streets further south and you will enjoy the dining there as well. Oh, I assume you have your horse, and the Marin stable master will take excellent care of your mount."

Then Sam added, "The Pony Express office is three streets north on the opposite side. I will head over there and ask for the contents of any mochila that arrives with locks broken to be weighed and keep you informed."

"Thanks again Sam."

CHAPTER SIX

1861

The Nevada Territory separated from the Utah Territory and adopted its current name.

The Pony Express became the Central Overland California and Pikes Peak Express Company.

Liam settled into the Marin Hotel after he sent an update to Jeremiah and enjoyed a long hot bath. Creena was in the hotel's stable, rubbed down and provided with a double portion of oats. He then became aware that he had not eaten since morning and set out for a good meal.

Dressed in his black broadcloth suit, pressed white shirt and black string tie, he decided to forgo belting his dual .44's and left his room with his .38 neatly hidden in his shoulder holster. The hotel butler had cleaned and polished his black gentlemen's heeled western boots. He looked more like a successful cattle baron than the Chief Inspector of the U.S. Marshals Service.

Liam decided to go to the hotel bar for a pre-supper beer, quenching his thirst and picking up on any gossip that may prove useful. The bar was busy with patrons, mostly men and some women, and it reminded him a little of the Willard in Washington. Nostalgia flooded through him thinking of his father and mother and their residence in the Willard; now with their passing his residence was occupied by his house servant Martha and her son Joel. He committed to write a letter to them both and to keep them, his only remaining family, in his prayers.

The suited bartender approached Liam as he reached the bar, "What may I get for you, sir?"

"A beer would be a good start, please."

"Coming right up, sir."

Liam watched as the bartender pulled the adorned lever, drawing the beer into the thick glass mug and used a wooden stave to wipe the foam from the ridge. Then he slid the mug down the bar gauging the speed as an expert would; it stopped directly in front of him. Impressive, he thought privately.

He was surprised that the beer was chilled and very refreshing. With the mug in his left hand to allow his right hand to be free, Liam turned leaning his back to the bar and scanned the occupants. Most were well dressed and clean, unlike the bars in Virginia City. There was faro, poker tables, and roulette deeper in the bar. Cigars were the smoke of choice but a few pipes were present. No doves were in evidence; it was obviously a very respectable establishment and people seemed to keep to themselves in hushed private conversation.

Liam's sense was that he would learn nothing here, so finishing his beer he ventured off to enjoy a good meal in the hotel's restaurant before retiring for the evening.

The next morning, he sent a telegram to Trent Masters, the Deputy U.S. Marshal who had helped him solve the murder and fraud crimes in Virginia City, with a brief asking him to travel south to the Castle Rock Pony Express station and make inquiries. Also, he asked him to check the route from Castle Rock through Paiute Pass. It would be a few days' ride for Trent so he determined to meet each Pony Express rider when they arrived.

Sacramento was abuzz with activity. The gray cloudless sky and cool still air was welcomed by both animal and laborer. As Liam walked to the Pony Express office, he took in the character of the city. He could see as well as feel the organization and structure, the citizens' camaraderie and pride and the commercial success. It was clear that communication with the east was a critical element of that success and therefore, the importance of routine mail from the Pony Express.

Soon the iron rails would span the United States and its territories from New York City to San Francisco, and many points in between, carrying people, goods and mail. Liam concluded that would provide added stimulus to the growth in California and Oregon, and would likely be the demise of the Pony Express.

Liam spotted the Pony Express office on the opposite side of the street, crossed, walked up the stairs, and entered into a beehive of people clamoring for their mail. He decided to stay back and watch the goings-on. It appeared that when the mail arrived it was sorted geographically and then alphabetically by last name, with each letter having its own box. People would simply wait their turn and then, getting to the postman, would ask if there was mail for their last name. Many were walking away in despair having received no mail, some reading their mail with excited faces.

With the office now empty, Liam walked to the weary postman and asked to speak with the Postmaster, explaining who he was. The postman turned and yelled, "Clayton, there is a U.S. Marshal here to speak with you!"

Moments later Clayton appeared and said, "Hello, Marshal. Sam told me to expect you this morning. Our rider arrived earlier than expected and when the town's people see a rider arrive, they come many and fast. Coffee?"

Clayton was a small thin man, bald with spectacles perched on his beak-like nose. His light gray wool suit was showing its years of wear.

"Coffee would be welcome, Clayton," Liam said as he extended his hand and introduced himself.

They walked to the back of the office and Clayton said, "In case you were wondering, the mochila was intact, Marshal. Sorry. But, if one comes in without the locks, we will weigh the contents before the sort and distribution. Sam told me of your idea."

"Thanks for the information, Clayton. How long have you been with the post office?"

Handing Liam a tin cup of hot coffee, he replied, "I opened this office, Marshal — been with the Postal Service eleven years now. I welcomed the first Pony Express rider in April of 1860; it was quite exciting."

Liam sipped the coffee, noting immediately it was not of the quality he enjoyed in the Police Chief's office. "It is good to have someone of your experience to help with this mystery. What do you make of it?"

Clayton was an energetic sort, constantly fidgeting with something, now his tin coffee cup. "Well Marshal, I can vouch for each rider. They are loyal and solid men, even if they are boys. I trust 'em, Marshal."

Nodding, Liam asked, "Do you think they were robbed?"

"I can tell you this, they all had a hell of a lump on the back of their heads and some needed the doc to stitch them up," Clayton replied, indicating with his left hand to a place on his head just above the back of the neck. "And, the locks were missing, so somethin' happened."

"Some suspect the Paiutes. What do you think?"

"Well it all happens in Paiute Pass, so it's a thought… but I doubt that, Marshal. The Paiutes are nomadic, moving constantly to find what food there is in that part of the Great Basin. If it was Indians, I don't think they would have interest in the mochila. They would be interested in the horse, the rider's six-gun and clothes, and none of them were ever taken. It sure is a mystery."

Liam took his last gulp of the dishwater coffee and added, "Yes, it is. When do the riders arrive?"

"They come in twice each week now, late morning usually. The next will arrive in three days, I 'spect."

"I'll be here then and would like to talk with the rider. Where is the rider that came in this morning?"

"We have quarters here," Clayton said pointing to the second floor. "He is likely finishing his meal and looking forward to dropping into his bunk. Want to talk with him, Marshal?"

Clayton led Liam up a creaking wood staircase to the second floor. There he saw a small cook kitchen, a table and four chairs and four bunks. There was a Chinese woman stirring the contents of a pot, presumably on an iron stove that Liam couldn't see, and one boy sitting at the table shoveling what looked to be a beef stew into his mouth.

"Avery, this here is a U.S. Marshal and he would like a word with you," Clayton said, and then turned and went down the stairs back to the post office.

Liam introduced himself and was invited to sit. "Coffee and stew, Marshal?" Avery asked. He was about sixteen years old, short and thin but muscled, with sandy hair and blue eyes. It was clear that he had not yet bathed, with trail dust covering his face, red wool shirt and dark blue Levi's.

"I reckon you're here bout the robberies, Marshal. I'll tell ya what I know. 'Bout two months ago, I was hit in Paiute Pass. Strangest thing. One minute I was a-ridin', slowed down cuz the trail narrowed and forked to the right. Next thing I knowed, I was waking up on the trail with a whopper of a head. My hoss was ground hitched, standing near me. I didn't see or hear nothing. The mochila was still on my saddle so I climbed into the saddle and continued ridin', my head poundin' with every step of my hoss. It was night when I came to and didn't see the locks were missing until morning at the station."

"Ever had trouble with Indians?"

"You bet, Marshal, mostly the Utes and Shoshone now cuz the Paiutes settled down after the Paiute War back in May and June. Never in Paiute Pass," Avery replied between spoons of beef stew, some leaking from the corner of his mouth.

Liam thanked Avery and headed down the rickety wooden stairs into the post office, deep in thought but looking for Clayton.

"Clayton, do you remember the contents of the last mochila that came in with missing locks?"

Rubbing his chin, Clayton responded, "Let me see now, there was an assortment of post cards, letters, some banking documents as I recall. Oh, there was an envelope for the Army, Fort Point in San Francisco, I believe."

Pondering the new information, the suggestion of an idea began forming in his mind. "How does that mail get from here in Sacramento to San Francisco?"

"At times it will stay with the rider and he would travel down the river on the steamer. Sometimes it is placed on the steamer and the captain delivers the mail to the San Francisco post office."

"One last question Clayton, do you remember who sent that envelope addressed to Fort Point?"

"Hmmm, it was either the War Department or Treasury, can't rightly remember for sure."

The sun was high in the azure sky with goose feather clouds pointing eastward when Liam left the post office. Someone hailed from behind him and turning, he recognized it was Police Chief Sam Oaks. He stopped and waited for Sam to catch up.

"Mornin', Liam," Sam said. "How did it go at the post office?"

"Pretty much a confirmation of what we already know. But, I have an idea I am working on. I was just going to have a bit of luncheon, join me?"

Liam and Sam settled into a corner table at the Marin hotel's dining area and ordered sandwiches and beer. The conversation was a rehash of what they knew and then Sam changed the subject, "Well, it will be a few days until your marshal has scouted the Castle Rock station and Paiute Pass. Want to do some marshaling in the interim?"

"Need some help, Sam?"

"Might be the other way around, Liam," Sam said with a grin. "Ty Smithers runs several thousand head north of here on the T Bar S. He came in this morning, complaining of rustling. He's been losing a few head here and there, but lately they have been losing a few hundred at a time. When I can, I look into these things, but I really don't have the time and my jurisdiction technically ends at the city limits."

"I see. I will look into it. How far is it to the Smithers' ranch?"

"Oh, it will be about a two-hour ride, it is a beautiful ride. I'll go with you, show you where it is and make the introductions. On the way I will fill you in on the history. I have an idea who is behind this."

"Thanks Sam. Can you leave now?""

"Thought you would ask that, our horses should be saddled and ready," Sam said with a chuckle.

"I need to send a telegram to Jeremiah before we leave," Liam said. He wanted some additional information to nurse his idea a bit.

Deputy U.S. Marshal Trent Masters was less than a day's ride away from the Castle Rock station. He was pondering the wire he received from Liam, thinking that nothing fit. Multiple robberies with little or nothing taken all at Paiute Pass suggested the possibility of Indians, but the horse, six-shooter and clothing were not taken. The rider was left alive, not killed and mutilated. How a rider was knocked unconscious while on horseback without the rider hearing something, let alone seeing something? He would talk with Horace Wellman, who had just transferred from the Rock Creek station as the new Castle Rock station manager and then head out to Paiute Pass.

The hills were alive with the color of fall. Poplar and aspens were preparing for winter and their burnt orange, brown, yellow and pumpkin-colored leaves were gently blowing across the trail. Liam recognized the scent of apples and asked Sam, "Is there an apple orchard nearby?"

"You have a good nose, Liam. Yes, just west of us over that rise yonder. There's Cortland, Paula Reds and Macs, and they are delicious!"

Riding side by side Liam asked, "Sam, you mentioned there is some history here and that you have an idea of who might be behind this?"

Taking a few minutes to organize his thoughts and then replying, "This is peak rustling season round here. The beeves have had the spring, summer and early fall to fatten, so they are at their weight now. There has been blood between Smithers and the Carlton outfits for a few years. Smithers has been an icon in these parts for over fifteen years. He runs the ranch with his three sons — good boys by the way. They all keep their noses clean. The Carltons, well that's a different story. Old Man Carlton is just that, old, and losing control of his five sons. He lost his wife 'bout six years ago and she was the ramrod of that outfit. It took the heart out of the man. Good woman too. He pretty much stays in the ranch house now. Their ranch ran about five thousand head before she passed and it has dwindled to about two now, maybe less. The boys drive a thousand or so to the San Francisco stockyards when they need drinking and whoring money. So, the natural increase just hasn't kept pace and the whole outfit is in steep decline. I suspect the boys are behind this and Liam, they are a caution. Jed, the oldest and the self-appointed ramrod, is quick to rile and lightning quick on the draw. If you brace him, he'll draw on you. I think his brothers are afraid of him."

As they crested a rise on the trail Sam reined up saying, "That's the T-S ranch. Pretty isn't it?"

It was, Liam thought, as he surveyed the field stone ranch house nestled in the valley facing the rising sun. There was a large barn, several corrals with horses at play, a smoke house obviously in use now in preparation for the coming winter months, a large bunkhouse and several out buildings — all efficiently laid out, beautiful and tranquil. They started down the trail heading for the ranch house.

Sam helloed the house as they approached, and a tall man dressed in Levi's, blue shirt and brown leather vest stepped out on the porch. He had a holstered pistol but no rifle, obviously not expecting trouble or possibly recognizing Sam's voice. Shielding his eyes from the low sun and sighting Sam, he said, "Come on in and set Sam, coffee's hot."

Sam and Liam looped reins over the hitching post and stepped up to the porch. Sam shaking hands with Ty, said, "Ty, this is Chief Inspector Liam deBláca of the U.S. Marshals Service."

Extending his hand to Liam said, "Ty Smithers. Welcome to the T-S Ranch Mr. deBláca. Come on in and set."

The ranch house was larger than it appeared from the trail, and the room into which they walked was cavernous and filled with soft leather sofas and chairs, side tables, wool carpets and a large stone fireplace. It looked and smelled like a successful ranch. Ty motioned them to the sitting area and a woman entered with coffee and mugs on a wooden tray.

"Mr. deBláca, this is my wife of more than forty years, Sally."

Standing with his hat in hand, Liam said, "I am very pleased to meet you, Mrs. Smithers."

Sally set about serving the coffee while Liam took in the rest of the room. Then, sipping the steaming rich black coffee, Ty broke the silence speaking to no one specifically, "I assume you are here to look into my missing cattle."

Sam placed his mug on the table and replied, "Ty, I brought Liam up to date. So, he knows the history and has cattle and rustling experience. You know that I really don't have jurisdiction beyond the city limits. But, Liam has jurisdiction everywhere, in every U.S. state and territory. And he is a very capable man."

Ty, as well as Sally, now looked directly at Liam, "Thank you for the help, Mr. deBláca. I don't begrudge someone taking a cow when they are hungry, a man has to eat, but rustling hundreds — that's too much. It is hurting the ranch. I can't afford to let this go on, Marshal. But, I don't want my sons getting into gunplay with the Carltons — after all they're cattle ranchers, not gunslingers. We want to do this legally."

Liam took a long pull from his mug, enjoying the rich coffee while organizing his thoughts and then replied, "I respect that, Mr. Smithers, and I agree completely with your thinking. After all, we suspect the Carltons, but we don't have solid proof. Not yet. I intend to pay a visit to Old Man Carlton tomorrow. We'll have a talk and I will look over their stock. If there is any T Bar S stock on their range, it will be proof enough to arrest them and stop the bleeding. I'm pretty good at detecting a brand that has met with a running iron."

Sally jumped in, "Marshal, you are welcome to stay the night with us and leave first thing in the morning. The Carlton place is just an hour's ride northeast of here."

"That is right kind of you Mrs. Smithers. I accept. It will give me a chance to meet your sons, I hear they are fine young men."

Sam said his goodbyes and Liam took Creena to the Smithers stable, rubbed him down and forked some hay into the manger. Later that evening, Liam enjoyed a delightful family meal that brought back memories of his close family ties and their suppers at the Willard in Washington. Before retiring for the evening, he thanked Sally for a wonderful meal and hospitality, and said he would be riding out before dawn.

The gray pre-dawn was cold and eerily still. Liam had coffee with the cook in the bunkhouse, which was in close proximity to the barn. Creena was rested and energetic and took to the trail with vigor, but Liam held him back a bit to keep an energy reserve should he need it later in the day. He wanted to be at the Carlton ranch just after sunup.

The trail was wide and well-traveled by both horse and wagon. Liam kept to the trail's center to avoid the wagon wheel ruts which were deep enough for Creena to turn an ankle. He was the lone traveler at this time of morning and he could feel the sun's heat on the right side of his face before he could see its light. He guessed that the Carlton ranch was about another twenty-minute ride. The tall poplars were guarding the trail and intermittently began letting the sunrise beams peak through.

The wooden sign off to his right with *Carlton Ranch* painted on it stood to the left of its road to the ranch. It was weathered gray and drooping forward off of its post, the top nail having failed to do its job — the first indication of the fading outfit.

Liam stopped when the ranch house came into view. It was a small wooden affair, perhaps a few rooms with a loft, a stone fireplace to its left, an uneven porch on its front and a roof with shingles missing. There was a smoke trail from the chimney, probably breakfast coffee, showing that the house was occupied. There were two corrals, with several horses standing three legged and a weathered barn.

Liam stopped about twenty-five yards back and 'helloed' the house. A few minutes later the door opened slowly and an old man stepped unsteadily out, a Winchester cradled in the hollow of his left forearm.

"State your business, mista!"

"U.S. Marshal, Mr. Carlton. I am here to talk with you."

Carlton stayed as he was, Winchester still cradled, obviously thinking. Then he let the rifle drop from his left forearm, still being held in his right hand but barrel down and said, "Come on in and set, coffee's aboil."

Carlton waited at the open door until Liam looped reins over the hitching post and walked up the two stairs and then simply nodded when he saw the badge on Liam's vest and said, "Marshal." Then he turned and led the way into the house.

The interior was in conflict with the Smithers' ranch. It was smaller, dirty, smelled of must and onions, and was sparsely furnished. Liam concluded instantly that the Carlton outfit was well down at the heels. There was no conversation and the sons were not in evidence. Liam waited for Old Man Carlton to break the silence.

Carlton looked to be nearing seventy, not the late fifties that he was led to believe. He walked with a limp that seemed to emanate from his right hip. He was dressed in soiled Levi's and a stained, faded red shirt. His feet were without boots and the socks were leaking toes. His gray white stringy hair was greasy, his eyes red-rimmed and he had a bushy gray beard that evidenced tobacco and last night's meal.

Handing Liam a tin cup with hot coffee he asked, "So, what's this about, Marshal?"

Liam took a sip of the coffee, nodded his thanks and replied, "Looking into reports of rustling. Have you lost any of your herd lately?"

"Shit Marshal, I ain't been out of this house is years. Damned hip won't let me ride and walking is purely pain. My son Jed ramrods the ranch these days. You'd better be asking him."

"Sorry to hear that, Mr. Carlton. Where can I find Jed?"

Carlton sat gingerly in a horsehair-stuffed chair, spilling a splash of coffee on his faded shirt that he left unaddressed. He was obviously a thinking man and seemed to be worrying.

"We don't see a U.S. Marshal in these parts much. What brings you here?"

"I am down in Sacramento on another matter. This is serious matter as well, and I have the time and the duty. I'll look into it."

Nodding, he seemed to make his decision after looking at Liam's two tied-down .44s. "Marshal, I lost my wife a few years back and it knocked the sand right out of me. Then my horse stumbled and threw me, breaking my hip and I was done. My sons are all I have, but I ain't been much of a father lately. You understand me, do ya?"

Liam did understand. Carlton either knew or suspected that his sons were the rustlers and he was asking Liam to let it go. "I think I do understand, Mr. Carlton. My father and mother were murdered a few months back so I know what it is like to lose family. I'll make a commitment to you right here; if your sons are involved I'll let them go with a warning this time but only if they return the cattle and commit to stay off the outlaw trail from now on. If they don't, I will arrest any of them that have been involved and turn them over to the county judge. The judge won't go lightly on cattle rustlers."

Carlton was nodding in contemplation and said, "You look like a man of your word, and I'll hold you to it. Jed and the boys should be here any minute for breakfast and coffee. You are welcome to wait."

As Carlton was talking, Liam could hear the distant horse footfalls at a medium lope getting louder as the seconds ticked by. Not wanting to be obvious, Liam placed his cup on the table, stood and reached over to Carlton, extending his hand and said, "You have my word." Then he discretely lifted both thongs from the hammers of the .44s.

Liam was aware that Creena would alert them of a visitor and being an unknown horse would put them on edge if they were the rustlers. So, he remained standing, easing to his left away from Carlton to have a clear field of fire. Always be prepared, he thought privately as he heard boots on the steps.

The door pushed open abruptly and who he assumed was Jed walked in; stopping just inside the door, preventing Carlton's other sons from entering. Mistake Liam thought, over confident probably.

Carlton remained seated but turned, facing the door and said, "Jed, this is a U.S. Marshal. He's lookin' into some rustling in these parts. Come on in. He wants to ask you a few questions."

Liam watched Jed closely for 'tells' and concluded Jed hadn't determined how to play this out. Jed was about two inches' shy of six feet, muscular and wiry, looked to be about thirty and wore a tied-down Colt. He had alert gray eyes, long brown hair and a tense hairless face.

"I don't think so, Pa. Marshal, you're on Carlton land, private property. I don't need to talk to you. You got two choices, forked on that animal or tied across the saddle. Now, git."

"Jed, threatening a U.S. Marshal was the wrong decision. It tells me you have something to hide. Are you and the boys involved with rustling?"

"You ain't leaving here alive so's it don't matter none. We took back cows that been taken from us, that's all."

"If that is the case, all you need to do is show me the cattle and the brands will verify your story and I'll be on my way," Liam said watching Jed intently for his tell. And it came, a twitch in the right shoulder...

Jed drew and cleared leather before Liam drew in response. Two shots sounded, one seemed an echo. Liam waited longer than he needed because of his promise to Old

Man Carlton and paid the price as Jed's bullet hit his upper thigh. Liam's bullet hit Jed where he aimed; the right shoulder, causing Jed's Colt to fall to the floor. Acrid smoke filled the small house, the shots still ringing in his ears.

Carlton lunged for his son Jed while screaming, "Marshal, you gave me your word!" But, seeing that his son was shot in the shoulder, and very well placed so as not to do any permanent damage, he realized that the marshal had indeed kept his promise.

Old Man Carlton jumped up as fast as he could and yelled at the boys as they pushed their way into the house, "Put your guns down, put 'em down! Jed's only hurt but he deserved to die!"

Liam was still standing, .44 in his right hand with five rounds left, blood dripping down his right leg to the floor.

"Boys, the marshal promised me that if you returned the cattle and stopped riding the outlaw trail, he would let you all go. He gave me his word and seein' that he could have killed Jed here and didn't, he's a man to ride the river with. Put 'em down, now!"

Somewhat reluctantly, they obeyed their father and holstered their guns and looked after Jed. Only then did Liam holster his .44 and looked at his wound. It was a through-and-through and luckily didn't hit the bone, but would need attention. For now, he tied his bandana tightly around the wound to stem the flow of blood.

Then Liam looked to the boys and Carlton and decided that there was hope to bring the family back to the side of the law if Jed was out of the picture. It was a risk, but for a family, he was willing to take that risk.

Looking at Old Man Carlton's sons, Liam said, "My commitment to your Pa is still available to you boys, but Jed will be doing some time in prison. Jed, you are under arrest for attempted murder and cattle rustling. I'll be taking you to Sacramento as soon as we fix that shoulder wound enough for you to travel. Now, you boys need to make a decision. Return the cattle and make the commitment to go straight, or I will need to arrest you as well. What will it be?"

Old Man Carlton sat down again with a grunt and said, "Kent, you are my ramrod now and damn it, you will straighten out! This outfit has gone to hell over the last years. It's my fault. I should have reined in Jed. He led you down a bad trail. Now, you can make the right decision and follow the marshal's advice. What will it be?"

Liam thought he saw relief in Kent's face as he finished attending to Jed's shoulder, but was it relief that Jed wasn't killed or that he would be free of Jed?

Kent looked at his Pa and then nodded to his younger brothers standing behind him, who all nodded back, apparently in agreement. Turning back to Liam he said, "Pa was always a good judge of a man. He says you're a man of your word. I am as well, we all are. We will return the cattle to the T Bar S this afternoon and we will go straight. We were never happy with Jed's path, but he was the oldest and the ramrod. Now, that will change. Pa, we will rebuild this outfit and make you proud. You have my commitment, Marshal. And my thanks for sparing Jed." Then he extended his hand to Liam who took it willingly.

Jed, strained and in pain yelled at Kent, "You gutless dandy!" Kent didn't respond.

Liam pulled his .44 shucked the spent round, reloaded and handed Kent a set of cuffs while instructing him to bandage Jed's shoulder and get him on his horse and tie his ankles along the cinch.

As Liam limped out the door Old Man Carlton stopped him, tears in his eyes, and said, "Thank you Marshal. You have saved what family I have left."

Liam swung into the saddle and reached for the lead rope of the horse with Jed forked on that Kent was handing him. The boys said their goodbyes and then Old Man Carlton stepped out onto the porch to have a last word with Jed.

Looking at Kent, Liam said, "A good starting point to bring this outfit back to life is to put some pride into that Carlton Ranch sign. Make is stand for something and stand behind it."

Stepping down off the porch to Jed forked and tied on his horse, Carlton said, "Son, it may not appear now that this is a good thing for you, but it is, mebe the best thing for you and for our family. You got a chance to turn your life around son, but you need to accept it. I will step up as the father you have needed and I am sorry I have not been there since your ma died. You set this right and you have a place here when you come back." Old Man Carlton then turned and limped back into the house, closing the door behind him but opening the possibility of a new life for his sons.

Liam decided to stop at the Smithers' T bar S on the way to Sacramento to update Ty and Sally on the outcome of the rustling investigation and to expect the return of the rustled cattle. Sally also cleaned and dressed both Liam's leg wound and Jed's shoulder wound. Jed kept to himself perhaps embarrassed of being treated so well by the very people he had robbed. Ty had already arranged to be neighborly with his sons to visit the Carlton Ranch and help the boys get the outfit back on its feet.

Trent Masters sat his horse on the rise above the Castle Rock Pony Express station taking its measure. The station was small with just a wooden station house and, close by, a corral attached to a horse shelter. The house backed to a steep ridge and fronted the trail. Beyond lay a field of dry grass and, judging by its height, most seemed to have been cut and laid into the shelter for winter feed. He saw no well and assumed it was dug within the house itself as a safety measure in case of Indian attack.

Trent 'helloed' the Pony Express station house as he neared and was greeted by a short man cradling a double-barreled scattergun. But, after identifying himself, he was invited in for coffee.

Horace Wellman, the stationmaster that had transferred from the Rock Creek station, was a short and stout man nearing fifty years of age. Horace had bushy gray hair that met with equally bushy mutton chops. He was wearing long johns under bib Levi overalls, both as clean as Horace himself. He spoke with a Scottish accent in short sentences with clipped words.

Sitting and enjoying the rich coffee aroma, Trent asked Horace, "What can you tell me about these robberies?"

Jumping into Trent's last word, Horace replied, "Noten Marshal. Tese boys are good boys. They come thur here fast. Take da pouch. Throw on rested hoss. Then they be off."

"Are the locks tested here?"

"Nope. But I see 'em. Dey are there."

"Any Indian trouble lately?"

"Some ask for food. We give some. Paiute war over now."

"Who do you think are doing the robbing, Horace?"

"Bandits, not Indians. You want some food?"

Trent was surprised at how good the savory venison stew and freshly baked bread was, so much better than his trail grub. There was little conversation over the meal as Horace offered to water and feed Trent's horse, knowing that he would be headed to Paiute Pass after the meal.

"Thanks for the information and food Horace and for caring for my horse. Tell any riders that come through that I will be on the trail. Give them my description so they won't get spooked if we meet."

Trent decided that he would travel the Pony Express trail heading to Paiute Pass. He had decided there were only two possibilities, Indians or bandits.

Trent began thinking. Paiutes, sometimes said to mean "true Utes" inhabited most of this region and their mountain brothers, the Shoshoni, the northern region. They were a poor tribe, largely as a result of the barren land they occupied, and therefore weak. In many cases Paiutes embraced the white man's occupation of their land because it offered them work as laborers which provided money for goods, clothes and food. The whites usually avoided the "Digger Indians" as they were called due to their digging for roots as a food source.

The horses weren't taken during the robberies and a Paiute definitely would have taken and probably eaten the animal. It would have been a feast by comparison to the roots they subsisted on. The skin would have been harvested for clothing or additional coverage on a wikiup. No, he thought, it is unlikely to be Indians.

What are the bandits doing, if indeed it was bandits? Was something stolen that had gone undetected? Perhaps they are just looking for information? How are they disabling a rider? He decided he would know more once he reached Paiute Pass later in the day and, being in Indian country, he needed to be alert and focus on his surroundings.

The land was like the venison stew he'd enjoyed earlier in the day; it had a bit of everything. There were lava fields, tall rock hills with some that could be called small mountains, small meadows and periodic stands of poplar and aspen. The trail was well traveled and therefore easy to navigate.

Trent saw not a soul. There were shoed horse tracks in both directions, but no Indian pony tracks. But being a born and raised Texan, he knew that when you don't see Indians is exactly when you should be most wary.

He judged that Paiute Pass was about an hour's further ride and with about three hours of daylight left he decided to press on and camp near the pass for the night. As it turned out, he came upon Paiute Pass in less time than he had expected and he decided to use the last of the sunlight looking for a camp near the pass.

The pass was tree-lined with sprawling limbed poplar and cedar, the cedar spewing its rich menthol-like aromas. Many of the trees had limbs that spanned the trail as it constricted, creating a tunnel-like feeling at times. He spotted a path to the right heading off the trail and instinctively took it. The path led to a small secluded bench with adequate grass and a gently running stream. He was not the first to camp here, as evidenced by the coals in a small fire pit near a rock reflector. Normally, that would suggest he move on, but being here to investigate, he decided to stay but roll his blanket well away from the fire area.

The night was cold but quiet, except for the cedar and poplars speaking in agitated bursts by the unpredictable wind. Morning broke cold and gray with a suggestion of snow in the air. Having poured the last of the hot coffee from the charred pot on the remaining embers, he swung into the saddle and headed out to look over the pass.

Trent decided to make three complete passes, the first on the trail itself, a second through the trees to the north and the last through the tree on the south side of the trail.

He estimated the trail's elevation to be between two and three thousand feet above sea level. The footing was of hard-packed soil, sand, and finely crushed stone. It was solid and echoed each of his horse's footfalls; moving in stealth was near impossible with an iron shoed horse, especially a Pony Express rider in gallop. To the right, the elevation grew and to the left it fell off, sometimes several hundred feet. From the beginning of Paiute Pass to its end, Trent failed to discover anything unusual, so he turned right, heading up and into the trees above the trail to head back eastward.

The trees along the north side of the pass were dense but no so much that Trent couldn't pick his way through on a makeshift trail looking for sign. He was rewarded almost immediately, picking up the tracks of two shoed horses, but the tracks were many days old, perhaps weeks old. They were heading the same way Trent was heading, west to east, so he pushed on, more carefully now.

It was deadly quiet, not even a bird invaded the environment which Trent assumed was a warning of an approaching storm. Suddenly there appeared several horse apples along the left side of the trail near a shallow opening where the two horses had obviously been picketed for some time in the past.

Trent reined up and ground hitched his horse, setting off afoot to investigate. He found where a small fire had been used for coffee, the pit deep enough so as to prevent its discovery from a distance. Boot tracks led from the fire to the trail and back. Following them he made his way to a ridge about ten feet from and twenty feet above the trail. He was recalling that this was the area where the cedar and aspen branches actually extended over the trail, sheltering it from the shy above. And then he saw a rope.

The dark horse hair rope was tied to the trunk of a strong cedar. Trent untied the rope and found it tugging against his hand and let it pull free. He heard it first and then saw it seconds later; a large ten-foot cedar log easily a foot-thick swing down parallel over the trail, suspended on either end with rope. It looked to be a large swing, the log a substitution for the typical board seat.

It all came together in Trent's mind as he struggled down the slope to the trail. The cedar log was still swinging well over his two inches' shy of six feet height. He was thinking, the riders are all of similar size and riding similar size horses, therefore their head would be within inches of each. The rider telegraphed their approach with galloping footfalls. The only real challenge was timing the release of the cedar log to hit the rider in the back of the head as he was riding by. If it missed, Trent was thinking, the rider would likely not even realize the danger that was so close at hand. The rider never knew what hit them because the log was pulled back into the trees before the rider regained consciousness.

The "how" mystery was solved but the "why" was still alluding them. Trent cut down the log to prevent another robbery, or at least make it more difficult. He then put pencil to paper, detailing his discovery for Liam that he would give to the next Pony Express rider for delivery in Sacramento, which would arrive ahead of him.

Winter was coming. The gusting breeze brought cool clean air, causing Liam to exhale a visible mist as he walked to the Pony Express office. The rider was due in by mid-day and he was determined to be there when he arrived.

The Pony Express office was a beehive of activity and Liam concluded that the rider must have arrived early. He waited as the people retrieved their mail, as he had done three days before. Then he approached the desk and asked for Clayton, the Postmaster.

"Marshal, I've been spectin' you. The rider arrived a few hours early. The pouch was intact, all the locks there and locked. Sorry. But, the good news is there was no trouble on the trail." Clayton said.

Liam was not disappointed at all. In fact, it was what he had expected after reading the telegram yesterday from Jeremiah.

"But, I have somethin' fir ya, Marshal." Clayton said, smiling and reaching into his vest pocket and retrieving a piece of paper and handing it to Liam.

"Thank you Clayton. What is this?" Liam asked.

"Seems your deputy flagged down the rider west of Paiute Pass and asked him to deliver this to you personally. He passed it to me before falling asleep upstairs."

Trent had tied the paper tightly closed with a green pine needle, knowing the needle would be broken if the folded paper was opened. Breaking the pine needle and unfolding it, he concluded it was not opened previously. He devoured the results of Trent's investigation because he now knew the "how" and the telegram he received earlier yesterday morning provided the "why".

Sitting in Police Chief Sam Oak's office, enjoying his rich black coffee, he brought Sam current. "Sam, we have this thing figured out. Now we need to determine who is behind it. Trent, my Deputy U.S. Marshal, found out how the riders were rendered unconscious without warning or seeing who did it. Seems there was a log that was released by a man, timed to swing down behind the rider as he slowed to take a switchback. He wouldn't have seen or heard anything."

Sam listened intently and then offered, "Okay. Swinging behind the rider in the same directing he was traveling would likely knock him out but not kill him; makes sense. So, clearly Indians are not behind this."

"Absolutely correct, Sam. So, that was how it was done. I received a telegram yesterday from Jeremiah yesterday that confirms why they are doing it. Seems that the U.S. Army has changed how they send their payroll to the western forts. It is moved by train to St. Louis and then secretly transferred to the Butterfield Overland Stage Line to Fort Yuma in southern California. There it is split for the southern forts and scheduled for guarded transport to the northern forts. The schedule is sent by Pony Express to the forts in San Francisco; all in secret. Because of the risk of robbery, these stages are heavily guarded and they send several Trojan horse stages to confuse potential bandits. But, with the schedule known by the bandits, the stage becomes an easy and very predictable target."

"Liam, I thought the stages carrying payrolls and other valuables are fortified and very heavily guarded by an Army troop. It would take quite an outfit of bandits to take that stage."

"Yes, and that worries me greatly. This is well organized by a patient man, a thinking man. I can only assume, like you have, that they have the resources to take the stage. This is a quarterly payroll and general operating cash for two forts, Fort Point and the Presidio; nearly five hundred thousand dollars."

Sam whistled.

"I have a suspicion, Sam. This could be a Confederate terrorist group trying to weaken the resolve of the remaining US Army's western theater. As soon as Trent arrives, I intend to visit Fort Point in San Francisco and have a look at those secret scheduling documents."

CHAPTER SEVEN

1861

Fort Hatteras at Cape Hatteras, North Carolina, falls to Union naval forces beginning the first Union efforts to close Confederate southern ports along the Carolina coast.

Lexington, Missouri falls to Confederate forces under General Sterling Price.

The Butterfield Overland Stage Line within California starts at Fort Yuma at its border with the Arizona Territory, and then heads north stopping at a series of twelve stations ending in San Francisco and covering about eight hundred and fifty miles. The stage line allows for a scheduled travel time of one hundred seventy-nine and one half hours, about seven and one half days.

Overland operated stages specifically for the transportation of people, along with their luggage and sometimes carrying a strong box with valuables. The other stage, known as an express, was deigned to carry gold, silver and cash, and to protect against robbers the coach was fortified with heavy planking and iron plating. The express stage was escorted by troops or by private employees as an added deterrent to robbery.

Two stage stops south of San Francisco in Gilroy, a man sat in the Dusty Saloon drinking a beer while taking in the details of John Butterfield's published stage schedule. The saloon was in full raucous energy with poker and faro tables filled by the post gold-rush miners, the bar full and smoke thick enough to cut with a knife. The man sat alone, undisturbed, and his body language telegraphed that was what he wanted.

His size and attitude gave the correct impression that he was not one to take lightly, but his cold gray eyes, the type that send chills up your spine when they light upon you, was why most men gave him a wide birth.

The bartender thought he was the only person the man had exchanged a word with. He had been in the saloon several times and each time sat alone. The bartender walked up to his table and asked, "Another beer, sir?"

The man shook his head ever so slightly from left to right; lifting the mug to his lips and taking a last mouthful, he rose and walked from the saloon to his horse, lifting the reins from the hitching rail and stepping into the saddle in one smooth motion. He walked his horse east out of town, feeling the warm setting sun at his back.

The fire in the center of the camp was larger than most trail fires, but they were not concerned about Indians and the camp was well sheltered from the Butterfield stage road. There were two large coffee pots and one pot bubbling with beef stew.

An imposing brown bearded man called the eleven men to the camps center and said, "Men, Major Seth Meyers would like a word. Major?"

The Major's cold gray eyes met each of the men's very slowly in succession before delivering his remarks. "Men, each of you is a trusted and loyal Confederate soldier. You are very capable. I know that and Sergeant Major Slayer knows it as well; that is why you were selected for this duty. We will soon have an opportunity to deliver a very serious blow to the Union Army and I intend to make the most of that opportunity."

The men began to look to each other with smiles on their faces before the Major went on. "There will be an express stage coming through Pacheco Pass very soon; I will share the timing in a few days. It will be well guarded, most likely cavalry but it could be civilians, so it will be dangerous. Some of us may lay down our lives in the taking of that stage, so I am going to tell you why it is so important. It will be carrying $500,000 in gold and currency, the operating funds and payroll for Fort Point and the Presidio in San Francisco."

The men broke ranks, hailed and clapped. "Our job is to take that stage and deliver the gold and currency to a schooner that will be waiting off the shores of Monterey about sixty miles west of us. If we can't make the schooner, we are to bury the money, keeping it out of the Union Army's hands. I intend to make that schooner because our army is in desperate need of that cash to pay for food, clothing and arms."

Major Seth Meyers paused for a moment to let the magnitude of the terrorist operation settle into the minds of his men; and then went on, "This is our biggest operation yet, and as I said in the beginning, it will be dangerous and some of us may not make it through. So, anyone that wants out, sing out now and there will be no hard feelings. I won't order you to report for this duty; you must do it voluntarily; do it for our fellow Confederates, our brothers and fathers. They need this cash desperately."

Sergeant Major Slayer stepped into the group's middle and said, "Let's do this the easy way men, raise your hand if you volunteer for the operation."

All hands immediately rose without the slightest hesitation.

Liam deBláca and Trent Masters traveled on horseback southwest from Sacramento to Benicia, located on the northeastern coast of the San Pablo Bay, and then on a steamer with their mounts to San Francisco. Their first stop was Fort Point.

Fort Point was the largest west coast fortification and stood at the entrance to San Francisco Bay within the Presidio compound. It was built where the sixth governor of California, Jose Joaquin de Arrillaga, built his fortified adobe fort in 1794. The US Army Engineers took possession of the property and built Fort Point in 1853, a near replica of the east coast Fort Sumter. It was the only brick fort west of the Mississippi.

The Fort Point Sergeant of the Guards had been alerted to expect Chief Inspector Liam deBláca, and immediately escorted them directly to the office of Colonel Albert Sidney Johnston, Commander of the Department of the Pacific.

Colonel Johnston was a serious man in his fifties, trim, about six inches shorter than Liam's six feet two, and sported a mustache resembling a Texas Longhorn. His uniform was immaculate and his posture remarkably straight for a man in his later years. He was a West Point man, obviously a man of stature and education.

The colonel extended his hand in welcome to Liam first and then Trent and then said, "I understand this is time sensitive and serious. Please have a seat and fill me in, Chief Inspector."

Concluding that the colonel was all business, he provided all the information that was relevant to the Fort Point operating cash express stage.

Liam finished his brief by summarizing, "Colonel, the security surrounding the operating cash shipment has been breached. My belief is this is a Confederate rebel group action. Therefore, if I am correct, we can expect a well-planned operation carried out by motivated and trained gorillas. And, I am confident that I am correct."

The colonel processed the information very quickly. "I understand. You have the express stage schedule which is normally kept very secret, for obvious reasons. The stage will be well guarded with a cavalry troop. One troop will take the stage from Fort Yuma to Los Angeles and a new troop from there to Fort Point. The second leg will be the longest and most grueling leg as it skirts the mountains. Water can be problematic and robberies are common, although mostly focused on the passenger stages. What is your plan, Inspector?"

"We know the timing, but we do not yet know the location of their planned attack on the stage or who is behind this, but I have suspicions. My first objective is to determine the likely locations for the attack and to do that I will talk with the stage drivers. That may also give me added information about who is behind this." Trent was nodding, concurring with Liam's approach.

Colonel Johnston's face conveyed his displeasure. "Chief Inspector, I was expecting a good deal more from you than that. If they succeed and we lose the operating cash, the impact on us will be catastrophic! Morale will plummet and there may be desertions. We simply cannot afford being substantially understaffed in our support of the war. And, to make matters worse, time is running out! I want daily reports from you!"

"Colonel, your concerns are my and Deputy Marshal Masters concerns." Then standing, indicating that the meeting was over, Liam said, "I will keep you informed, but as a courtesy as this is my operation, Colonel, and I do not report to the Army."

Liam and Trent went directly to the Butterfield Overland stage depot. On the way, riding side by side, Trent commented, "Liam, that is one tightly-strung officer!"

"Sure is, but his concerns are all too real. We need to determine the likely spots for this robbery to occur, and fast."

"You told the Colonel you had a suspicion as to who may be behind this. Care to share?"

"The express stage with the $500,000 in operating cash and gold is schedule to leave Fort Yuma on California's southern border on November 24th which will bring it into San Francisco on December 1st. There are very few that know the schedule and there will be several dummy express stages carrying little cash as a diversion, preventing onlookers from figuring it out. The scope and planning lead me to believe this is a Confederate undercover operation. Keeping that cash from the Colonel, and worse, getting control of that cash for their needs would indeed be catastrophic."

Trent whistled, "I hadn't thought about that angle! But, I reckon that it all rings true. That would explain why the robberies have stopped; they got the information they wanted. Since today is November 15th, we best make the most of these nine days."

Liam added, "As I indicated, I think they are a group involved in espionage, and they could only operate with anonymity. That would suggest they are dressed in typical western attire to blend in, and are secreted near the location where they intend to take the stage. But they need access to supplies and a way to retrieve information, either in person or by mail. Telegrams are a possibility, but only if it were done in code. So, they need to be within riding distance to a town."

Trent pondered this for a few minutes and added, "That all reasons well with me and may help us triangulate their general location."

At the Butterfield Overland stage depot, they learned that the stage drivers were likely washing the trail dust down at the Gold Rush Saloon, located several streets to the south.

The Gold Rush Saloon was in conflict with its surrounding environment. It was a no-thrills old-west-type saloon that the locals called an eye sore but it was the most comfortable place for the stage drivers being old west trail men. Pipes were the smoke of choice, beer and whisky the drink of choice and poker the game of choice. There were dozens of hard looking men sitting at various sized tables and bellied up at the bar, all apparently comrades.

Trent felt right comfortable; the saloon reminded him of his Texas heritage. Liam and Trent walked to the bar, flagged down the bartender and each ordered beer. Liam then asked the bartender, "We are looking for the Butterfield stage drivers. I would take it kindly if you point them out."

"I see your badge Marshal. Are you expecting trouble?"

"Not at all sir; we just need some trail advice is all."

"Okay, I'm happy to help you then, but no trouble please. The locals will close us down. Your best bet is to talk with Curley. He is the big guy in the fringed coat over there by the poker table," the bartender replied, motioning the direction with a nod.

"Give me another of what he is drinking, please."

Curley looked up as Liam and Trent approached his table. He was a big man with a mop of curly brown hair, alert brown eyes and clean-shaven face, probably nearing forty years of age. He was well muscled with broad shoulders with a thick neck. It was Curley that spoke first with a deep somewhat-raspy voice, "Problem, Marshal?"

"Not at all Curley. This is Trent Masters, Deputy U.S. Marshal and I am Liam deBláca. We're told that you're the man to talk with about the stage road," Liam said as he offered him the beer.

Curley, sized them up before responding, "Have a chair, men, and tell me how can I help ya?"

Liam took a long pull of beer, using the time to organize his thoughts. He didn't want to tip his hand. "We are looking into the Butterfield stage robberies. Where are the spots where you are most vulnerable, most on alert for robbers?"

"Well Marshal, I been driving the trail for over two ya's now; I seen my share of outlaws and happy you be lookin' inta this. Dar be two places; Tejon Pass near Fort Tejon, and Pacheco Pass east a Gilroy. Now, the Army bein so close to Tejon have helped up there."

Trent jumped in and asked Curley, "Tell us about Pacheco Pass. Why there?"

"That pass is purely hell. Hell on me and my boys and double hell on the horses. Worse ifin' it be a heavy express stage. It be about fourteen miles long with half of that up a long slow grade. So, the animals are winded; the stage is slowed to a crawl. Usually my boys are behind it pushing just to make the grade. And, when we get to the top, about fourteen hundred feet in el-e-vation, we gotta stop and rest; everyone and the animals are plum worn out. We are sittin' ducks. The animals and my men need water so's we are sittin' there for a good thirty minutes."

Liam asked, "What is the terrain like?"

Curley chuckled and then responded, "Well, the pass is rocky, sandy and dry. To the east you got desert for a while and then forest as ya get closer to the San Joaquin River. To the west, rocky, sandy, dry for a bit and then it is wooded as you git near the Salinas River. There be hundreds of places to hide out where you would only be found if ya wanted to be found. There be a dozen places where we could be attacked. It is hell there boys, but there ain't no better route."

Liam and Trent looked at one another in recognition that the Pacheco Pass was the likely location for the planned robbery.

"Much obliged Curley. You've been a help. I will have the barkeep send over another beer," Liam said.

Liam and Trent didn't need to discuss where they were headed next. Gilroy. The trail south went along the western shores of San Pablo Bay, then on to San Jose where they would stay the night. From there it would be a day's ride to Gilroy, a total of seventy miles. Pacheco Pass would then be another twenty miles due east of Gilroy.

The town owed its name to John Gilroy, a Scottish seaman who had jumped ship to recover from scurvy and fell in love with the area and the Mexican people who lived there. He eventually married Maria Clara, daughter of his new employer, ranchero Ygnacio Ortega. Upon Ygnacio's death in 1833, the rancho was divided among his three children, including Gilroy's wife Maria Clara. Gilroy, or "Old Gilroy" as it was known to the locals, grew up around Rancho Ygnacio Ortega.

The predominant language of Gilroy was still Spanish although the majority of the residents spoke both English and Spanish. Sombreros were the head covering of choice and adobe was widely used in building to maintain a cool interior. The streets were empty, short of a few horses here and there at a hitching rail. Guitar music echoed off the adobe walls from somewhere. The smell of spiced roasted meat floated in the hot static air.

Liam felt both at home and relaxed as well as alert and on guard. It was the foreign environment and an unknown feeling that left him uncomfortable. For Trent, the born and bred Texan, it was an everyday occurrence and sensing Liam's lack of comfort, he took the lead.

"Liam, after we check in with the sheriff, how about I introduce you to good Mexican food?"

"Well, I certainly am hungry after that ride. There is the Sheriff's office," Liam responded, pointing off to the right.

The sheriff was sitting outside in an old oak chair with the chair's front two legs off the porch and his sombrero tilted low on his head. He pushed the brim of the sombrero up with his left index finger just enough to see the two approaching riders, but not so much as to allow the setting sun to invade his shaded face.

"Evening boys, what can I do for you?" the Sheriff said in perfect English elocution.

Liam studied the man wearing the star. The voice had emanated from beneath the sombrero and the face was hidden in its shadows. Although difficult to guess a sitting man's proportions, he estimated his five-foot-seven frame carried about one hundred sixty pounds. He was in tan colored Levi's, white shirt and a matching tan vest. A single holstered gun, most likely a Remington, was tied to his right thigh.

"We are U.S. Marshals looking for the town sheriff. Do you know where we might find him?" Liam responded in a neutral but friendly voice.

The man lifted his head to take in the two visitors but his face remained shadowed. "You're looking at him. The name is Rafael Diaz and I have been the sheriff for nearly nine years. What brings you to Gilroy, Marshals?"

Trent looked to Liam when the sheriff said nine years, and they both concluded correctly that Sheriff Diaz must be good at what he does to last so long in the same job.

"Robbery Sheriff, stage robbery. We are looking into the Butterfield Overland stage robberies," Liam said.

The sheriff pushed his sombrero back and allowed the sun to bathe his face. He was of Mexican descent with coal black eyes that matched his hair and neatly trimmed pencil-thin mustache. "Have you boys had supper as yet? If not, I suggest you take rooms at the Villa Hacienda just south of here and stable your horses there as well. Perhaps we can become acquainted over a meal at the Hacienda."

"Much obliged, Sheriff, for the suggestion. Shall we meet at seven?" Liam suggested.

"I will meet you at the bar at seven," The sheriff replied as he tilted his sombrero back down, shading his face from the setting sun.

The Villa Hacienda was a two-story saloon, restaurant and hotel of adobe construction that was spotlessly clean and well maintained inside and out. The rooms all had glass windows and feather beds with freshly laundered sheets.

Liam and Trent were standing at the Hacienda's bar enjoying a beer when Sheriff Diaz entered. Much can be learned about a town and its sheriff when the sheriff enters a bar. Do some patrons abruptly leave? Does the conversation lower to whispered tones? In this case, there was literally no change in the patrons' behavior, and that is a very good sign, one of respect.

"Sheriff Diaz, we were not formally introduced earlier today. I am Liam deBláca, Chief Inspector of the U.S. Marshals Service and this is Trent Masters, Deputy U.S. Marshal," Liam said, gesturing toward Trent.

"It is a pleasure to meet you both, and welcome to Old Gilroy."

"Would you care to join us for a beer before supper, Sheriff?

"Thank you, but no. My choice of libation is tequila," Diaz said, as the bartender delivered a cut crystal shot glass half filled with the clear liquid. "To your health, gentlemen," Diaz said as he lifted the glass in salute and then drained the tequila in a single swallow.

They were soon seated in a quiet corner of the Hacienda's restaurant and feasting on tamales, tacos, and beef roasted with fiery hot peppers and onions. Diaz continued with tequila while Liam and Trent stayed with beer to accompany their meal. The conversation was casual and friendly until coffee arrived.

Diaz asked, "How can I be of assistance to you, Liam?"

Liam had decided to hold back the real mission until he was confident Diaz could be trusted. "As we mentioned earlier, we are looking into the stage robberies. The drivers indicate that Pacheco Pass is the worst place for them. What do you think?"

Diaz enjoyed a long pull on his coffee mug, organizing his thoughts before responding. "The pass is surely a favorite location. The long grade greatly tires the animals and it is very slow going. There is quite literally nowhere for the stage to run and there is no satisfactory alternate route. The Army considered a permanent outpost there to act as a deterrent but with the war upon us they lacked the resources. I would agree with the drivers' suggestion."

Trent asked, "Have there been any strangers in town recently, especially a large group of strangers?"

"Trent, I am sure you understand that we host a good many travelers, those heading to San Francisco from the south and those heading to Los Angeles from the north. Old Gilroy is an oasis to escape from trail food. To your question, señor, large groups no, perhaps a few groups of two or three. Strangers many but none that stand out as menacing."

Liam was so deep in thought that he was unaware the waitress was asking him if he would like more coffee. Something didn't fit. He felt strongly that they were missing something vital, but what? The express stage should reach the pass on November 27th and tomorrow was the 22nd, so there was time to rethink this from the beginning.

"Sheriff, would you be kind enough to make inquiries with the general store or mercantile to learn if any stranger has been purchasing supplies multiple times; supplies for a dozen or so?"

"Marshal, I will do as you ask first thing in the morning."

"We are riding out to the pass tomorrow, would you care to join us, Sheriff?" Liam asked Diaz.

"I will meet you at the stable in the morning after making inquiries. It will be a pleasant four-hour ride. Thank you for your company this evening, gentlemen." Sheriff Diaz excused himself to make his evening rounds.

Trent waited for Diaz to leave before commenting to Liam, "Interesting man, that Diaz. I judge him to be formidable and happy he is on our side. But, I sense you are not entirely convinced."

"Five hundred thousand dollars is a mighty big temptation, so I suggest we play it close to the chest for now."

Sergeant Major Slayer was drilling his men hard in a remote location that was very similar in layout to that of Pacheco Pass. Their plan was to deploy five men on each side of the trail with Major Meyers and himself forward of the attack zone. One man would be left to tend their horses lest the gunfire spook them to the point of pulling their picket pins.

It would be a blood bath. Without warning, all ten men would open fire on the army troops. They assumed the troops would be riding in a standard column of twos, and they would set up in a line with each taking aim at their assigned number in the column starting with troops forward of the stage. Then shifting by five for their second shot should there be more than ten in the column. Slayer and Meyers would take the stage driver and shotgunner.

With the troops neutralized and the stage in their control, the plan was to backtrack south down the trail about ten miles, rest the animals and then proceed west over rougher terrain heading for the Pacific Ocean and the waiting schooner. They would not rest until reaching Monterey Bay, a grueling ride of at least forty-eight hours that would be hard on animals and men.

Major Meyers had four positions planned for the possibility of pursuit and capture. A detail had been sent days ago to dig four large holes along their planned route to bury the large strong box containing the cash and gold. Their goal was to deliver the cash to the Confederate schooner but they would do everything possible to avoid letting the cash fall back into the hands of the Union Army.

Each of the large holes would be camouflaged after they passed that could fell the horse of anyone in pursuit. With the first horse down, the remaining pursuers would be more cautious, which would slow their pursuit.

Sheriff Diaz was waiting for Liam and Trent outside the stable as promised. He sat a massive black stallion obviously of Arabian blood with a classic Mexican saddle adorned with silver medallions. "I took the liberty of arranging for your mounts. Magnificent animal, Liam. As to your inquiries, yes there have been several suspicious supply purchases. All by the same person: tall, thin and a man of very few words. Always had a packhorse or two with no markings or brands. Not much more to add, I'm afraid."

This new information gave Liam and Trent added confidence that their thinking had been accurate.

They headed east toward Pacheco Pass three abreast at a casual trot, with the rising sun in their face. A slight westerly wind brought a faint sea salt scent that surfaced memories for Liam of County Kildare and his ocean voyage to America. The terrain was sparsely wooded and relatively flat. The Butterfield stage trail was packed dried earth and obviously well-traveled. As the ride progressed, the terrain evolved to rocky hills increasing in height as they rode.

Liam used the ride to think through the mystery; who were they looking for and what had he missed, if anything? Could he trust Sheriff Diaz? He replayed in his thoughts what was known: The Pony Express riders were not robbed; rather the timing details of the cash delivery locked inside the pouch were gained. The obvious goal was to hijack the stage and the likely location was Pacheco Pass. November 27th was the day the stage would crest the pass, four days from today. An Army troop would be escorting the stage and the hijackers would know that, which in itself suggests a large team would hit the stage by surprise. What have I missed? The uncertainty remained, haunting him.

Liam's thoughts were interrupted by Diaz. "We will start a gradual climb now, six or seven miles to the crest of Pacheco Pass. If this is the site of the planned robbery, the stage will be hit about a mile south of the apogee to prevent the spent animals from being spooked by the gunfire and running down the other side."

The three immediately reined up at the sound of distant shots. Liam suggested, "Those shots are easily a few miles away to the south. Diaz, is there a stage scheduled through here today?"

Sheriff Diaz rubbed his chin in thought, "Yes. This isn't an express stage so it will be carrying passengers and perhaps a small strong box. The rock walls through which the pass runs can sometimes play tricks on you, however. The echoes can confuse the direction and the distance. We are only a mile from the crest so two miles away is my best guess as well." Then digging spurs into the flanks of his stallion, Diaz was in full gallop toward the crest of Pacheco Pass with Liam and Trent following closely.

Diaz led them into a small alcove near the trail's crest and they dismounted and carefully climbed the ridge to survey the scene below. Intermittent rifle and pistol gunfire continued.

The stage was stopped about a mile from the crest with the stage driver and shotgun both lying at odd angles across the front bench, perhaps dead. Shots were coming from inside the coach holding the robbers at bay. There were four bandits, two north of the stage and two south, all with Winchesters.

Liam took control. "Trent, you work your way behind the two on the north, I will take the south. Diaz, you stay here and take out any that try to escape."

Diaz added, "Be very careful of diamondbacks in those rocks. There are plenty of them and they are mean. Good luck, amigos!"

Knowing they would need stealth to creep up close behind the bandits, both left their rifles in the saddle scabbards, relying on their pistols.

It was slow and difficult but they moved as quickly as they could, aware that the passengers likely had little ammunition left. The plan relied on catching the bandits unaware from their rear. Liam moved in a low crouch from boulder to boulder. He was well above and behind them now and picked up his pace, being careful not to cause a rockslide that would surely alert the bandits below. The last twenty yards would be the most treacherous as there was little in the way of cover and lots of loose gravel that could give him away. He decided to stand and palm his right .44 and carefully tiptoe closer.

Now within easy pistol range he planted his feet and yelled, "Don't turn around! Drop your rifles now! You turn and you die where you stand! U.S. Marshals. Do it now!"

Both bandits froze and turned their heads, facing each other with questions on their faces, not knowing how to play this very unexpected turn of events. Then one dove to the right and the other to the left, turning their rifles toward Liam.

Liam didn't wait and fanned two shots, both center chest hits. The one bandit rifle shot went wide and high but both were down, not moving. Liam ran over and kicked both rifles away and pulled their pistols before checking their pulses. One bandit was dead and the other would likely soon join his friend.

Carefully he looked over the rocks and watched Trent covering two bandits with raised hands walking toward the stage.

Alerting the stage occupants, Liam yelled, "You in the stage, U.S. Marshals here. We have the four bandits and are coming over. Don't shoot! Do you understand?"

From inside the stage a man responded, "Alright, but come slow so's we can see your badges!"

Liam walked out slowly and a shot rang out, followed by another. The first shot ricocheted off a rock to his left, coming from an elevated position close to where Diaz was positioned. The second shot was from Diaz, hitting a fifth bandit that Liam hadn't seen. Diaz waved an all-clear and Liam continued to the stage.

There were five people in the coach, three women and two men. "U.S. Marshal Liam deBláca at your service. U.S. Marshal Trent Masters is coming up from the south with two bandits under arrest. Sheriff Diaz of Old Gilroy is coming down as well. Are you hurt?"

The women were crowded onto the coach floor with the two men each holding a pistol, covering their respective sides. "We are unharmed, Marshal. You arrived just in time. We have only two rounds left between us. The driver and shotgun may need your help; I think they were hit by surprise first."

Liam climbed the coach to check on the driver first, then the shotgun. Both were hard hit in the chest but alive. The driver had wrapped the reins around the stage break handle to prevent a runaway in hopes of saving the passengers.

Trent had arrived with the bandits and had cuffed them to the rear wheel.

"Trent, we need to get the wounded to Gilroy fast. How are you with a rig this size?"

"I can handle it, Liam. Let's get them on their backs on the roof. It will go easier on them."

"OK. Diaz and I will follow with the bandits forked on their mounts or tied over them. I will bring your horse as well. Get moving!"

Arriving in Gilroy later that afternoon, Trent updated Liam and Diaz. "The doc says that the driver has a good chance but the shotgun didn't make it. Butterfield will have a replacement crew here tomorrow morning. The passengers were a little shaken up but they are all fine."

Liam turned to Sheriff Diaz, "Diaz, thanks for watching my back today. Join us for supper tonight at the Hacienda and I will fill you in on what we are really doing here."

"Marshal, I suspected you had held back some important details," Diaz said smiling.

Major Meyers and his men had just finished a full supper of venison steaks and potatoes. There was no liquor allowed in the camp and everyone was sitting around the fire awaiting orders for the next day.

"Men," Meyers started, "We have pushed you hard over the last few days, and the Sergeant Major and I thank you for your hard work. Tomorrow is the day before we take the stage. You will invest that day resting and caring for your weapons and horses."

The men murmured their satisfaction with that order.

Continuing, Meyers said, "The day after tomorrow we will take our positions in the early morning, several hours before the stage arrives. There you must remain still and quiet. Surprise is our advantage. Take a full canteen with you. When you hear me take out the driver and the Sergeant Major take out the shotgun, you are to immediately assume firing on the troops. Focus first on the troops in front of the stage, one shot to the number in the column that you have been assigned and make it count, center chest. Then, if there are more soldiers, your next number."

The men were all quiet, knowing this was what they have been trained for, knowing the importance of success.

"There is to be no mercy. None! Your friends, brothers, fathers back east are hungry, cold and short on ammunition. Your homes are being burned to the ground by the Union Army; your stock and crops confiscated. This all by the same army we will confront and conquer. Our success will not only fund the needed supplies for the Confederacy, it will demoralize the Union, not just here in the west but in the east as well. Each of you individually hold the key to our success, and men, we will succeed. I have complete confidence in each of you. Now rest. Dismissed."

Seated at a corner table in the Hacienda, Liam, Trent and Sheriff Diaz feasted on spicy jerked chicken, roasted vegetables and corn. Each were thinking about the attempted stage holdup earlier in the day and the likely similarities to what they may be facing the day after tomorrow. It was Liam that spoke first.

"Sheriff, let me fill you in completely." He told the sheriff everything from the Pony Express robberies to their belief that it was a Confederate terrorist group, as well as the amount of cash and gold being transported.

Sheriff Diaz nodding jumped in, "And with that much money involved, you didn't know who you could trust, am I correct, amigo?"

"Yes, and we apologize. But surely you can understand. We simply didn't know you," Trent added.

"You did the right thing, Marshal. I would have done the same," Diaz said. "What is our next move?"

Liam took the lead responding to Diaz, "We have several challenges to work through very quickly. Trent and I figure that there will likely be around a dozen Confederates to contend with; we have no way to alert the stage or escort already in route; our priority is to protect the gold but I would like to find a way to also protect the troopers and the stage drivers. And we are three, assuming you will back us, Sheriff."

Diaz didn't wait to respond, the smile on his face stretching his pencil-thin mustache, "Amigos, I am with you! I haven't had this much excitement in sometime."

"Thank you Sheriff. Three against twelve is almost a fair fight," Liam said with a chuckle.

Trent was deep in thought and pensive before clearing a space on the table. Liam and Diaz watched as Trent began breaking off pieces of bread, placing them within the space. He then removed the cap of the salt shaker creating a thick line of salt between the bread pieces and then placed the cap several inches away from the bread.

"Here is how I see it," Trent said. "The Butterfield stage trail through Pacheco Pass is represented by the salt, the bread the cliffs on the north and south sides and the salt shaker cap I will get to in a minute. Similar to the holdup today, I 'spect that they will have at least five soldiers secreted on the north and five on the south side. Their job will be to take out the Army escort. Now, they don't know how many of our troops will be in escort. My judgement is that there will be more than the typical six but not so many as to draw unusual attention. So, maybe ten or twelve, perhaps half leading the stage and half trailing."

Liam nodding, "That makes some sense. What is the salt shaker cap?"

Sheriff Diaz jumped in, "They need to stop the stage so that must be the long shooter to take out the driver and shotgun. With the stage going up the grade, the team will stop if not being driven. Am I right amigo?"

"That's how I see it," Trent said. "And, they will likely attack some distance before the top of the trail to dissuade the animals from running."

They were all analyzing the crude diagram on the table and deep in thought. Each were aware they were missing something, perhaps more than just one thing. It was Diaz that broke the silence.

"When the party opens, probably from the long shooter, the north and south sides will open fire. There will be one hell of a lot of shooting. Most horses nearby will be spooked. Where will the Confederates secret their horses? And, if they are trained troops as you judge, they won't risk picket pins to hold them. There will likely be a soldier managing them."

"Good thinking Diaz. That is what I would do," Trent acknowledged and moving the salt shaker to the south side of the bread.

Again, they were in silent focus before Liam posed a question. "Let's assume they are successful and took control of the stage. What would be their next move? Where would they take it? It is a long way from Virginia or the Carolinas. Try for Texas? A cavalry troop could easily catch them."

Again, they were all focusing on the table. Diaz sipped his tequila while Trent took a long pull on his beer. Several minutes passed before Liam picked up the pepper shaker, removed the cap and dumped a large quantity far west of the bread.

"The only reasonable hope of getting the gold out of the country is to do it fast and that means taking the stage due west to the Pacific. My thought is there must be a ship awaiting them," Liam said.

"Sheriff, how far is it from the Pass to the Pacific?" Trent asked, placing his beer back on the table.

"Maybe seventy to eighty miles. They could do that easily in two days over trails that are not well traveled. The tough part will be when they make the coast. It is mostly cliffs and gold is heavy."

Diaz added, "I think we can alert the stage, amigos. I could send one of my deputies with a dispatch from you, Marshal. It would be too late to reroute the stage because they will have passed the last intersecting trail."

Trent jumped in with excitement, "Why didn't we think of that? Good thinking, Diaz. But, will they believe it or think it is a trick?"

It all began to take shape in Liam's mind. It was the lawyer's logic that helped him take disparate information and construct a defense quickly.

Liam swallowed the last of his beer and said, "Okay. Here is the plan for us to think through. I will write a message with all the facts including the breach in Pony Express security and our contact with Colonel Johnston at Fort Point. It should be enough. I will ask them to stop about a mile or so from Pacheco Pass, secure the stage and send as many soldiers as possible to assist in the capture of the Confederates."

The server approached and looked at the mess on the table with a blend of interest and disdain before asking if more drinks were needed. With two beers and one tequila requested, she left for the bar and Liam continued.

"The message will ask for your deputy, Diaz, to lead a split force behind where we expect the Confederates to be on the north and south sides. This needs to be executed quietly to catch them unaware. Trent, you will secret yourself above the Confederates on the north, and I will be on the south side in case the U.S. Army commander doesn't believe my message. Sheriff, you will work up behind the long shooter and it will hinge on you taking out the long shooter first. We will await the Army but, and this is important, if the party starts for any reason before the Army escort arrives, we all jump into action. Diaz, take out the long shooter and Trent and I will take out as many of the Confederates as we can. What do you think?"

The server placed a beer in front of Liam, another in front of Trent and a tequila in front of Diaz and removed the empty mugs and glass. Not a word was spoken until she returned to the bar.

"That leaves the soldier holding their animals unattended, but he will probably think that the rifle fire is his band taking the stage and remain where he is. Then, we could take him after the party is over. It is a good plan, Liam," Trent said.

"Agreed, amigos," added Diaz.

The next morning found Liam and Trent in the Hacienda enjoying a breakfast of eggs, bacon, roasted tomatoes, biscuits and gravy with black coffee when Diaz and one of his deputies walked through the door. The deputy was taller than Diaz, with alert eyes and a confident manner.

"Amigos. This is Deputy Childs, Clinton Childs." Diaz added, pointing to Liam, "This is Marshal Liam deBláca of the U.S. Marshals Service and this is Trent Masters, Deputy Marshal."

"Nice of you to help, Childs. Please pull up a chair and join us."

Trent sported an unusually large smile that caught Liam's attention. "Trent, you seem rather happy all of a sudden."

But it was Clinton Childs that responded to Liam. "Marshal Masters and I have seen some action together, some years ago back in the great state of Texas. We were both Texas Rangers then, Trent's path was to the Marshals Service, and mine to sheriffing. Trent, you sure are a sight for these tired old eyes!"

Trent, still with a broad smile on his face but now nodding to Clint said, "Pard, I never thought our paths would cross again, but by the grace of God I'm happy they did, and now especially." Trent turned to Diaz and continued, "Sheriff, you have one of the few men I trust with my life right here. I am guessing that you have filled Clint in on our operation?"

Clint jumped in, "Yes, he did and I am proud to be backing your play, Trent, and yours too, Marshal. My horse is saddled and ready to ride. Need to be making tracks ifin' I'm to get to that stage."

Liam took the sealed envelope from his inside jacket pocket and handed it to Clint. "This letter has all the details that Sheriff Diaz has shared with you from how the marshals uncovered the hijack timing to the likelihood that they are Confederate rebels. However, the escort commander may think it is a trick. If I were him, I would consider it. All I ask is that you do what you can to persuade him that it isn't and that we need some help to capture these rebels to prevent a future hijack. God speed, Deputy Childs!"

Clint Childs simply nodded and left the Hacienda. They heard the footfalls of Deputy Childs horse as he galloped south out of Old Gilroy.

Trent looked at Diaz, still with that broad smile on his face and said, "Sheriff, you chose well, very well. Clinton Childs is a very good man. I owe him my life."

Sergeant Major Slayer called, "Fall in!"

It was several hours before sunup and the weather was brisk. Then men were shaking the life into their limbs and wiping the dust from their eyes, finishing their coffee as they lined up. Major Meyers was leaning on a large poplar off to the side with a mug of coffee in his hand. It was Sergeant Slayer that addressed the men.

"This is the day you all have been awaiting, men. Pack only whatcha' be needin'; for three days. We be movin' fast after taken' the stage, so travel light. Be ready to move out in thirty minutes. That will git us to Pachinko Pass before sunup. Two full canteens fir each of ya. Water your mounts well. Okay, assholes and elbows now!"

***

Several hours later, Liam and Trent finished their early morning breakfast and retired to their rooms. In preparation, both were cleaning and rechecking their weapons for readiness. The process was so automatic that it allowed for a period of deep introspection. It was to be a life and death day; who lives and who dies was to be counted at the end of the day. Their plan was well conceived but anything could go wrong. They both knew well that a plan was just a starting point because unknowns were always plenty and caused the plan to be instantly modified or even discarded entirely for improvised action or reaction.

Their horses were well watered by the Hacienda's hosteller and awaited them at the hitching rail. Sandwiches were in their saddlebags as well as an additional full canteen.

Liam had both .44s loaded, all six chambers. His .38 was in the shoulder holster, loaded in all five chambers. His twelve-inch Bowie was sheathed and tied on his back belt, and the modified Henry fully loaded with twenty-two rounds. His right and left jacket pockets carried a handful of extra ammunition that he hoped he would not need.

He was dressed in tan broadcloth pants with a fringed buckskin jacket over a brown shirt in hopes of blending in with the natural color of Pacheco Pass. Liam was thinking through the telegram he had sent to Jeremiah earlier as he was putting two extra boxes of .44s into his saddlebags when Trent walked out of the Hacienda.

"Looks like you are ready for war, Liam."

"You too, pard."

The sounds of a horse approaching caused them to turn to see Sheriff Diaz approaching. "There is death in the air, amigos. Let's pray it is not our own."

***

Sergeant Major Slayer supervised the placement of the five Confederate soldiers to the north and south of Pachinko Pass where the Butterfield stage trail turned from the north to the east toward Old Gilroy. Each man was secreted before sunup with a canteen, their rifle and extra ammunition. They would now await the stage which was expected near high noon.

Major Meyers and Sergeant Slayer then split up and found good vantage points to take out the stage driver and shotgun. They, too, now lay in wait. It would be Major Meyers that would fire the first shot at the driver that would start the bloody ambush and hopefully breathe new life into the Confederate Army.

The three cantered in absolute silence save that of the horse's footfalls, each alone with their thoughts and worries. They were badly outnumbered and if Clint was unable to secure the help of the Army escort, it would be up to them. Their only edge was the element of surprise and they were each hoping it would be enough.

Sheriff Diaz took the lead and veered off the trail heading due south, finding an old game trail. It was narrow and required him to take the lead with Trent and then Liam following. It was a rough trail, not used regularly, with frequent fallen rocks and tree limbs, but well concealed to the higher elevation where they were heading. They were benefited by being well hidden and raising no dust but it was slow going.

An hour after taking the game trail, Diaz abruptly stopped and motioned with his hand to dismount very quietly. In a whisper Dias said, "You and I will leave our mounts here. We are near the south side of the Pass. Trent, you will continue for another mile where the trail leads to the Butterfield stage trail. Then, cross the pass carefully and make your way above the north side. We will give you an hour to get into place and before we move. Good luck, amigo."

"Rider approaching from the south, Captain! Look like he's alone!"

"Thank you, Sergeant. Weapons at the ready! Hold the stage and put someone on the top of the stage to get a better view."

Deputy Childs was moving in a gallop, but as he neared the stage and the escort he slowed to a cantor. As he came close enough to be heard, he yelled out, "Deputy Clinton Childs with a dispatch for the commander. Can I come on up?"

Captain Shelton was an experienced officer and was well aware of the importance of the stage's cargo. A veteran of several Indian campaigns, he took immediate protective action.

"Sergeant Dorsey, deploy a protective perimeter in those rocks on both sides of the stage. Driver and shotgun get down please, but lock the break."

"Come on in Deputy, hands where we can see them and no sudden moves," the captain warned.

Childs did as was asked and walked his horse, cat hopping up onto the Butterfield stage trail and approached the Captain. He was comforted to see that the captain was a salty, middle-aged man of experience.

"Captain, I have been sent by the Chief Inspector of the U.S. Marshals Service to personally hand you this dispatch. May I remove it from my pocket?" Childs remembered the captain's warning, no sudden moves, and kept his hands on the saddle pommel.

"You may, but carefully and with your right hand, Deputy," the captain said noticing his six-gun was tied to his right side.

Captain Shelton took the sealed envelope from Childs, and before opening and reading the contents, asked the lookout on top of the stage for a report. Hearing that there were no other riders in sight, he opened the dispatch and after digesting the contents handed it to his sergeant. He sat his horse with both hands on the pommel, sizing up Childs with steel gray intense eyes before he spoke.

"You're the deputy sheriff of Old Gilroy where we are to lay over tonight. Who is the sheriff?"

"Well sir, that would be Sheriff Diaz. He and two U.S. Marshals are at Pachinko Pass right now and intend to take out those rebs by themselves ifin' you won't help."

"How do I know this isn't a trap, Deputy?"

"Well sir, that is what Marshal deBláca feared you might think. He said it would be what he would think. I can only give it to ya straight; it ain't a trap. It's on the level, Captain."

Captain Shelton was contemplating the options and they were few. Turning back was out as the animals wouldn't make it, and Fort Point needed the gold. Splitting his protective escort would leave the stage very vulnerable if this was indeed a trap. His thoughts were interrupted by the sergeant.

"Sir, Corporal Gussy has some information that might be helpful. Corporal?"

"Captain Sir, I know this man, well my pa does. He was a Texas Ranger and saved my ma and pa when the Apaches attacked our spread some years ago."

"Thank you, Corporal."

"Deputy, you know that Texas has sided with the Confederacy. Why would you want to help the Union Army?"

"Well sir, leaving Texas was right hard to do bein' born a Texan. But I couldn't side with the Confederates so I resigned my commission when rumors of the wars were spreadin' and traveled north to California where I met

Sheriff Diaz and now I back him. He is as fine a man as there is, sir, even ifin' he ain't a Texan."

Captain Shelton was continuing to size up Childs and asked, "What would you have me do, Deputy?"

"Well sir, speaking freely, I would secure the stage right here. Then, I would ask that you send four or six capable men to assist. You have the marshal's plan in the dispatch. That is all we would need but we need to move quickly. The location of the ambush in the pass is not more than two miles ahead so we could capture these rebs and be in Old Gilroy tonight."

Captain Shelton believed that Childs was on the level and thought the suggestion was his best option and made his decision quickly. "Sergeant, cut out five capable men to accompany you and the deputy on the double. I will stay with the stage."

"Thank you, Captain. We will send a trooper back when the party is over. Sergeant, I suggest you take three to the north and I will lead the other three to the south. Remember, there will be a U.S Marshal up there behind the rebs, so careful with your aim. Times a wastin'!"

An hour had passed, and Liam had to believe that Diaz and Trent were now in position. There were no shots indicating they were discovered, but he was unable to see them. Now, he would wait until the Army arrived to support the counterattack or until the stage arrived, indicating the commander thought his message was a trick. He prayed Childs was able to convince the commander because if they rode up the Butterfield stage trail, they would be cut to pieces in short order.

The sun was near overhead, its heat blistering his neck. The air was still, the quiet menacing. Below him were five Confederate rebels, tough-looking men all with their backs toward the Butterfield stage trail, leaning on rocks and cradling their rifles. They were well positioned and concealed from the trail but not from Liam's position. They were fully visible to him but that also meant they were facing directly at him, but keeping their heads tilted down, protecting eyes from the blistering sun. Liam assumed it would be the same for Trent on the south side of the Pass.

Another hour passed and Liam was fighting impatience. Sensing movement but hearing nothing, Liam turned to see a Union Army sergeant belly-crawling slowly between several large boulders toward him. He obviously had taken in the rebs' positions as he was moving with ultimate stealth.

Crawling the last twenty feet and then crouching beside Liam, the sergeant whispered, "You must be Marshal deBláca. Sergeant Dorsey at your service, sir."

"You are a very welcome sight, Sergeant!" Liam let out a long breath of relief.

"I have two sharpshooters, good men, positioned above with clear sight of the rebs, Marshal. They have selected their number one and two targets and Marshal, they don't miss. Deputy Childs has another two on the south side. What's the play?"

"I hope we can take them prisoner to learn more about their rebel operations, but if they don't surrender we are in for a fight. Then it is shoot to kill. I will open the party."

Liam risked a look over the rock hiding him from the five rebs below. Moving his head to the left of the boulder so as not to skyline himself, he looked north to where he believed Trent would be. But, he saw no evidence of Trent, Childs or the sergeant's men. He resolved to trust that they were ready.

Liam, taking a deep breath, stood, plainly visible, cupping his hands to his mouth, shouted, "You are completely surrounded by the Union Army and the U.S. Marshals. Drop your weapons, walk to the trail and lie face down. Do it now! This is the only warning you will get!"

A shot came from the head of the trail followed by several more. The first bullet tore through Liam's left arm, spinning him around, while the second hit the boulder in front of him spraying his face with bits of rock. Off balance he fell to the ground. He was in pain, bleeding but not out. Sergeant Dorsey quickly tied his bandana tightly around Liam's arm and said, "Well, you gave them rebs a chance and that's more than I would do. Now its shoot to kill. You gunna be alright?"

Gunfire from the sergeant's sharpshooters had started within seconds of the first shot. Both the north and south sides were mowing down the Confederates with almost every round finding its mark. The rebs had no chance as they had chosen their positions to be protected from forward of their fire and were wide open to the rear.

Liam said, "Looks like it went through the muscle, missed the bone, but I can still use my .44. Let's give 'em hell!"

Dorsey then shot one of the two rebs still standing on the south side as the fire continued from all sides except the head of the Pass. Childs' group along with Trent spent several rounds in seconds catching the rebs on the north side completely by surprise. The long shooters made short work of the rebs on the both sides with their backs open. Minutes after it started it was over. No Confederate soldier surrendered and all met their death quickly.

Acrid gun powder smoke clouds blossomed low in the air and meandered eastward with the gentle breeze. The shots' echoes began to fade but the ringing in Liam's ears continued. Deathly quiet ebbed over the Pass.

Diaz walked slowly down from the head of the pass trail, Winchester at the ready. Liam and Sergeant Dorsey having verified that all five rebs were dead, unsteadily made their way to the trail seeing Trent waving the all clear from the north side.

"Diaz, I suspect I owe you thanks for taking out the long shooter" Liam said.

"Two long shooters Liam. Both are dead."

"Sergeant, thank you again for the support", Liam said offering his right hand. "We suspect there is another reb secreted further south holding their mounts. Could I impose upon you to take a few men and take him alive?"

"Be de-light-ed Marshal. I will take two men and have the others bring the reb bodies down for you as well. And, thanks to you and your Marshals for what you did!"

"Sergeant, only two Marshals here. Diaz is the Sheriff of Old Gilroy and a man to ride the river with! Childs, as you know, is his Deputy."

Trent, Childs and the two soldiers walked onto the trail smiling, obviously relieved to be alive. Trent noticed the blood dripping from Liam's left arm and said, "We need to get the doc to look at that, clean the wound to prevent infection."

"It will keep until we are back in Old Gilroy."

Childs jumped in, "Liam, I told the escort commander, Captain Shelton, that we would send a trooper when the ruckus was over."

"Good thinking, please handle that if you would," Liam said feeling a bit lightheaded from the growing loss of blood.

Minutes later, Sergeant Dorsey and two troopers appeared with a dozen or more horses trailing, as well as a secured Confederate soldier. Liam said, "Good work, Sergeant! Now we have someone that will tell us about their operations. I can arrest him for attempted robbery but I suspect that Captain Shelton would like to interrogate him as a prisoner of war. And, if you don't mind, we will leave you here to care for the dead. Trent, Childs and Diaz will head to Old Gilroy. Need to get this arm look after."

"Thanks Marshal, happy to! And, if you ever need my help, just find me. I owe you all my life and the life of my troopers. We would have ridden right into the ambush ifin' it wasn't for you."

Liam was deep in thought while riding Creena back to Old Gilroy. Was it the Confederate rebel leader's hubris or lack of tactical training that left the rear unguarded? Had they placed even one lookout, he and Trent would likely have been spotted and the counterattack fail. He would never know but it was something to remember.

Liam had telegraphed Attorney Geeral Jeremiah Black as well as Colonel Johnston at Fort Point, but had not received replies as yet.

Liam, Trent, Childs and Captain Shelton were enjoying a sumptuous meal at the Hacienda, Diaz drinking his tequila, the rest beer. Everybody were in good spirits. The express stage was under heavy guard around the clock. All were relieved that the Confederate rebel's plan was uncovered and thwarted. The Union payroll would be delivered on time and, just as important, the Confederate Army wouldn't have the much-needed operating cash.

Sergeant Dorsey had searched the rebs as well as their saddlebags. Of no surprise to Liam, he found several telegrams in code that would be analyzed later by Union Army experts and more importantly, orders from the Confederate States Army, signed by Brigadier General P.G.T. Beauregard, confirming they were indeed Confederate soldiers.

Liam raised his glass with his right hand as his left arm was ailing, "A toast gentlemen; Today was one major success for the Union!" All raised their glasses in agreement as a boy walked through the door and approached their table. Liam recognized him as the telegraph operator.

"Marshal, this just came in for you. I thought you would want to read it immediately", he said while handing the envelope to Liam.

After reading the telegram Liam looked at Trent with a sly smile and slid the telegram across the table for him to read.

TROUBLE IN ARIZONA TERRITORY NORTH OF CONFEDERATE LINE STOP REPORTED BANDIT ACTIVITY STOP BELIEVED TO BE CONFEDERATE DESERTERS STOP WIRE WHEN YOU ARRIVE PRESCOTT STOP CONGRATULATIONS TO YOU FOR PROTECTHING THE EXPRESS

Trent was unsuccessful in his attempt to read Liam's mind; the meaning of that unusually sly smile.

Finishing the last of his beer, Liam asked Trent, "Ever been to the northern Arizona Territory, Trent?"

HISTORICAL NOTES:

September 24, 1789.

Many Americans are unaware that the United States Marshals Service (USMS) is a United States federal law enforcement agency managed within the United States Department of Justice. The office of the U.S. Marshal Service is the oldest federal law enforcement office in America. The Marshals Service is part of the executive branch of government, and today is the enforcement arm of the United States federal courts. The U.S. Marshals are responsible for the protection of court officers and buildings and the effective operation of the judiciary. The service also assists with court security and prisoner transport, serves arrest warrants, and, as is the focus of the Chief Inspector series, seeks fugitives.

The agency was formed by the Judiciary Act of September 24, 1789. The act specifically determined that law enforcement was to be the U.S. Marshals' primary function. Therefore, it appropriately defined Marshals as law enforcement officers. The text of Section 27 of the Judiciary Act that reads:

And be it further enacted, That a marshal shall be appointed in and for each district for a term of four years, but shall be removable from office at pleasure, whose duty it shall be to attend the district and circuit courts when sitting therein, and also the Supreme Court in the district in which that court shall sit.(b) And to execute throughout the district, all lawful precepts directed to him, and issued under the authority of the United States, and he shall have the power to command all necessary assistance in the execution of his duty, and to appoint as shall be occasion, one or more deputies...

The Marshals Service itself, as a federal agency, was not created until 1969. It succeeded the Executive Office for United States Marshals, itself created in 1965 as "the first organization to supervise U.S. Marshals nationwide."

In a letter to Edmund Randolph, the first United States Attorney General, then President George Washington wrote:

Impressed with a conviction that the due administration of justice is the firmest pillar of good Government, I have considered the first arrangement of the Judicial department as essential to the happiness of our Country, and to the stability of its political system; hence the selection of the fittest characters to expound the law, and dispense justice, has been an invariable object of my anxious concern.

Many of the first U.S. Marshals had already proven themselves in military service during the American Revolution. Among the first marshals were John Adams' son-in-law, Congressman William Stephens Smith for the district of New York, another New York district Marshal, Congressman Thomas Morris, and Henry Dearborn for the district of Maine.

From the earliest days of the nation, Marshals were permitted to recruit Special Deputies as local hires or as temporary transfers to the Marshals Service from other federal law enforcement agencies. Marshals were also authorized to swear in a posse to assist them in manhunts and other duties on an ad hoc basis. Marshals were given extensive authority to support the federal courts within their judicial districts, and to carry out all lawful orders issued by federal judges, Congress, the Attorney General or the President of the United States.

The marshals and their deputies served writs (e.g. subpoenas, summonses, warrants), and other process issued by the courts, made all the arrests, and handled all federal prisoners. They also disbursed funds as ordered by the courts. Marshals paid the fees and expenses of the court clerks, U.S. Attorneys, jurors, and witnesses. They rented the courtrooms and jail space and hired the bailiffs, criers, and janitors. They made sure the prisoners were present, the jurors were available, and that the witnesses were on time.

When George Washington set up his first administration, and the first Congress began passing laws, both quickly discovered an inconvenient and large gap in the constitutional design of the government: It had no provision for a regional administrative structure stretching throughout the country. Both the Congress and the executive branch were housed at the national capital; no agency was established or designated to represent the federal government's interests at other localities. The need for a regional organization quickly became apparent. Congress and the President solved part of the problem by creating specialized agencies, such as customs and revenue collectors, to levy tariffs and taxes, yet there were numerous other jobs that needed to be done. The only officers available to do them were the marshals and their deputies.

The marshals thus provided local representation for the federal government within their districts. They took the national census every decade through 1870. They distributed Presidential proclamations, collected a variety of statistical information on commerce and manufacturing, supplied the names of government employees for the national register, and performed other routine tasks needed for the central government to function effectively.

Individual deputy marshals, particularly in the American West, have been seen as legendary heroes in the face of rampant lawlessness. For example, Marshals arrested the infamous Dalton Gang in 1893, helped suppress the Pullman Strike in 1894.

U.S. Marshals also have the common law-based power to enlist any willing civilians as deputies. In the Old West this was known as forming a posse, although under the Posse Comitatus Act, they cannot use troops for law enforcement duties while in uniform representing their unit, or the military service. However, if the serviceman or woman is off duty, wearing civilian clothing, and willing to assist a law enforcement officer on his/her own behalf, it is acceptable.

The United States Marshals Service (USMS) is based in Arlington, Virginia, and, under the authority and direction of the United States Attorney General, is headed by a Director, who is assisted by a Deputy Director. USMS Headquarters provides command, control and cooperation for the disparate elements of the service.

The U.S. court system is divided into 94 federal judicial districts, each with a district court. For each district there is a presidentially-appointed and Senate-confirmed United States Marshal that function within the district. Senior Deputy USM's working in special assignments requiring highly skilled criminal investigators often receive the title of "Inspector". The titles of Senior Inspector and

Chief Inspector are also sometimes used in the service for certain assignments and positions within the agency.

See: _www.usmarshals.gov/duties/factsheets/overview.pdf

The Pony Express:

The Pony Express was a "fast mail" service delivering messages, newspapers, mail, legal documents, bank notes and sometimes small packages from St. Joseph, Missouri, across the Great Plains, over the Rocky Mountains and the Sierra Nevada to Sacramento, California, approximately 1,900 miles in under ten days. The mail carriers traveled by horseback, using a network consisting of 120 riders, 184 relay stations, 400 horses, disbursed along the mail route.

In 1860, riding for the Pony Express was difficult and very dangerous work. Riders had to be tough and lightweight and aged fifteen to eighteen. A famous advertisement allegedly read: *'Wanted: Young, skinny, wiry fellows not over eighteen. Must be expert riders, willing to risk death daily. Orphans preferred.'*

Pony Express stations were, on average, ten miles apart along the route. This was roughly the distance a horse could travel at a full gallop before tiring to the point of hurting the animal. The express rider carried a horn in the early days to alert the station of his approach but in later days the galloping horse could be heard from some distance. The rider would quickly change to a fresh horse that the station hosteller had readied, taking only the mail pouch called a mochila (Spanish for pouch) with him. The mochila was unlike a saddle bag that sat behind the saddle but rather draped over the center of the saddle with the saddle horn protruding through a hole in the mochila with the rider siting upon it securely. It was limited to twenty pounds of mail.

There were two types of stations, relay and home. The relay station provided quick food and water along with a fresh horse while the rider traveled his average seventy-five miles a day. The home station was where the rider, having completed his daily travel, rested for the next day's ride.

The riders were paid one hundred dollars a month, more than double the typical wage for the time in recognition of the dangers they faced each day.

Butterfield Overland Stage Line:

Once the mail arrived in Sacramento, California, it was sorted with local mail sent to the post office. Mail going north was bagged, sealed and sent to the Oregon Stagecoach Line run by the H. W. Corbett Company. Mail going south was bagged, sealed and delivered to the Butterfield Overland Mail Stage Line with service all the way to Fort Yuma at the southernmost tip of California.

Stagecoach was the preferred means of extended travel in the far west with rail service just beginning its expansion. There were generally two types of stagecoaches; one that catered to passengers and intermittently carried a strong box with cash, gold, silver or other valuables and an express stagecoach that was specifically designed to carry cash, gold, silver, bank notes – anything of significant value – but did not carry passengers and was always accompanied by a heavily armed escort.

In this book, I take license to expand the duties of Chief Inspector of the United States Marshals Service by order of the President of the United States. While there are several historical accuracies cited within the work, this is a story of fiction.